Stripped

By Falkman and Gouldthorp

Stripped

By Falkman and Gouldthorp

FOREWORD

My experience of Rave Alexander tells me that he is
a highly intuitive person who shoots straight from
the hip, and is ruled by his feelings both in business
and matters of the heart. The first time I met Rave
was in the bar at the Stromonoff Hotel by the river
in the centre of Ljubljana. It was late in the summer,
very warm and the place was crawling with tourists
and locals who had chosen to dine outdoors that
evening. I had been invited to dinner with an
international businessman from one of the Nordic
countries within the EU. The invitation had come
from the head of the supranational bank which was
formed by the EU when the bank sector had crashed
a number of years earlier. I had accepted the
invitation and arrived as arranged in good time. The
man sitting on the other side of the table was tall
and thin. In his early forties and with a touch of
arrogance in his smile. He wore an expensive Saville

Row suit without a tie but his shirt was buttoned up to the collar. He reminded me of an Iranian envoy without a beard. By his side sat an attractive lady, Slovenian or Russian, with blond hair and all the right attributes. She introduced herself as Elena and was his lawyer. Rave smiled and, from nowhere, I felt sympathy towards him – my interest was aroused. Rave Alexander was made of flesh and blood.

Following the bank crash in Slovenia, various interested parties began greedily acquiring companies that had fallen upon troubled times during the crisis. The newly-formed EU bank involved itself with the struggling companies and tried to sort out their problems as quickly as they could in order to sell them back onto the private market. Rave and I founded a company together and initially bought hotels, property, leasing companies and the like. The market started to tick over, albeit slowly, and little by little the country began to recover.

Everyone has a story. I have one and so does Rave. This book is not only about passion and love but also about the workings for the intelligence services where everyone has at least two identities, and sometimes three.

In this business, you quickly realise that you know nothing about the person you have in front of you despite the apparent reality of what you see. You always need to know who you are dealing with. I know for a fact that I will make Rave disappointed if he finds out who I actually work for. I also know that I can't be sure who he works for either. And yet, despite this, I feel secure in the knowledge that I can trust him.

Stripped is the first book in a series of three. It is a hard-baked story of love and betrayal, and the cold war which many believed had died out. The reader will find out that fact is stranger than fiction. I would like to wish every success to all those involved and that the trilogy about Rave is fruitful for him and his friends.

See things as they really are.

Now is not the time to shed any tears.

Laibach, 20 January 2020
Carl August Randall

CHAPTERS

(From book 2 in the Rave trilogy)

Chapter 1

THE ST. PETERSBURG DAYS

Sophya feels the flood of passion building up inside her body between her beautiful thighs – like a ticking bomb beginning to approach its point of detonation.

'Come and take me now. Kiss my lips, my fingers, my shoulders, my hair. I want you so much. I want your love and your affection,' she goes on, almost pleading.

She leans forward over the window sill, her legs wide apart, and throws back her hair wildly in an open invitation. She stands naked – her skin is soft and tanned as her hair settles over her shoulders and back.

'Now,' she says as her breathing becomes even more intense and her body stiffens. 'Take me now!'

When did this start? This passion, this lust for sex. I can't remember when she made me realize for the first time that she really wanted to go all the way with me. Now when we make love, she does so with all the power and passion of a young married Russian woman.

Through the open window, the light, powdery snow falls slowly, sparkling in the winter sun and gently settling on the roof of the ice-blue Nikolsky Cathedral. The trees are bare. The sounds of the traffic and the crowds of people on the pavement below are muffled by the snowflakes.

Her slim body trembles as the cold night air sweeps into the room, and she is wet and can hold back no longer. I take her with both hands and suddenly, finally and explosively, release my all inside her. She trembles again, then the fire within her gently subsides and her body becomes soft and relaxed. Then, within a few seconds, she almost absent-mindedly looks out over St Petersburg's rooftops.

Her husband is dead. He was murdered. On the very day Sophya and I were together for the first time on one of the summer beaches just outside St Petersburg. It was a beautiful summer's day in July. A fantastic day - in fact, a day that I will always remember but a day which ended in tragedy for Sophya and her family.

The police said they found her husband's body in a small alley in a run-down area on the outskirts of Moscow. They believed, however, that he was murdered somewhere else and was moved there later on. I knew none of the details, neither did I want to. I could see that she was clearly upset by his death but, at the same time, she did not seem particularly surprised either. Perhaps this was the Russian way. Nothing shakes them. They just put their heads down and get on with their lives. She certainly knew what kind of life he was involved in, but she never discussed potential enemies, motives, or the circumstances surrounding his death with me. The most difficult part for her was to explain to her daughter Anna that she would never see her father again.

The police were formal, efficient and discreet. They knew who her husband was and what his profession was. They kept their meeting with Sophya very short. It seemed to her, from the impression she got from the police, that they would never find the killer, or even try to. Yet they seemed to know more than they said. Such things happen in Russia and life goes on anyway. Ordinary people are completely at the mercy of the authorities; totally unprotected by the law. There is no one to help you or defend you if you get into trouble with the powers-that-be. No international movements, no news magazines or television companies prepared to fight for your rights. Individuals just disappear, swallowed up by mother Russia.

In her apartment, after the police officers had left the apartment and her daughter had finally fallen asleep, we just stood there, in the heat of the night, looking at each other without saying a word, and I slowly stroked her hair, over and over. I looked at my watch and realized it was time to go, but I couldn't just leave her there. It actually felt good to be able to comfort her a little, to take away her thoughts from what had just happened to her husband, so I stayed on playing with her hair and ears.

And now, on this wintery day in St. Petersburg, I walk around the apartment and look for my clothes. My socks have found their way under the bed but eventually I'm fully dressed. Again, my glance falls upon Sophya for a few seconds, until I am ready to leave the apartment. She is completely relaxed with her naked body. She loves the old houses in this part of St Petersburg. Outside, on the street, people go about their lives without any great urgency. They stroll along before stopping to speak to one another, sometimes in small groups; walking and talking; waiting for the green light at the pedestrian crossings. Respectable, decent Russians.

**

She closes the window and effortlessly glides onto the couch in the living room where she slowly lays back and stretches out in her nakedness, fully exposed, wearing nothing but a smile. Everything with her is perfect.

'Rave, why do you have to go so early?' she asks with a questioning look as she turns her beautiful face towards me. 'Let's go and have dinner somewhere. I'm starving'.

'I'm sorry but I can't stay tonight, Sophya. I have to attend a meeting at the Consulate. Some boring old politicians from Sweden are here on a visit, and too few guests have been invited for me to be able to decline. I'm just as sorry as you are, perhaps even more so ...'

I look at her one last time; at her straight black hair resting on her shoulders, her cool blue eyes, her thin lips and delicate nose set into her round face. Her figure once again takes my breath away as I admire every inch of her body from top to toe.

I leave the apartment and take the stairs down to the street where my car is waiting. The newly-fallen snowflakes whiten up what is otherwise a rather grey, dirty city and one which is still largely unknown to me. While the black Mercedes slowly make sits way through the traffic to the Consulate, I decide to make myself quite conspicuous during the mingle and to make a good impression on the most important guests. That way everyone will remember that I was there. Then, at the first suitable opportunity, I will make myself scarce and get out of there as quickly as I can.

As I feared, dinner is a dreadful event. It's a 'zombie-like' affair made up of half-dead, fat bodies wearing suits. Among the invited I see the number 2 from the Swedish Consulate in the company of Sweden's Foreign Trade Minister. Everyone smells of sweat, too much coffee and too many cigarettes, and they are 'gender invisible'. It's actually hard to see who's a woman and who is a man, apart from the fact that some of them wear ties and some don't.

Through an interpreter, a fat heap of flesh with a tie says something that is supposed to be a funny Russian joke to another heap of flesh without a tie, and they both burst into polite laughter.

One of the guests, a cheaply-dressed Russian with sweaty hands, who runs a company in the woods where he produces cheap clothes hangers, takes the opportunity to complain about the tax burden in Russia to the Swedish number 2. Even by Russian standards, the burden is very tough, he argues. The truth is that he and his company would have chronic problems paying their taxes wherever they did their business irrespective of the country they were in. His business idea is to minimise his taxes, maximise the subsidies, and exploit his staff through low wages and slave-like employment conditions up to and beyond the point of moral decency. Like many of his fellow businessmen, he wants to squeeze his costs so much that he is able to swim in the profits. No flying business class flights or expensive hotels for him. He hates everything which has some class about it. He becomes extremely animated and rubs his Alcantara jacket up and down against the back of his chair so violently as he tries to explain his situation that I begin to think he might burst into flames at any second. All the static electricity he generates from rubbing his jacket up and down makes his hair stand on end.

I think I'm going to die sitting there at the dinner table, but finally, after two hours, it's all over. I fly out onto the street, throw myself into the car and tell the driver where to take me.

'To the Maximus, and don't take any prisoners.'

When I arrive at the nightclub, I ask the barmaid if all the girls are in. And all the girls laugh. It's a well-used joke.

'Of course, we are! My name's 'All' and everybody else's name is 'All' too,' says the girl behind the bar. They know how to make jokes and smile to keep their customers happy.

After a couple of cold beers, I'm ready to go home and get some sleep, but on my way out of the club, I catch sight of my old friend Christian Silver sitting in a private booth, and as usual he's clearly enjoying the moves of the private dancer who's gyrating in front of his face, in time with the music.

Christian, is an English aristocrat with a Japanese mother, who has lived in St. Petersburg for many years, making a living by translating Japanese paperback porn for the Russian market. Years before, he lived in Torquay, England, and worked as a teacher of Japanese at a minor university. His now deceased wife, a humourless, obese, dragon of a woman, called him Chrissy because she thought his real name was too masculine.

Following a severe car accident, mercifully for Christian, the bane of his life passed away and, with her death, he became a free man once again. He made a great effort to get his life in order, and decided to flee the drudgery of Torquay and move to Russia of all places. Christian, a talented linguist, quickly added Russian to his arsenal of languages and started his own business collaborating with a publishing company in Japan where he developed an interest in the special paperback porn culture that exists only there.

He established contact with a Russian publisher in St. Petersburg and his company has now become quite successful. The Russians are increasingly starting to like the Japanese porn culture. Sometimes, however, Christian's ideas about the extent of the shock factor in the language of the books clash with those of his Russian publisher. He thinks that Christian tends to tone down and clean up the language to avoid the worst and most obscene vulgarities so as not to alienate the readers. The Russian publisher knows best however, and insists on including the genuine Japanese raw vulgarities which his readers, he argues, are only too pleased to read. This means that Christian is constantly on a collision course with his publisher and, consequently, always short of cash since his publisher makes him wait excessively long periods for payments.

But tonight, he looks to be in a good mood, maybe celebrating something for all I know. A slight, slender girl who could be his daughter is sitting on his knee. She's one of his favourites. She comes from the region of Karelia and, as a good Finn, she knows how to work her customers so that they are completely satisfied by the end of the evening.

Christian is actually a sexual predator or, as they say in Sweden, a sex addict of insatiable proportions who never gets enough. And he has the time of his life here in St. Petersburg when he's got money to spend.

I wait until he sees me and then I give him a wave. He points to the bar, so I cross the floor and order two vodkas. Christian comes out of the booth looking very pleased with himself. We hug each other Russian-style, and drink down the shots in one. When it's time to leave, he asks for a lift home because, of course, he has no money left for a taxi.

'No problem, my friend,' I say. 'We're heading in the same direction, so let's go. Tomorrow's a new day.'

'Rave, you're a real kill-joy. The night is young. What would St. Petersburg be if everyone was like you? There would be more action in the Lubyanka prison than here,' he laughs, before setting off, head held high like a true aristocrat towards the waiting car outside.

Anton, the driver, looks at him with a raised eyebrow but says nothing as Christian stumbles into the back seat. After closing the doors, he drives us away into the St. Petersburg night.

The streets are empty, cold, dark, and snow-covered. Christian continues to brag about his adventures with women and his various projects that never come to anything, but it's always interesting to listen to him when he's in full flow.

'We should buy some old submarines from Thyssen, then scrap them and sell the scrap in Shanghai. We'd make a fortune with the first shipment. We can get a letter from the navy as security so it'll be completely risk free. You can fund the whole deal Rave. I've spoken with thirteen different banks in China but they've all said no,' he continues, 'but I can't do business like you can! So, my friend, are you in?'

'This is just another of your crazy pipes dreams Christian. This time next week, you'll have forgotten all about it and you'll be working like crazy on something totally new and different. You're nothing but a dreamer! Just get on with finishing your porno paperbacks and don't forget to kiss the publisher's ass so that you'll get paid. I'm telling you as a friend.'

Suddenly I feel very tired.

Anton drives through the quiet streets, the sound from the tyres hushed by the newly-fallen snow. No one says anything. Christian has run out of conversation and doesn't bring up any more business ideas.

Anton parks and waits outside the house where Christian lives. Rubbish, empty vodka bottles, junk, wild dogs, broken balconies and cracked facades are what we see. This is the real Russia. I know a girl who lives here in the same neighbourhood. Those living here sleep three or four people in a single room. I can smell the sweat, the stink of over-cooked vegetables and the decaying rubbish. I see a drunk slumped in a dark doorway. The elevator, a death trap if ever there was one, is hanging as usual from a single rusty wire, like an old street lamp that has seen too many winters.

Christian disappears into the filth of the building. Anton starts the car and we drive off.

He takes a different route to the one that I'm familiar with. I don't know where we are. After a while, rather abruptly, Anton turns to me and says that he has to check the tyres - the warning light says that something is wrong.

He gets out of the car out and I'm sitting there alone, by myself. Then, I hear him talking to someone and now there is a group of men around him; men who have suddenly appeared on the street from nowhere. Maybe it's the police who want to check our papers, or maybe they just want money there and then, on the spot, for no particular reason. The police are just as hungry as all the other poor people in this country. Not everyone in Russia is a billionaire.

'Please step out of the car,' I hear someone say.

'Anton, what's going on?'

Anton gets back into the car again, looks straight ahead, and says nothing.

'Please get out of the car,' I hear again in bad English.

Something feels dangerously wrong. Anton is clearly scared. He doesn't answer my questions and refuses to look me in the eye. I get out of the car as requested.

I'm frightened but I know that I mustn't show any fear. That will only make things even worse.

At that moment, I feel that Russia and St. Petersburg are remote places, totally empty and devoid of people, far away from everything, and I'm terrified. I'm on my own now. Nobody will come to my defence. I'm in the hands of these men, whoever they are.

The questions come thick and fast.

'Your papers, please! What's the purpose of your stay here? How often do you come to St. Petersburg? Who do you work for? Do you pay tax in St. Petersburg? Do you know that prostitution is illegal in Russia? We've been shadowing you since you left the nightclub. You're well known there, and you're a good friend of Christian Silver. What is your relationship with him? We know you're familiar with his black deals and the business he's involved with!'

'Fucking capitalists,' someone snarls. The man is dressed in a filthy uniform from the 60's. Some sort of grey-black thing that wasn't even nice when it was new. There's nothing on the jacket, no badge or decoration that can identify who he works for. He is probably a Russian nationalist who hates Westerners. His head is shaped like an American football, he has pig eyes and he weighs at least 120 kilos.

'You come here and fuck our daughters. Then you take all our raw materials out of the country really cheaply, process them in the west and keep all the profits for yourselves.'

He pushes me hard and I fall backwards, down onto the snow. He lifts me up and hits me straight between the eyes with his clenched fist. I feel my nose break, blood spurting across my face and I fall back down onto the snow.

'I don't know what you are talking about,' I shout lying in the snow. 'I don't know what you want. Anton, tell them who we are for god's sake. Explain to them!'

I'm lying with my head down on the road. The men are standing around me. They start to come closer. I spit it out a loose tooth and then I wet myself. I get very cold very quickly, and there's not a car on the street or a soul in sight at this time in the small hours.

I wonder if Anton chose the route himself or if he received orders from someone else?

'A courier will come to The Firm tomorrow carrying a large amount of cash. Tell the clerk to accept it and count it without question and then pay it into the designated account. You are working for us now, you understand; helping Russia to rise up and be great again. Is that absolutely clear?'

I'm still on my stomach in the snow and I say nothing. A few seconds pass. 'Is that absolutely clear?' he yells in my ear and I answer him 'yes'. The two men tower over me, before one of them pulls me up onto my feet, ties my hands together and laughs.

'We'll teach you a fucking lesson, you rat,' he snarls and then he spits in my face.

The man binds my hands together and then ties me to the tow bar on our car. Then he takes a step towards Anton and produces a revolver and holds it against Anton's head.

'Drive forward slowly,' he orders, 'at walking speed.'

Anton starts the engine and begins to drive forward, slowly. I can't believe what is happening. They are going to kill me. The rope almost brings me down as it tightens with a jerk and I start to walk behind the car. The Russians behind me laugh again.

'Anton, stop,' I scream, 'For god's sake STOP!'

The Russians laugh again and tell Anton to pick up speed, and now, I'm starting to run - faster all the time. I'm afraid of falling and I'm terrified.

The car goes even faster and I'm running as fast as I can. They tell Anton to go even faster, and that's it! I lose my balance, crash onto the ground and get dragged along on my stomach in the snow. I scream out as pain shoots through my body, but no one hears; no one comes to my rescue. In any case, no one would ever dare to do anything even if they saw what was going on. They know what it's all about.

By now, my face is covered in blood and I can't see anything.

'Anton, Anton, stop for fuck's sake! You're killing me!'

But the car just goes faster and faster, now around a corner. I'm being thrown around from side to side, my head hits a kerb stone and I'm bouncing and spinning all over the road. I lose my coat and jacket and my shoes are dragged off. I feel my arms being pulled from their sockets and my hands and wrists are in shreds. I cry out in agony, a long desperate shriek of unbelievable pain.

Then everything goes black.

***

The next time I open my eyes, I realise that I am in the American hospital in St. Petersburg. My body is covered in bruises and my head is heavily bandaged. My body aches all over and it is painful to make even the slightest movement. Someone knocks on my door and in comes my secretary, Miss Top, wearing an almost indecently short skirt because she wants to please me. She always wants to please me.

'Rave, here's your new passport, your new credit card and your new Russian phone. And now that you appear to be on the mend, I hope we can get together very soon,' she says suggestively.

■■■

I ignore her invitation. If she ever finds out about Sophya, she'll tear my eyes out.

'Nothing,' I say, looking at Miss Top, 'but nothing of this must come ever out. No one at The Firm must get to know about this. Not least, those bastards in Stockholm. We can't have their useless security guys running around here interfering with our entire organisation. They'd bring in an entirely different kind of team given half the chance!'

'Also, tell Mr. Flogel to come and see me - in person, as soon as possible!'

Miss Top, now sitting on the bed, looks at me with her sad, questioning eyes, hoping that I will suggest something romantic with her but I gave her a cold look so she turns her head away.

'Please go now. And be sure to do exactly what I have asked you to do.'

I roll over in the bed and bury my head in the pillow. I can feel a headache coming on. My head is wrapped in bandages and maybe talking to Miss Top today has been too much for me. I feel exhausted.

I pick up my new phone and check the date. It's January 3rd. I'd been here for a week without knowing it. I lie there thinking about what to do with Anton when I get my hands on him. A few evil ideas come immediately to mind.

***

The following morning, Flogel, my lawyer from the

law firm Ram & Stache in Moscow, visits me in my hospital room, wanting to know exactly what has happened to me and why.

Flogel has lived and worked in Russia for over 20 years. During this time, he has flown back and forth to Sweden regularly to see his children grow up during their school years. But nobody really knows who Flogel is —or what drives him?

No scandals or gossip have ever leaked out among the small Swedish colony living in St. Petersburg where everyone otherwise knows each other very well. However, no one really believes that he is as white as he seems. Professionally, he is knowledgeable, honest, helpful and always accessible. The perfect support for a Swedish businessman in Russia.

'Rave, absolutely dreadful what happened. But I don't suppose you want to report anything to the police, do you?'

'No, certainly not. It was probably the police who did it, or people working for the police. None of this can be allowed to come out, you understand. And under no circumstances can the security department in Sweden get a whiff of this. Listen. Those guys who nearly killed me, told me to take their money, deposit it into an account and push it into the banking system. That's what it's all about, Flogel. So, can you find out what we have to do next

– how we are going to deal with the situation? And then – another thing. We have to find my driver Anton. Find out if he is involved or not, and how much he was paid. Then, if necessary, we'll deal with him the Russian way.'

'Okay, Rave. I'll put my men onto this and find out who's behind it. And depending on what we discover, we can decide on how to proceed. If it's who I think it is, then we have to do what they want. We'll stake out Anton's home. Sooner or later, he'll show up. Then we'll squeeze him dry and find out what he knows. I'll be in touch.'

Flogel looks at me with a strained expression, gets up and leaves the room, and once again I am on my own. This time in a sterile hospital bed.

Chapter 2

I AM RAVE

I am Rave. Rave Alexander. The Swedish son of immigrant parents. According to some, a somewhat self-centred man, more focused on myself than concerned about others. Of course, that's not true. I come from a background where people learned at a very early age that in order to succeed, to get what you wanted, to enjoy the good things in life, then you needed very sharp elbows. Nothing and no-one could stand in your way. Nobody was ever safe - they were all replaceable. Expendable. Out with the old and in with the new. Success in life meant a new house, a new car, and a new wife. New and exciting, all in the blink of an eye. Everyone wanted to make the social journey up the ladder to a better life. And it was driven by money; money they believed would make them happy.

My parents were born in Moldavia to Hungarian/German parents. They had no education at all and came to Sweden during the war where they worked as circus performers and helped out with the animals. The three of us travelled the length and breadth of Sweden together. Life on the road was tough and I got to see every dead-end place where nothing ever happened, apart from when the circus came to town.

My mother never felt at home living in a circus caravan and my father drooled his days away over the trapeze artist Vera. Vera had a muscular body, was short, extremely strong and agile, and when performing, she always wore a beautiful, sparkling leotard costume. The costume was secured with hooks down the back and Vera often let me stand on a stool and help her hook up and unhook her costume. She wasn't in the least shy about showing off her body.

I must have been about 5 years old and it took me all my strength to get the hooks into place on her back. I remember the feeling I had when I touched her skin. Her dark hair was always gathered in a bun when she performed but there were always a few strands which hung down at the sides and I used to touch them gently and play with them when I stood on the stool. Vera smelled a little of vanilla and I loved the smell of it. I still do.

Even then, as a young boy, I knew that I liked Vera a lot. She was the first love of my life and I have searched ever since in my adult life for someone who looked and felt like Vera, sometimes getting close but never quite finding her completely. There was always something missing.

One of my father's duties was to feed the lions. His arms were covered in scratches and bites from their teeth and claws. One day when I was six, he was attacked by a lion for no obvious reason at all, completely out of the blue, and he died in hospital later the same day. Imagine the impact that had on me. I was unable to understand the whys and wherefores but I knew that my father was no longer with us.

They said he died of wormwood poisoning. His ever-present mistress Vera comforted him until the end. Later, it transpired that a mountain ranger from the city of Östersund, had fed the lion with contaminated, poisonous meat. The meat didn't kill the lion but the poison was transferred to my father with fatal outcome when he was bitten on the arm while giving them their food.

We tried many times to find the ranger, who it transpired was both a kind of animal rights activist and a hunter of elks and deer. So, on the one hand, he strongly objected to wild animals being caged up all their lives and forced to perform in circuses and, on the other hand, he was a lover of the great outdoors and all the pursuits including hunting game which went with the lifestyle. His efforts to kill the lion were intended to show how cruel circuses were in the way they treated their animals.

After my father's death, his phone stayed disconnected and he was never at his office in Östersund, but it seemed he spent days hiking in the Swedish mountains or flying out in a police helicopter with the local police officers to remote lakes in order to fish in peace and quiet – all during working hours. The police did nothing because he was their friend and they thought that the worthless scum at the circus should all go back home to Bulgaria, or 'wherever the fuck they came from!' They thought that the mountain ranger was a decent guy and a good fishing companion. No wonder they turned a blind eye.

Mother was neither interested in father nor the mountain ranger. She quickly understood that there was no money to be had by hunting down the mountain ranger. There was no money in father's will either she discovered, when his 'estate' was read out to the family. So, she left the circus, retrained as a nurse, and we both went to live in a boring small town in the middle of Sweden.

One cold day in February, for no particular reason at all, standing ankle-deep in wet snow in a cemetery on the outskirts of the town in which my father's ashes had finally been buried, I decided that when I died, I too would die in the arms of a strong, beautiful woman who had a slight touch of the scent of vanilla on her body. The idea filled me with inner warmth.

In Russia, many years later, I got the chance to hook up and unhook a ballerina's costume. Her name was Ekaterina. Her father was a Muslim and her mother was Jewish. She came from some isolated town far away in Siberia. She was dark-haired and her family was originally from a small state by the Black Sea. She was a well brought-up family girl but far too young for me in her mother's eyes. Both she and her costume carried the mild scent of vanilla.

My flirtation with Katja was short-lived and intense, but I still have some of photos and drawings of her tucked away, and my memories of her still remain.

***

Growing up in the small town, I spent all my time with my mother. She was now a nurse but worked as little as possible to be at home with me until I started school – like mothers usually did in those days. I used to help her with everything. I was good at stretching the bed sheets with her: that was my favourite chore. I loved being with my mother.

One day I was introduced to a little girl called Cass. Cass was the neighbour's daughter and probably about two years younger than me. The routine was always the same. In the morning, after breakfast, I decided what we would play. Mum called Cass's mum and told her what idea come up with. Then Cass came over, ready to play whatever I'd chosen.

One day I decided that we would play Indians. I was dressed like Sitting Bull and Cass was dressed as a squaw, in a yellow leather costume with yellow leather fringes. She looked really great in her costume. Another day, I decided that we would play football. I was the 'Swedish' goalkeeper and Cass looked like something between a cheerleader and a football player. She was the perfect playmate who happily joined in with whatever I wanted to do.

One day in August, when I was 7 years old, mum took me to school for the first time. It was a nightmare. Having to obey orders and follow the school rules, and meet all the other pupils. I couldn't decide anything for myself any more. Other boys would come up to me and tell me what we would play and what we were going to do. It wasn't good at all. In fact, I hated it. Things started to get tough and I realised that I was starting out on a life that was completely new to me.

I just wanted to go back to my safe life with my mother, where I could build my dreamworld and decide what to do. But that time was now over, gone forever, and I had to get on with my life towards adulthood.

As a young man, I always felt a bit left out. It wasn't easy for me to make new friends.

Later on, I was always out partying or getting up to mischief in the town with my friends. But I really didn't fit in all that well and I was a bit of an outsider even within the group. I was always a bit different. I can't remember trusting anyone, apart from my mother.

I don't know how it is to be young today, but I felt back then those who worked with children and youngsters weren't particularly interested in them, and in some cases enjoyed the power that being a teacher gave them. It was quite normal to hear a teacher insult a pupil in front of the whole class and to make derogatory remarks in public. No-one talked in those days about coaching or building self-confidence for those students who needed it or who had the potential to go on to higher education.

Never once, during my 12 years at school, did I hear or see a grown-up praise a student publicly for something that he or she had done. The kids that didn't have any support from their parents at home didn't stand a chance. They were probably actually talked out of applying for higher education.

School wasn't particularly hard but it was a cold, sterile place in which to be. But on Friday and Saturday nights it was a different story, and there it was the strongest who made it and the others who went under. I saw a spotty guy wearing glasses, standing in the queue at the hot dog kiosk on a Friday night get beaten up for absolutely no reason at all. And I was chased and beaten on more than one occasion, by bigger, stronger boys on the way home from school.

One night, I remember, a gang of louts took over another local hot dog kiosk. They went behind the counter, and caused havoc. They threw sausages and everything they could lay their hands on at each other and onto the floor. They threw bar stools through the windows and absolutely wrecked the place. The staff in the bar retreated into the backroom and waited for the police to arrive which they did after half an hour had elapsed.

The place looked like a battlefield. Walking through the town at the weekend, late at night, was not to be recommended in those days. Yet we did, now and then. One Friday night, on my way home in the early hours of the morning, I was walking across the football pitch, beside which were some apartments for 'young, single men' that were basically one room flats - among others, guest workers from Finland who worked in the steelworks for varying periods of time lived there.

I saw my friend Diamond Jim coming towards me, so we stopped and started chatting in the dark.

'Let's sneak up on the Finns and steal their booze,' he suggested. 'They're probably so drunk now that they won't notice anything.'

'Yeah. Good idea. Why not!' I answered, so we turned and started to sneak closer to the apartment building.

We could hear a faint murmur from guys speaking Finnish as we got closer. The sun was beginning to rise by now and they'd probably been drinking all night and were tired. We opened a side door, and looked down a long corridor with lot of doors off to the left and right. Jim smiled at me as his face brightened up. He loved doing things like this even then, and the time he spent at a youth correction centre later in life did nothing to deter him from continuing in the same vein.

Without making a noise, we gently tried the first door. It was unlocked and opened without a sound. Diamond Jim nodded and I was into the room and out again in the corridor in a flash with a bottle of Finnish Koskenkorva in my hand.

'No, no, no, Rave. Don't be such a coward! Go back and take everything you can find,' Jim whispered. It sounded like an order.

I went back into the room again and started looking around for a second time.

Suddenly I heard a man shouting at Diamond Jim.

'Oj, you, what do you doing?'

With the bottle of vodka in his hand, Jim started running down the corridor with the man close behind him.

'Stop, you fucking Swede! Come back with our vodka you bastard!'

I was pretty frightened. I opened the window and climbed out only to see Jim running across the football field with a herd of furious Finns after him, screaming and shouting in Finnish. Faces began to appear at the windows in the neighbouring houses, and someone must have called the police because they arrived on the scene within seconds. They must have been patrolling in the area. It was none less than police chief Arnhof himself who got out of his Volvo Amazon to take command of the situation. He started by telling the local residents to 'shut up and go to bed'. Then Jim reappeared, running flat out across the football field once more, with the horde of furious, intoxicated Finns in hot pursuit, running down the hill and straight towards the Volvo Amazon. They were like a pack of hounds chasing a fox.

Arnhof evaluated the situation in a split second and decided to beat a hasty retreat back into the police car, an operation which he completed successfully within seconds. Having locked the car, he called for reinforcements on the police radio.

'Radio car 2, radio car 2, I am in Lammeboda. Send three more cars immediately. People here are rioting!'

I made my way home through a small wooded area, climbed over the back fence and entered the house through the back door. My mother was asleep.

A couple of days later, I met Diamond Jim in the local playground where he could usually be found selling cannabis to the other kids.

'What happened to you last night?' I asked him.

'It was fun. I drank with the Finns all night. You missed something.'

***

Diamond Jim always told a good story, but I knew that he'd been driven home in a police car to keep him from being beaten up. I smiled to myself. We both sat on a swing and said nothing. Then a couple of classmates from school turned up. Renée and Ingela. They lived in the area and we knew each other well. Renée lived right next to the playground and you could see her house from where we were sitting.

As a 12-year-old you sometimes think and react to good looking girls like an older teenager. As I watched Renée on the swing, she went higher and higher. Her short skirt fluttered and lifted all the way when she swung forward. She was wearing yellow panties. I moved a little closer, but not too close. I didn't want to get her feet in my face, but I stood in front of her. She laughed as she swung forward and nearly touched me with her feet. As she reached the top of the swing, I took a step forward and went underneath her skirt and grasped her yellow panties which slipped down her legs and came off completely as she swung backwards.

What a beautiful sight it was for a boy of 12. I held her yellow panties in the air almost like a trophy feeling very pleased with myself.

'What the hell do you think you're doing, you nasty little creep?' It was Renée's mother who had seen everything from her garden patio.

'This, you old tart!' I said, still waving Renée's panties in the air like a flag.

I threw the panties back to Renée and she ran home to her mother who was standing on the patio still shouting at me. Renee turned and gave me a little wave before her mother took her inside the house where she stayed for the rest of the day.

Thinking back now, it strikes me that many of the men and women from this small Swedish backwater of a town didn't live beyond the age of 30 or 40, with alcohol and drugs often ending their lives prematurely.

And actually, growing up in the small town was tough. So, I decided to be tough too; as tough as the rest, if not tougher. I made friends with boys who were lower down the pecking order than I was and they looked up to me. Sometimes they were new arrivals in Sweden. One boy had Austrian parents and couldn't speak any Swedish, had no status, no money and no contacts. So, I took him under my wing and he became a loyal follower.

On a warm June night, at 2 in the morning, I left the town's hotel where our school's graduation party had just come to an end and saw Renée standing by the door in the main entrance, smiling in my direction. Her skirt was very short and she was giving me the come, but I didn't stop. I had decided to leave the town and all the people who lived there.

I had no contacts and no money. What I had, however, at my early age, was an understanding of how ordinary people thought and behaved. How people were steered by their own vanity and that this could be used to exploit them in order to get what you wanted. The hard life on the road had given me insights into how people functioned.

It was only after living in Stockholm for a while that I realized that Stockholm was in fact a reasonably safe place in which to live. When we went out at the weekend, the trouble-makers in Stockholm didn't have the same power as the gang leaders did back in my small home town; not on the streets nor in the discos. I loved living in my new city.

Chapter 3

I AM SOPHYA

In my world, a man who takes risks is a beautiful man. A man who plays for high stakes is a man with the financial wherewithal to take care of me and my offspring and give us a luxury lifestyle, if he survives – unlike a man with more 'normal' ambitions. He may be fat, ugly, unpleasant and totally lacking in scruples but, at the end of the day, he's the one who comes home with the meat.

I am classical Moscow-Russian beauty with all the attributes that go with the part. My parents are the epitome of Russian architypes. My father was a high-ranking military officer and my mother was a proud and highly respected housewife. Old school, loyal traditionalists. We are not very impressed by the 'new' Russia and the tensions between Russia and the rest of the world. We are Muscovites and Soviets.

When the Soviet Union fell and Latvia was talked about, my father said, 'You never ever give back a country!'

This attitude is shared by many in Russia, both

young and old. People are divided over many different issues, but, when it comes to foreign policy, they are completely united in their support of their country.

As a child in Moscow, I learned languages, danced ballet and played the piano like most other girls of my age and background. My parents kept a very close eye on me at all times, especially during my early and mid-teens, and made sure that I didn't bring any Western decadence into the family.

In Russia, a daughter traditionally lives at home until she finds a boy who can be accepted by her parents, after which the wedding takes place in a church and then the young couple move together.

In reality, women 'come of age' at 18, get married at 19, become pregnant at 20 and divorced at 21. Sadly, the whole country is swimming in single mothers who are 19 years older than their only child. These beautiful, young women fill page after page with photos and biographies of themselves on dating sites in search of a new man. Unfortunately, they hardly ever manage to find one and, if they do, they can't always hang on to them.

But not me. I'm different. I'm married to a Russian diplomat called Juri Sachenov who is 2 years older than me. We met during my time as a student. I was studying languages in Moscow and 'living the life' at university after the constraints of home life. Ballet and piano were replaced by amateur dramatics and listening to modern western 'rock'. I made so many friends both female and male in my free time that there was never a dull moment. I really enjoyed acting and playing a role on stage. It was really liberating to play someone else and to distance myself from my own feelings in order to be convincing in the part.

Naturally the world of drama and theatre was sexually liberated as well, and my innocence disappeared very quickly. We became even wilder over time as we lost all our sexual inhibitions with each other. The parties were usually vodka-driven and the combinations of male/female, male/male/female/female, one on one, one on two, two on three were constantly changing. You name it – we did it! I soon discovered my preference which, traditionally enough, was one on one, male/female.

Every male I slept with was the result of careful selection. No aimless drifters or penniless paupers for me. I wanted men with the lust for sex games in bed but also with an iron will to succeed in life. Men who were not afraid to take risks. It was a great learning experience which would stand me in good stead later in life.

One day, after rehearsals, I was approached by a smartly-dressed woman with long black hair in a pony-tail who wondered if I had time for a quick chat, so we went to the cafeteria and ordered something to drink. Tea, as always. She introduced herself as a talent-spotter for students who were ready, willing and able to serve Russia in unconventional ways. She'd clearly done her homework and knew everything there was to know about my family, my upbringing and my life as a student.

Of course, as the daughter of a military officer, I was immediately interested in her proposal which involved taking a year off my language studies and attending a training school just outside Moscow to learn the trade of 'serving the state'. My ability to take on theatrical roles and to 'play the field' in bed had been noted and I was 'perfect' she said for the work.

So, I said 'yes' and went away to train as 'a resource' for the state; someone who would do as they were instructed when the time came, with no regard for their own feelings, for the good of Mother Russia. I completed the training with the best grades and flying colours; top of the class! - particularly when it came to the female art of seducing a man, and pulling the right triggers to take him to paradise. Tall, short, fat or thin, young or old, attractive or not, they could all be played to order. And I was a natural.

I then resumed my studies, and student life continued as before. Lectures, studies, parties and concerts – with my eyes always open for a good-looking man with all the right qualifications.

Following the long, dark winter, spring finally arrived and, as we did every year, we made plans for a week's break in Yalta down on the Black Sea.

Yalta was buzzing at this time of the year with students and holiday-makers from all over Russia. There was always so much to do in addition to the daily walks up and down the seafront Lenin Embankment where people would gather and talk; to see and be seen. The climate was just wonderful, and Yalta was fascinating as the place which had attracted the Russian aristocracy and gentry in the 19th century.

During the spring break, Yalta also attracted young naval officers who were serving with the Russian navy and based in Odessa. Their leave was arranged to coincide with the spring break and it was an opportunity for them also to see and be seen, in their splendid naval uniforms. The prospect of meeting an attractive female student to seduce was as exciting for them as it was for us to contemplate falling into bed with a young officer in uniform.

On the third day, we decided to make a morning visit to the White Dacha. The residence and gardens were built by Anton Chekhov who lived there until 1902 and it was there he wrote a number of plays like The Three Sisters – all very interesting if you're interested in the theatre.

Having had our 'fix' of culture, it was then time for the Lenin Embankment and time to show ourselves off on the 'cat-walk'. Occasionally in life, but not frequently, things fall into place and this time it was my turn to get lucky. After strolling with the girls for a while, I broke away to buy myself an ice-cream and joined the queue. After a few seconds I could 'feel' the presence of someone close behind me and, looking round, I saw a good-looking young man in full naval uniform who removed his hat, bowed his head slightly and wished me a very good afternoon. I faced the front again, blushing madly, thinking to myself 'Wow! Where did he come from?'

When I had ordered my ice-cream and it was time to pay, the man stepped up beside me and said, 'My name is Juri Sachenov and I would very much like to buy you your ice-cream, if I may?' I was rather surprised by his unexpected offer over a mere ice-cream but managed to say 'Well yes, thank you very much!'

He then ordered an ice-cream for himself and the two of us strolled along the promenade, away from the others, in the sunshine, past the white facades and palm trees, enjoying our ice-creams and chatting about who we were and what we were doing in Yalta.

Juri, it turned out, was a Muscovite like me and was planning to study at the Diplomatic Academy of the Russian Foreign Ministry in Moscow when he had completed his military service. His dream was to become a diplomat and get rich like his father and to see the world. Really, I thought! How very interesting!! A man with some real plans and ambition. This could be what I've been looking for – a ticket to a better life outside Russia! One day he told me a story from the time when his parents were living and working as diplomats in London soon after the end of the Second World War. It seems that when Juri was 9, his parents were hosting a reception at the embassy. Lots of guests were invited to the gala dinner, as was the fashion in those days. At some point in the early evening, Juri was sent downstairs to the basement to fetch more champagne. As he opened the cellar door, he saw the body of a fat Russian general, General Gogol, hanging from the ceiling with a rope around his neck and an orange forced into his mouth.

His beautiful English wife, Countess Beaton was carefully lowering the dead body to the floor so as not to make any noise. After first staring in disbelief, Juri turned on his heels and ran back upstairs to join the assembled company as quickly as possible. As he hid his head in his mother's skirt, she hugged him and said, "Why are you running so fast Juri? You look as if you've seen a ghost!" to which the guests all smiled sympathetically.

The images, he said, still troubled him in nightmares, and he'd never found out why the General was strung up in the cellar.

I told Juri about my life as a student in Moscow, and my plans and hopes for the future. He nodded and smiled in the sunshine, and I could see that he was enjoying my company and also that he was feasting his eyes on my breasts which were well displayed in the warm weather. I made no effort to cover them up but moved closer, making myself more available to him.

'I hope you are able to join me tomorrow Sophya? There are some interesting places in Yalta I would like to show you, if you have the time to come along?'

'Why not, Juri? Tomorrow is a free day so I'd be delighted to join you.'

***

The following morning, we met again as planned on the promenade and made the journey up to the Saint Hripsime church which sits high up on an outcrop of rock overlooking the Black Sea. The views were wonderfully spectacular and totally unforgettable, and we strolled and talked in the sunshine, sometimes hand in hand, sometimes not.

After lunch, Juri suggested taking the cable car to the Darsan Hill to get another panorama over Yalta. The car was built for two and was rather cramped, and we laughed as we scrambled aboard and tried to lock the door. The ride to the top was once again spectacular and we sat in the warm sun, his arm across my shoulder and talked more about our plans for the future.

On the way back down, I couldn't stop myself. 'Juri,' I said, 'what a lovely day we're having. You make me feel so alive.'

I quietly put my arms around his neck and his arms embraced me as we had our first kiss together – short and gentle at first, then longer with more passion and only ended as we neared the end of the ride.

After we'd stepped out of the cable car, he told me that he and his fellow officers were staying at the Villa Elene Hotel in Yalta and that a spring ball would be held there on Friday.

'Perhaps you would like to be my guest at the ball,' he said, and I said 'yes', straight away, without having to think for a second. I knew a little about the history of Yalta's best hotel and I would have been mad to turn down Juri's invitation to see it, given that he was clearly interested in me and I was enjoying the attentions of this stylish man in uniform.

I told him where I was staying with the other students, and he said he'd send a car to pick me up at 6.00 pm on Friday.

My girlfriends helped my find some new clothes and shoes for the ball and, when Friday came, I felt a little like Cinderella, and ready to meet Juri again in the most magnificent hotel in Yalta. Juri arrived in a taxi at 6 o'clock precisely and we drove to the hotel sitting in the back seat, holding hands, and talking excitedly about the evening's activities.

Upon arrival, the naval officers in all their finery and their invited guests all looking so lady-like and refined mingled together in the magnificent reception hall, sipping the chilled champagne which was readily available before proceeding into the main state dining room for the next event of the evening. Once seated they were served an exquisite 5-course meal which was interspersed with speeches and toasts, followed by more speeches and more toasts, after which a male-voice choir from the naval base in Odessa came onto the stage and gave a rousing performance of traditional Russian patriotic songs which were received with huge applause and standing ovations. Juri and I sat opposite each other, but we spent almost as much time looking at each other as we did watching the performance.

It was then time to adjourn into the ballroom where a naval orchestra was waiting to play for the assembled company. Juri escorted me in and we sat down with some of his fellow officers and their guests and ordered more drinks. The noise levels rose as everyone spoke over the sound of the orchestra and the sound of bursts of laughter could be heard from tables around the room as the officers recounted stories of recent mishaps and embarrassing moments at sea. I was more and more taken by Juri as the night progressed and when we took to the dance floor, he held me very close and told me how beautiful I looked and that he was the happiest man in the room with me by his side.

As the ball drew to a close, Juri leaned towards me and suggested that we go outside to admire the view. Standing on the balcony overlooking the Black Sea on that beautiful warm evening, I could feel the power of the attraction between us growing. We were drawn together into an embrace and a kiss which lasted for several minutes. His arms were around me, on my shoulders, around my waist, on my breasts, constantly exploring.

My arms too were constantly moving, up and down,

exploring Juri's body beneath his uniform. When I touched him below his waist, I could feel from the firmness of his shaft that he was much aroused and ready for me.

We made our way to his room without speaking, both knowing what was shortly going to happen. The balcony doors in his room were open, allowing the warm night breeze to move the lace curtains. Beyond that, there was nothing but the sea and the sound of the waves breaking gently on the beach.

Within seconds we were both lying naked on the bed, kissing and touching one another. When Juri entered me, it was a gentle action, slow to start with but then picking up the rhythm as we both moved together as one. Juri was so affectionate in his passion, I understood that this was very special for him. Even at my younger age, I had much more experience of bringing men on than he had of satisfying women – my student days and the special training I had gone through to serve my country were the big difference – but Juri's feelings, I knew, were for real

When morning came, we joined the other officers for breakfast on the balcony and made small talk of no real

Chapter 5

THE MEETING THAT CHANGED MY LIFE

I hated it. I hated the company I worked for and every little corner of the corporate empire with its culture of clandestine social networks, gossip and rumours regarding conspiracies and nepotism. I hated all the ass-licking cocksuckers who fawned around to ingratiate themselves with the CEO, with no self-respect or sense of how they were demeaning themselves.

The Firm made me want to vomit. It was a company operated by people with all the right skills and social status, who crawled over one another, like freshly caught crayfish in a bathtub, trying to get to the top of the pile. Every morning was spent in the company of Gauk as he held his master-class in the art of pure humiliation. He put the hangers-on through an infinite number of routines designed purely to see how low they were prepared to grovel. It was his revenge for all the times he was the last boy left to be picked for the football team back in his school days.

The meeting began with the gathering of the worshippers in Gauk's office which was cluttered with an endless number of glossy car magazines. Usually over half of those in attendance had absolutely no need to be there at all. They just wanted to see and be seen. Be visibly a member of the inner circle. Some of them actually arrived in the early hours of the morning and waited outside Gauk's office like temple dogs, to ensure a good place in which to position themselves and do Gauk's bidding.

While they waited nervously for their master to make his entry, Gauk sat reading his precious car magazines in his private men's room. Not only because he wanted everybody to wait half an hour longer as a demonstration of his power, but also because expensive cars and expensive magazines were two of his passions in life.

On this particular Monday morning, everyone was there in Gauk's office. Chimney, Mushroom, Ash, Garbage and Poisonous Spider all pushed forward to get closer to the chair in which Gauk always sat. They congratulated themselves on the deals they'd closed or the meetings they had set up for future business, and would try to outdo each other with stories about the trips and meetings they'd made with Gauk to show how close they were to the great man himself. Little Poisonous Spider always tried to get additional airtime by telling the story about his family and how they helped to build the town they came from, how they donated money for a new library 'which, by the way, bears their name, and which was inaugurated by none other than the Prime Minister's wife.' He recounted the same story every time and no-one ever listened, but still he kept on telling his story and to show what fine citizens he and his family were.

Chimney knew that he was a nobody. He got his nickname because a chimney is all smoke and no fire. The fire always had to come from somewhere else. If anyone had evaluated his true worth to The Firm, he'd have been gone a long time ago. His best weapon was his CV which showed that he had been a dependable ass-licker under a number of different CEOs.

Mushroom was short and slightly overweight, and a little green in the face. He was an outsider with a good heart, although he drank too much too often, and never or rarely took any form of physical activity. He had great empathy for other people however, and created good relationships both inside and outside The Firm with colleagues and clients alike. The problem was that he seemed to attract the shaky deals to himself like a magnet, and although his deals always looked good when they were signed, they soon turned sour and become a problem, eventually often turning into major financial losses. This gave the Risk Assessment Manager the enjoyable opportunity of gloating over the loss and telling everyone how stupid they all were. He always knew best – particularly with the benefit of hindsight.

We were now 25 minutes over the announced time and there was still no sight of Gauk. The magazine had an interesting article about a new Jaguar and its new CAT shock absorber system. Gauk just had to finish reading the article before making his entrance. And then, without warning, the office door opened and there he was.

An overpowering smell slowly but surely registered in everyone's nostrils which was reminiscent of a whore-house on a rainy day. Little Poisonous Spider had inadvertently poured on too much Paco Rabanne, purely out of nervousness, and was now polluting the air in Gauk's office. Gauk swayed across the floor and finally settled in his usual seat.

The atmosphere in the room changed instantly from being the survival of the fittest while they jostled for positions to a sort of dancing exhibition- a choreographed line dance. In a twist on musical chairs, the gathered company began to move slowly round in a circle in an effort to acquire the chair which was closet to Gauk. Everyone was on their feet. Chimney was first in line, and as a former ice-hockey player, he knew how to use his elbows in a crowd.

Gauk's second man was Ash. He was everybody's doormat. They all walked over him, especially Gauk himself because, theoretically at least, Ash could be Gauk's successor. Ash was tall and gangly with a handshake like a wet piece of toilet paper and a face like a pineapple. When he walked with his sad, shuffling steps, it looked as if the carpet was holding him back and he had to make an effort to lift his foot for the next step. He was employed solely to echo Gauk's statements. His success was down to the fact that he participated in all of Gauk's meetings whatever the purpose, and nodded his head in agreement when he saw that Gauk was in favour of something, and having licked a little more ass, he trudged away to the next meeting.

My dream, which I now wanted more than anything else, was to leave The Firm well and truly behind me; to get away and start again - somewhere else – with something completely different.

***

One day, a female acquaintance of mine who worked at the university told me about a Russian woman who wanted to improve her Swedish and was looking to be matched with a Swedish man who wanted to learn to speak Russian. I spoke a little Russian but I was quite interested in learning some more. I was very curious about who the lady was, so I decided to go ahead and a meeting was set up. Maybe, I thought, she was someone who could take me away from The Firm? Perhaps it was written in the stars? We can't always control our own destinies, can we?

Her name, I heard, was Sophya Sachenova and she was from Moscow. She had lived in Sweden for a couple of years with her husband Juri and their daughter Anna. It seems she worked quite a lot, nights too, and she wondered if we could meet and speak Russian and Swedish together, drink a little tea and maybe even dance as well.

We decided to meet in the bar of the Grand Hotel. I knew that first-class hotels always impressed Russians. They hungered for everything which glittered.

The meeting was set for the following Wednesday evening. It was cold and dark. A typical Swedish winter night. The streets were quiet with dirty snow ploughed up on the pavements. The waters of the Baltic in front of the Grand Hotel were frozen over and the sightseeing boats had been taken out of service until the following season.

I wore a dark business suit, a tie and black shoes and sat down at a table near the stairs and waited impatiently for the mysterious women I was going to meet to appear. My head was full of ideas about what the meeting might lead to. Did she really want to her improve her Swedish? Probably not! So why then had she contacted me?

And then, there she was. She walked slowly up the hotel staircase, like a cautious little vixen with her senses fully activated, wondering where to take the next step. She was tall and slim, with long slender legs. She had dark hair cut with a straight fringe, big, round, blue, innocent eyes and the stealth of a cat. She was wearing a slightly nervous-looking smile.

I waved her over to join me at my table and I could see that all the men in the bar, mainly fat, bored businessmen, were clearly envious of my company as she headed in my direction. I stood up, and greeted her politely as we shook hands rather formally. Her name, she said, was Sophya and she told me that she was the wife of a Russian diplomat. Then I ordered some drinks. Tea for her and a single malt whisky for me. The conversation was rather slow to begin with as we switched from Russian to Swedish. She told me about herself, her family and her situation in general. But within a matter of minutes, the ice was broken and the conversation flowed much more freely. Her husband, she said, didn't do anything very special in life other than work and didn't have any fantasy dreams for the future. It seemed to me, rightly or wrongly, that she was rather bored with life and maybe looking for new friends, for new adventures.

As the conversation went on to other lighter things, and without thinking about it, I found that I was falling for her and her female charms. She was one of the most beautiful, interesting people I had ever met. As she sat there in front of me, everything about her was wonderful. The way she spoke, the respect she showed me, the way she moved her hands and adjusted her skirt, how she touched her hair – even the way she drank her tea. I was captured by her - hook, line and sinker.

After two hours, which felt like 5 minutes, Sophya

sat back in her chair and smiled a smile which would have melted the iceberg which sank the Titanic.

'So, Mr Rave Alexander, shall we break up this delightful evening, much though it feels as if it has just begun? I hope that this will be the first of many occasions where we can meet and talk.'

'The feeling's mutual I assure you,' I replied, with a slight bow of the head.

When we stood outside the hotel a short time later, we both knew without mentioning it that we soon would meet again. I closed the door of the taxi and Sophya said 'Dobroynochi' and then disappeared into the night, leaving me standing there alone with my head spinning. I pulled up my collar against the cold, thrust my hands deep into my coat pockets, and slowly made my way home.

Next morning, as I walked through the office with a real spring in my step. Gauk bellowed something at me down the corridor– an insulting remark about my red tie, but I couldn't care less about Gauk. I walked quickly past the coffee machine and then into my office where I found a letter waiting for me, propped up on my desk. It was from Sophya. How on earth did this find its way here, I thought, as I opened the envelope and read the letter.

Dear Rave,

It was a pleasure to meet you last night. I am free this afternoon. If you have time, we can go for a walk in the Old Town?' Shall we say 3 o'clock at the German church in the Old Town?

Best regards,
Sophya

She must be from a different planet, I thought, if she imagined that I could drop everything and go for a walk in the middle of the day. She obviously had no idea what went on in a normal place of work. Nevertheless, I decided to meet her in the Old Town as she had suggested.

It was difficult to concentrate on anything while I waited for the time to pass but, eventually when it was approaching 3 o'clock, it was time to leave. I put my silver pen down on my desk, turned off my computer and left the office without informing anyone.

We met at the German church in the Old Town as Sophya had suggested in her short letter as the bells rang out three.

'I had a feeling that you'd have time to see me again today,' she said in her own blend of Russian and Swedish. 'You know how to prioritise your day!'

She wore a smart winter coat and some high-heeled knee boots. Sensible clothes for the snow. We walked around the German church chatting about this and that. The time flew by without us noticing. 'Five o'clock,' she said. 'Time for me to make my way home'- and after a rather formal handshake, she set off for the nearest subway station. I still didn't know what she really wanted. Perhaps she wanted to get me firmly on her hook first of all, which was something I definitely wanted to happen.

Chapter 6

A TRIP TO ST. PETERSBURG

Fast forward six months and it appeared that my prayers been answered. Not only had I become the good friend of a fantastically attractive Russian woman, but I had also been given the chance to a new start in my professional life. A new job, but in St. Petersburg, yet still working for The Firm; running the recently-opened office there to build up and develop our international business. Gauk of all people had invited me to a long lunch in one of Stockholm's most exclusive fish restaurants during which he outlined his plans for me to lead the business in Russia.

The Firm would make handsome profits, I would earn a small fortune, and it would look very good on my CV. He was convinced that I was 'the right man for the job' and he made me an offer that was almost too good to be true. He refused to take 'no' for an answer - which was no problem for me since this was the exit ticket I had been hoping for to get me out of the poisoned atmosphere of the Stockholm head office.

So here I was, at Arlanda airport, waiting to board

the plane for yet another routine flight back to St. Petersburg. It was the fourth time I'd made the trip in three months. I was still with The Firm but out of the immediate clutches of Gauk and his miserable minions, which was certainly a big step in the right direction.

I spent many waking hours thinking about Sophya, her husband and her daughter Anna. What was she thinking of doing with the rest of her life? How settled was she in her marriage and how much did Anna mean to her? Not least, what were her feelings towards me? We'd met a few times but all we had done so far was make small talk despite the feelings we aroused in one another.

A few weeks earlier, I had invited Sophya to join me on her own in St. Petersburg to see a performance at the Mariinsky theatre and she had accepted. I was overjoyed. I booked her flight tickets and reserved a room for her in the same hotel that I was staying in.

After picking her up in the company car at the airport and we drove to the hotel where she checked in and freshened up before getting changed for the evening's event. She said it felt strange to stay in a hotel in Russia – in St. Petersburg. Russians usually stay with friends.

We were going to see the ballet 'Giselle' at the Mariinsky, the greatest of all romantic ballets. Sophya looked radiant in her beautiful blue gown, while I work a smart dark suit.

'Rave, I love dressing elegantly when I go to the Mariinsky theatre,' she said as she admired herself in front of the mirror.

'You look really fantastic tonight,' I said enjoying her feminine shapes from top to toe.

'I've seen Giselle many times,' she continued, 'it's my favourite ballet, the one I love the most.'

'And I'm looking forward to seeing the Mariinsky theatre with you, Sophya.'

When our driver dropped us off, the sight of the theatre was truly impressive, illuminated as it was in green light. Quite majestic.

'What can you tell me about the theatre,' I asked as we made our way up the steps.

Sophya told me that it was built at the behest of Catherine the Great, and opened in 1783. The current conductor, Valerij Gergijev, she said, had very good relations with the Russian president,

Vladimir Putin. Gergijev had received substantial funding from the state to raise the quality of the orchestra's musicians and, she added in a derogatory tone, as a result, many of the musicians were now over-paid and complacent and were not working hard enough to retain their places in the orchestra.

'They played better before, in the time of the Soviet Union, when musicians starved. But in spite of everything, this is still seen by many as being the leading symphony orchestra in Russia.'

'Stalin decided to call the Mariinsky theatre the Kirov Ballet, after Sergej Kirov,' she added, 'but after the collapse of the Soviet Union, the theatre was renamed the Mariinsky theatre in 1992.'

After our tickets had been checked, we moved into the main auditorium to take our seats. I sat there in utter amazement looking around in sheer delight at the sight before my eyes, coming back constantly to the magnificence of the Tsar's box, with its elegant glue drapes and topped by the enormous Tsar's crown. What a masterpiece. It was fantastic to see how much work and dedication had been invested into creating this iconic building and its wonderfully decorated interiors in bygone days.

'I'm so pleased that we're here Rave, in this magnificent theatre. I don't like the new theatre at all. You know, the new one was built with bribes – 8.5 billion roubles in bribes. Money which could have been used to for other things,' she went on, now with frowns across her forehead.

And then, suddenly cheering, up she asked, 'Did you know that the premiere of Giselle took place in June 1841 in Paris?'

'No, I didn't know that.'

'Do you know the story of Giselle?' she asked.

'No, not really,' I answered feeling slightly embarrassed by my lack of knowledge.

'OK, well let me tell you. Giselle is a beautiful, young, peasant girl who falls in love with the deceitful and disguised nobleman Albrecht, who actually falls in love with Giselle despite being betrothed to Princess Bathilde. When Giselle discovers the truth, she dies of a broken heart.'

We sat spell-bound by the music and the dancers, and were completely absorbed by the ballet until the rapturous applause which marked the end of the first act, and we filed out with most of the audience into the adjoining glittering hall for some light refreshments. We sipped our chilled glasses of Shampanskoe, the Russian version of champagne, from Georgia, produced at a tenth of the cost of champagne in the West. Very drinkable in spite of its slight sweetness.

'Look around you, Rave and see how the fine people are dressed. Lovely clothes, fine shoes, elegant dresses and smart ties. This is what I love about the Russian theatre and the ballet. People dress up to see a work of art. It honours and shows respect to the composer who has written the ballet, it honours the dancers and the musicians who spend a lifetime of hours practising the steps they dance and the music they play. That's what I call style,' said Sophie rather proudly.

'Yes, you're right,' I answered. 'In the West people dress down when they go to the theatre. It's as if they don't care about the work that has gone into the performance. They don't really care about art.'

'But this is a good Shampanskoe,' I said raising my glass in a toast to lighten up the conversation.

We joked a little and finished our drinks as the bell ran to announce that the second act was about to start. After the final curtain, with standing ovations and thunderous applause, we left the theatre hand in hand feeling the afterglow of the ballet, and strolled along the footpath beside the Krykov canal. It was a wonderful evening and rather warm to be St. Petersburg.

We paused to admire the blue and white St. Nicholas Naval Cathedral.

'It was built between 1752 and 1762 and can hold several thousand visitors,' Sophya told me.

'I can see why they built the cathedral here,' I replied. 'It has a fantastic view over the Krykov canal and it's not far from Nevskyprospekt.'

'I really enjoyed the ballet with you Rave. It's so wonderful to be here with you in St. Petersburg. Thank you so much for inviting me. You're very kind.'

'Well, I'm just happy that you were able to make the trip. It makes me happy too!'

'And not only are you smart, intelligent and generous – you're also interested in culture. Isn't that amazing. We share the same interests - in theatre, opera, ballet, music, art, sculpture and architecture. Just think about cities like Vienna and Prague. They're wonderful cities of culture. I'd love to go there. I want to see the opera house and visit the cafés in Vienna. So, let's go the together? Why don't we?'

Sophya had a look of great excitement in her eyes.

I felt very flattered. I felt my spirits lifting to the sky. I felt like I was walking on air.

'Yes, of course, Sophya. I'd love to visit those places with you, and for once soak up some of the culture instead just meeting business people and then flying out. That would be really great!'

How many times had I visited places without having had any time to see them, I thought? I worked day and night for The Firm, but what about me, I thought, what about my life and my memories?

As we entered the hotel lobby, Sophya stopped, and turned to face me. She took my hands in hers and looked deeply into my eyes.

'Rave, this is so wonderful. You're such an attractive man. I love St. Petersburg, and, do you know what, I love you too.' Sophya said in Russian with a beautiful smile on her face.

'Yes Sophya. It feels as if we belong together, doesn't it?'

'But I'm so sorry Rave. I can't be with you in your hotel suite tonight – it doesn't feel right yet. I'm still a married Russian woman remember,' Sophya said as she diverted her eyes shyly to the ground.

'That's not important,' I whispered in her ear like a true gentleman.

'So, goodnight and sleep well, Rave.'

She came closer and kissed me gently on both cheeks, three times.

And with that, we walked off in different directions along the hotel corridor.

***

The following day I woke early and thought immediately of Sophya. Was she awake or still asleep? Did she like the roses I had sent to her room? How would she behave towards me today, I wondered?

Last night, at the theatre, she looked extremely beautiful in her classically elegant, figure-hugging evening gown and all her jewellery. People had looked at both of us, some in admiration of Sophya, and some in envy of me and my younger partner; mostly the older male tourists with their older wives. I smiled to myself over my good fortune.

I lay there and tried to imagine what Sophya was doing in her room. In my imagination, I could see how she washed herself, how she dressed and applied her make-up and spent time in front of the mirror getting ready to make her appearance at the breakfast table.

I called her in her room.

'Good morning Sophya, and thanks for a wonderful evening.'

'Rave,' she said in a gentle voice, 'Thank you for last night. It was wonderful and you behaved impeccably.'

'And as far as today is concerned, I'm wondering if you'd like to come with me today to Krestovsky island? We can have some lunch there perhaps? It's a lovely sunny day in spite of it being a little chilly,' I said somewhat nervously.

'Of course, I'd love to go with you to Krestovsky island, I really would. But first how about some breakfast? See you downstairs in half an hour?'

The dining room was full of breakfasters when I entered. They were mostly foreigners who were here to enjoy the city and all the cultural highlights which St. Petersburg had to offer. Sophya was already there sitting at a small table for two. Someone had placed a small vase with a long-stemmed red rose on the table. The sun shone through the windows and Sophya looked radiant as she looked up at me and smiled. For a split second I could picture her as if she wasn't wearing any clothes. I could see every sinew of her body, every curve of her figure, every delight of her silk-like skin. It made me shiver slightly.

When I sat down facing her, her hand came slowly across the table towards me. She covered my hand with hers and held it there. We said nothing. I used my free hand to read the menu, which consisted of eggs, eggs and more eggs. Some hotel restaurants took delight in impressing their guests over the number of different ways they could present your breakfast egg. This must be one of them, I thought to myself.

I ordered two three-minute eggs, while Sophya ordered kefir, tea, a sandwich, and an eight-minute egg with toast. We ate breakfast relatively quietly and then went upstairs to make ourselves ready for the day. Outside the hotel, my driver pulled up in the car and waited to drive us to Krestovsky island.

Slowly but surely, step by step, our friendship was developing. We'd been under the same roof for 2 nights and were enjoying breakfast together. Everything was still very correct and proper but how long would it take to become really intimate? Not much longer I thought.

Sophya was dark-blond with light porcelain-coloured skin, shared by many Russian women. It was a skin type which couldn't take too much sunshine and which simply liked to be bathed in the warmth of the day. She had slight shoulders and small rebellious breasts.

She was a classical Russian beauty. She was honest and had a certain distance to men which you only found in Eastern Europe. Women there were not the friends of men. Bu neither did they go around rubbishing their husbands or constantly sticking knives in their backs in public.

I well remember an anecdote I heard at a summer party at Gauk's summer house in the Swedish archipelago. Two of the guests, he said, a husband and wife, arrived in their Range Rover and the man drove the car down the steep slope leading down to Gauk's house where we were all gathered for a pre-dinner drink. The wife, however, an American lady, made her way down the drive towards us on foot!

When she reached the assembled group of guests, she told us all, in a very loud voice, 'You all know Borje! He can't drive a car to save his life! He's really hopeless. He's sooooo clumsy!' before laughing loudly, as Americans sometimes do. Only one or two of the guests joined in.

In Russia, women don't usually make idiots of their husbands in front of other people. Interestingly, this respect and the 'distance' between men and women often makes for good erotic relations. Women don't question their husbands in company but show them lots of affection instead. Men don't pick at their wives in public either. This is what Western men fantasize about when they think about Russian and East European women and it is why Western men find them so attractive.

As they say, 'A man who has never had a Russian lover has never loved.'

And the thought of a Russian lover, in the form of Sophya, began to burrow its way further and further under my skin. Somewhere along the way, I thought, I might have to pay a high price for my relationship with Sophya. It's always the same. As they say, 'there's no such thing as a free lunch' but, never mind, this lunch will have to cost what it costs.

Chapter 7

DINNER WITH MARINA

One evening in the middle of the week, some months later, I was invited to dinner by Miss Marina, a middle-aged Controller at The Firm, to her apartment on the 6th floor on Za Nevsky, at the far end of St. Petersburg's famous boulevard, Nevsky Prospect. She'd invited me so many times in recent weeks, I felt I had no choice but to finally accept her invitation.

My driver made his way slowly through the heavy traffic, just stopping along the way to allow me buy flowers for the hostess. As we drove along the skies opened and there was an almighty downpour which cleared the pavements in seconds as people scattered for shelter.

It's unusual to be invited to a Russian home. Occasionally it's because they don't have a home, but more often it's because they don't like to mingle with foreigners more than necessary, unless it's about getting money out of them of course. Still, I had nothing to lose by accepting her invitation. It beat yet another night alone in my apartment streaming movies.

When she opened the door and invited me in, she was wearing a rather skimpy kimono which left little to the imagination, unlike her dress code in the office which was always strictly no-nonsense business-like. But now her breasts were bursting out of her top like two melons and her voluptuous cleavage was impressive in its promised delights. After the traditional Russian greeting at the door, I stepped inside.

The apartment had just two small bedrooms, a living room full of heavy Russian furniture and a small kitchen which was actually very well equipped with all the latest gadgets. There was a large oil painting on a dirty yellow wall in the middle of the living room of one of Russia's beloved leaders from the thirties in full combat uniform.

It appeared to me, looking around, that the apartment had another resident; perhaps one of Miss Marina's relatives, a friend or something?

"You must be ready for a drink," she said, and after putting on extra red lipstick and adjusting her hair in front of the mirror, letting the kimono open up just a little, she walked into the kitchen and, to my surprise, opened a bottle of expensive red French wine.

She seemed to be full of life and joy, without the bitterness that was so common in women of her age in Stockholm.

85

She didn't lead the discussion, but waited for me to take the lead and then she just smiled or made a witty remark. The wine was loosening our tongues and she went back into the kitchen to serve up the food.

The dinner which consisted of typically Russian food was very enjoyable, and the conversation swung backwards and forwards; sometimes work and sometimes gossip. Towards the end of the meal, she said that she wanted to tell me something that had recently upset her and, of course, I was interested in hearing her story. I poured the last of the wine as she began.

'Rave. I want to tell you something that happened recently to my dear brother Ivan. He lives in Yekaterinburg in the Ural Mountains.'

'Really, I didn't know you had a brother. So, what happened to him?'

"Well, a couple of weeks ago, Ivan and his friends were out in one of Yekaterinburg's more luxurious restaurants. There are surprisingly many of them, what with the oil money and the black-market gangs. It's like a mini-Moscow down there in all sorts of ways, some good some bad. Anyway, there they were, having a nice evening, when they were suddenly in the middle of one of the worst shooting incidents ever seen in the city. It was like a horrible nightmare and I still can't believe what happened..."

Marina lowered her head, looked down at the table and started to cry. I began to fear the worst.

'Two men suddenly burst into the restaurant with machine guns and started shooting wildly around the restaurant. They attacked a table where four men were sitting and the place went crazy. Total chaos broke out. People screamed and shouted and tried to hide under the tables.'

'Who the two men were and what they were doing?'

'We still don't know. They moved quickly around the tables and shot anyone who tried to escape. My brother and his friends were sitting at the next table to the four guys and saw the gunmen empty their magazines into them. Their heads and bodies exploded and there was blood and brains everywhere.'

'In the middle of the madness, my brother was hit in the head by a stray bullet and that was it. He was killed instantly. Gone in a split second! We were twins and completely inseparable. We talked on the phone every day ....'

Marina fell silent, with her head in her hands, and began to sob.

"In the newspapers you could see a CCTV photo of the two men, without masks on their faces, walking out of the restaurant still holding their weapons. It feels like they got the OK from the police to do this - or from people higher up in the hierarchy. Perhaps they were doing society a favour by getting rid of the four men. Who knows? But my brother had nothing to do with this. He was just an unfortunate innocent victim of cruelty in Russia's underworld world. Men rule by creating horror and fear. That's Russia today.'

'The ambulance staff took a long time to arrive. They knew there wouldn't be any injured people to take care of, just dead bodies to remove. Nobody had a chance, and neither did my brother. It was a slaughter.'

'And what happened next?'

'Well, the police arrived at the restaurant eventually. The street was full of people and journalists as always on occasions like this. I guess that Yekaterinburg is at least as dangerous as Moscow, maybe even worse. There's a lot of money in circulation, and the judges and police officers are easy to buy.'

'My old mother called me late in the evening and told me what had happened. She cried all the time and I could barely hear what she was saying. She wanted me to fly down and take care of Ivan's dead body, so I did, directly in the morning, the day after the attack. We buried our dear Ivan within 48 hours. Mother was so small and frail. She just stood there and said nothing. All I could do was to put my arm around her.'

'The four dead men were wealthy Bulgarians and were in town on some kind of business trip. Perhaps they were looking for companies to buy locally. I don't know. Maybe the hit men thought they were Mafia, but they shot my brother and he wasn't Mafia.'

"And now, nothing will happen. No investigation. No arrests. No one will be punished. My brother's killers will go free. Of course, it will all go away, disappear for ever, like water under a bridge. This kind of thing can happen anywhere, anytime. Innocent people hit by bullets intended for other targets, and there's no way to stop it.'

And then, without warning, in the blink of an eye, Marina began to move her body, slowly, back and forth. She pushed her hips forward and started to gyrate. Her hands began to move slowly up towards her breasts and she moistened her lips. Then she bent slowly forward towards me and I looked far down into her kimono as her cleavage became fully exposed.

Russians never give up, I thought to myself, even in a situation like this. She's carrying on now as if nothing happened.

'And now', she said, 'I want to dance!' and she totally left the story of the restaurant behind her and moved on.

She began to move sensually around the room in time with the music and asked me if I would like another drink.

'Of course, I would, I'd love one,' I replied as I moved forward towards her, taking my first dance step.

'Drink and dance, Russian style. I feel so free now, Rave. I'm going to ask if the girl who lives with me wants to join us and maybe bring some brandy. Her name is Alice, by the way.'

Why not, I thought. It's a free world. Anything goes.

You didn't have to be a meteorologist to know which way the wind was blowing, and I was feeling good, and going with the flow. Ready to see what would happen. Drinking and dancing the Russian way.

Alice strutted into the living room from the other bedroom, wearing a pair of worn-out jeans and a skin-tight T-shirt. She laughed. She was in the mood for a party. She stood there in front of me. A small bag of bones with no buttocks and mosquito bites on her chest. She had dark, sharp eyes and she looked like she'd been trained by the FSB.

'This is Alice, my good friend Alice. She lives with me.'

'Hi Alice' I said, as she poured us all a large glass of brandy. Then she turned around, and without looking at us, she saluted and emptied her glass in a single sweep.

'Dance with him,' said Marina. 'Why don't you dance with him?'

I stood close to Alice, and felt her breath on my face, as she twined her arms around me and we slowly began to move around the room. As we danced around, I felt our bodies come closer together. Her lips were so near my neck and I felt them touching my skin very lightly with every step of the dance. We were dancing slowly, very close together now when Marina returned from the kitchen with more candles.

'Oh, it's so hot in here,' said Marina. 'Let's take our clothes off.'

She quietly stepped out of her kimono, and stood there naked, fully exposed in the candlelight. Marina was magnificently fully loaded. A well-trained woman with everything a man could want in a woman. She closed her eyes and caressed herself, first over her flat stomach and then lower down between her legs and around her erotic zones.

As I removed my clothes, I saw that Alice had beaten me to it and was already caressing Marina's breasts while Marina was taking Alice's buttocks with her two hands, and massaging them lovingly.

Marina's hands moved between Alice's thighs as they both became more excited and lost their inhibitions. The colour of Marina's face had turned from pink to magenta as became more and more aroused in her lust. I too became more and more excited and eventually I couldn't hold myself any longer.

'Clear the table and make some space,' I ordered. Marina and I eased Alice up onto the table where she presented herself to me, and I made my entrance with all the pent-up desire that had been locked inside, while the two ladies entertained each other as they had done many times before.

The following morning in the office, Marina and I did not have cause to speak to each other, working as we did in different parts of the building.

When she got home from work that night, she found Alice in bed in her room with one of her 'guests'. He was a Norwegian oil director. He usually visited Alice every Tuesday after making his getaway from Oslo after another yet uneventful weekend with his boring wife. Alice always met her customers in the apartment and Marina glanced into the bedroom and smiled to herself. She liked Alice's Scandinavian clients. They were always so nice and clean. They only came one at a time and they didn't give Alice a hard time.

It was nice to see that Alice was working hard and would be able to pay the rent again this month, she thought.

Chapter 8

THE POOL GAME

After work, on the evening after the meeting with Marina and her friend, my driver took me to the gym as I was feeling rather bruised after the tough workout the three of us had had together. After a light workout and some gentle massage, it was time to find somewhere to have dinner and Cafe Charlotte was my choice. A quiet, relaxed evening in a small, cosy restaurant was what I had in mind after my recent exertions.

Tonight, the place was only half full and I sat down at an empty table by the window. Next to me sat two girls who were deeply engaged in intense discussions about all the men they'd been with in the last three months, and there were many! 'What did they do?', 'What was it like?', 'Did it hurt?', 'How much did they pay?'

They fired their questions and answers at one another at great speed, and their answers were mostly interspersed with vulgar laughter. My bad Russian had trouble keeping up, but I could guess a lot of what they were saying from watching their faces.

One of the girls had a billiard cue case on the floor

beneath her feet. If she's got her own cue, I thought, then she must be good and play for more than just a beer on Friday night with friends.

'So, you think you can play pool,' I said in their direction.

The girls snapped their heads towards me and laughed a little, surprised by my cheek.

'My name is Irina. I'm from Minsk and I'm here to play some professional tournaments in St Petersburg this weekend,' was the reply I got together with a look designed to put me in my place.

'And I can play the trousers off your bony ass any day of the week,' I said provocatively.

The girl jumped straight to her feet, waving her arms around, and started shouting and ranting in Russian. I couldn't understand much of what she was saying. Her girlfriend laughed and seemed amused by the situation. She stood up and leant against me, showing off her big boobs that almost touched my hand and said that Irina wanted to challenge me immediately; she would thrash me and take the big grin off my face, she said.

'OK. We'll play for your panties. If you lose you take them off and put them on the pool table. And if you win, which is something you can only dream about, then you can keep them on and I'll give you 100 euros in cash. Do we have a deal?'

Irina was boiling with anger and about to explode again. She tugged at her short, crumpled skirt and snarled between her teeth, 'You choose the pool hall and we'll be there in an hour.'

She stared hard at me, but her friend just laughed and started getting ready to leave.

'Let's make it the pool hall on Petrogradsky Prospect,' I said. 'You can come with me if you like. I've got a car outside.'

When they nodded in agreement, I turned to make my way to the exit with the two girls with right behind me. Irina was verging on the hysterical, almost spitting her words out as she spoke. She didn't like the way I'd spoken to her and told her what to do, but she'd accepted the bet and wanted to show me how Belarusians played pool!

The black Mercedes pulled out slowly onto Nevsky Prospect and drove west towards Petrogradsky island. It always took a long time to drive anywhere in St. Petersburg. The roads just couldn't handle the volume of traffic.

I sat with Vladimiir in the front seat and tried to overhear what the girls were talking about in the back seat. It was another highly-animated discussion with screams, laughter and crying, with sometimes a worried look in my direction. Irina's friend looked at me as if she wanted to swallow me whole and then spit me out.

Once at the pool hall, the girls got out of the car and slammed the door shut. Irina was still so worked up that she was visibly shaking. She could hardly wait to get to the pool table to put me in my place for being so insulting.

The tables were all taken apart from the one closest to the reception which meant that everyone in the hall could stand and watch to see how the game was going. Perfect, just what I wanted.

Irina proudly removed her cue from its case, screwed the two parts together and chalked the tip. I could see from the way she handled her cue that she knew how to play. It was an American Meucci cue which must have cost her at least a month's salary, so either she had a sugar daddy or she had saved up and bought the cue out of her own winnings.

'Let's play nine-ball,' I suggested. 'It's a game of luck, so it'll be easier for you Irina!'

Irina didn't answer. She just stood there fuming, looking down at the green table cloth.

'I'll set the balls up and you can break if you want

to. First to five wins.'

I put the nine balls in the diamond-shaped rack. Ball number 1 at the front and ball number 9 in the middle. The balls had to be potted in sequence. The one who potted the 9-ball would win.

Irina broke off with huge force. The balls flew everywhere. The one-ball went down, the four-ball went down, then the white cue ball settled behind the three-ball which obscured the two-ball that was in the middle of the table. Irina took her cue and set up her next shot to jump over the three-ball. Pang, the white cue ball flew into the air and came down on the two-ball which disappeared into the corner pocket. Her girlfriend laughed and Irina looked at me with an arrogant expression. I began to realize that this was going to be a tough match.

Irina missed nothing and cleared the whole table apart from the nine-ball. Then she turned the white ball towards me and deliberately smashed it into the centre pocket thereby giving me my first point and a large degree of humiliation.

I stepped up to the table and potted the nine-ball without any problems and we started setting up the balls for the second round.

My turn to break. I struck the white quite hard too and the balls spread nicely with two balls disappearing but the nine-ball remaining. I planned my shots as carefully as possible to get into a good position for the next shot. I knew that if I missed a single shot then I'd lose. I needed to be lucky if she was going to take her panties off tonight!

I potted the four-ball, but then missed the five. Irina had a simple shot from the five-ball onto nine-ball and it was 1–1. Meanwhile, people from the other tables had stopped playing and had gathered around our table. I could see that they recognized her, and they knew that she intended to wipe the floor with me show me who was top dog.

After an hour, it was 4–1 to Irina, and then she played a trick shot where she played the white onto three cushions before hitting the nine-ball sweetly into the pocket. She turned towards me and stretched out her hand for her 100 euros, gave me a firm handshake, smiled and acknowledged the cheers of the audience, which she did by snapping her fingers.

'Well played,' I said, as I handed her the 100 euros.

'Now, would you ladies like a lift somewhere?'

'You played well too, Maestro,' she said. 'I like your style. it was a nice evening.'

Irina was delighted to stuff the 100 euros down into her bra. We all made our way to the car and Vladimir drove us back to the Old Town. After a few minutes, Irina leant forward from the back seat towards me.

'My little foreign boy! Maybe we'll meet another day. I'm sure you still want to see me without my panties, don't you? All wet and freshly shaved?'

We both laughed together. Vladimir stopped at the first subway station we came to, and the girls disappeared into the night.

Later, on the back seat, I found a small piece of paper with a mobile number and Irina's name. The mobile number had a Belarusian country code. On the paper she'd written, 'Next time we'll play for your manhood, right? Winner takes all"

Chapter 9

ISOPHYA IS INSTALLED

I really missed Sophya. In spite of all my female adventures, I missed her a lot! I hadn't seen her for several months, and we'd only talked once on the phone. It was just a short call and I suppose her husband was hanging around in the background and overheard the conversation. Ever since I first got to know her, I'd been thinking more and more about offering her a job here with me, in St. Petersburg. We'd discussed the idea, and now that I had found a position that would suit her, or rather, now that I'd created a position that would suit her, I invited her to join me in St. Petersburg again. Sophya accepted my offer and I made all the necessary arrangements. She then moved to St. Petersburg with her daughter but without her husband, and I was ecstatic about having her with me.

I employed Sophya in the accounts department at The Firm. I needed my spies there too, so I could find out what was really going on and what kind of business we were actually running. I was more or less convinced that it was something that I wouldn't approve of; something that would need smoking out.

Sophia was clearing interested in romance but we still hadn't gone 'all the way' despite the opportunities which had presented themselves. Actually, Sophya had warned me several times about getting too close to Russian women. She said they were fickle and dishonest.

However, I installed Sophya on the same floor as mine, and I enjoyed the close contact we had during office hours. Everyone in The Firm knew the score, but nobody said anything. They'd seen this happen before, and it was probably quite common in Russia. People in high positions pleased themselves and did what they wanted when it came to fixing jobs for their lovers.

We rarely met each other after work. She had a daughter to take care of and I was never invited to her home. She played it cool and let me do the chasing around the office.

At The Firm, there was always a lot of paperwork that crossed my desk for my signature. I didn't understand a word of what they said, so I was completely in the hands of my Russian staff who produced the documents. Why so many formal documents and so much red tape? Was it all really necessary? Presumably it was necessary in Russia. Thankfully Sophya helped me understand the procedures and the routines. She explained why they existed and so on, but I still felt that there was a lot of going on here that I didn't know about and didn't see. Things going on in secret behind my back. It made me feel uneasy.

Every time I travelled to Moscow, or anywhere for that matter, my secretary asked me when I would be back. I got the feeling that, as soon as my back was turned, things started happening and we did things for our customers which we shouldn't. Sending money from Russia to the EU was a popular financial service that could also be highly profitable, particularly if you didn't ask the customer where the money came from.

Garbage was Gauk's right hand. Always in a a bad mood, he was an overweight alcoholic who looked as if he might drop down dead at any minute. He visited us from time to time, and always for the same reason. Namely, to spy on me and send home distorted reports to discredit me and get me fired. Garbage was hated by everyone at The Firm, and survived only because of his close connection with Gauk. He had to be 'tolerated'.

He'd had several heart attacks and a minor stroke a few years ago. Talking to him was a breath-taking journey where he moved at breakneck speed between lots of different subjects, touching down on one topic very briefly before he was off and touching down on the next and so on until he'd forgotten where he'd started. Afterwards he didn't remember what it was we had talked about.

But Sophya was my saving grace. Although she remained distant and cool, not flirty at all, she always left the door open little, enough for me to see the light shining through, and that was good enough for me.

***

'Come on now little Rolf. Hurry up. The taxi will be here in 20 minutes. It's going to be so nice to travel to Geneva with my sisters. We haven't done anything together, just the three of us, for over six months.'
'And now my little darling, about food. There's a lovely salmon pudding in the oven that I bought for you at the supermarket yesterday. Just for you. All you need to do is to warm it up in the oven. And don't forget to feed little 'pussikins' while I'm gone will you!'

She climbed into the front seat of the taxi, gave Rolf a quick wave, then took out her mobile phone started to speak to someone, presumably one of her sisters, while looking vacantly straight ahead as she chewed on her chewing gum. The taxi disappeared around the corner.

Rolf was 50 years old and a postman in Stockholm. His friends at the Post Office call him Roffe. As he prepared for work, he carefully buttoned up his grey work shirt which had to last a long time. The cost of his work uniform was deducted from his salary. When he started working as a postman, he told his work mates that his wife was 'an academic' and they were all suitably impressed.

Roffe made himself ready to leave. He only had a short bus ride every morning out to the sorting centre at Haga Norra. As he got onto the bus, he decided to tell his work-mates about his wife's trip to Geneva during the coffee break to see their faces turn green with envy. Being married to his wife was almost like being married to a celebrity.

Rolf ended up in the middle of the crowded bus, standing squeezed between three heavyweight Viking yobs and an evil-looking middle-aged mother with small twins in a pushchair. She sneered at Rolf when she saw his cheap postman's uniform.
Then one of the Viking yobs leant towards Rolf and stared him in the face.
 'Are you a copper? Yeah, you are! You're a fuckin' copper, aren't you?
One of the others then started circling Rolf, pushing into him and eyeballing him while pulling on his grey police-type uniform. Rolf looked out the window and tried to to focus on something else. He didn't want any trouble. Suddenly the youngest and biggest of them, jumped into the aisle in front of Rolf with an iron pipe in his hand.

'Right then, you pig, let's see what you think about this.'

He circled closely around Rolf waving the pipe in front of his face shouting 'you can't touch me; you can't touch me!'' while recording everything on his mobile phone. The atmosphere on the crowded bus was tense to say the least and no-one made a sound. When the bus overtook a young female cyclist, everyone in the bus conveniently diverted their eyes to the cyclist and followed her progress for an unusually long time. Nobody wanted to see what was going on inside the bus. They were all too scared to look.

'Excuse me,' said Rolf politely to the yob. 'I'm getting off at the next stop. Excuse me.'

Rolf pushed towards the doors and eventually stepped out onto the pavement with the sound of the abuse from the yobs still ringing in his ears. His pulse was racing and he was feeling very shaky but he was safe at least.

He'd escaped from the bus and could now breathe a huge sigh of relief. He'd been lucky, he thought. He'd got off the bus much earlier than usual, and he'd have to walk the remining distance but it was well worth it. He was still in one piece.

He started walking towards the Haga Norra terminal at a brisk pace and his head began to clear and he could regroup after all the verbal abuse. Soon he'd tell his mates about his wife's trip.

***

Now that I had employed Sophya in The Firm, and she was living with her daughter Anna and her mother who had moved from Moscow to be closer to her daughter in St. Petersburg, I spent a lot of time trying to think of how to handle Sophia's husband Juri. Gauk now wanted to grow the Russian desk in the organisation in Stockholm and maybe Juri Sackenov could be the right man for the job, I thought to myself. Naturally he had no idea what we did in the company, but that was immaterial. He had good contacts high up in the Russian hierarchy. Not to the very top of course but high enough. If you were 'under protection' in Russia, you could do practically anything you liked. But if you were on the outside, things could go very badly wrong. But certainly, it might be worth having a quiet word with Sackenov and the fact that there were about 700 kilometres between Moscow and St. Petersburg was one major added bonus!

A couple of days later, I give Sackenov a telephone call from St. Petersburg and gently introduced myself while he listened to what I had to say. It was half past eight in the evening but he was still working. A real workhorse. Finally, I broached the subject of the vacancy we were looking to fill in Sweden, and when he murmured his interest, we continued to talk a little more.

He wasn't the cuddly bear he might have appeared to be to some. He knew that our business was highly lucrative with high salaries and very generous compensation packages for those who delivered; for those who were willing to take the risks. I could see his round face with his baby eyes in front of me as we discussed the intricacies of the business. He murmured his interest as we proceeded and no difficult questions came up as we chatted. He was up for it, it seemed. I knew we'd have to pay at least two salaries if he took the job, the second one for the assistant he'd want to recruit to do the work he'd been employed to do. That was how it worked in Russia. We end our conversation amicably by agreeing to discuss matters further by phone at the same time the following day.

The next evening, when we talked again, his tone of voice was friendly and interested. He was surprisingly open to my ideas, given that I knew he was a KGB officer. He appeared totally unsuspicious to my approach and actually rather flattered that I had headhunted him. When the time was right, I popped the question.

'Shall we have a meeting at head office next week when I am back in Stockholm. My secretary will call to book a time.'

'Very good. It would be an honour for me to work for you, Mr Alexander'

* * *

At the embassy in Stockholm, the staff began to pack up for the day and got dressed for the walk down to the underground station. When they had all left the building, Sackenov made himself comfortable at his desk, opened up his PC again and entered a security code while putting on his headphones.

After a couple of hours of listening to the sound of silence, Sackenov could hardly stay awake. He couldn't make any calls to anyone including Sophya in case something 'interesting' started to happen. He eyelids became heavy but he just had to stay awake. Another hour went by. The clock showed 00:47. Still completely silent. Then suddenly he heard a voice he recognized.

'Sandra, it's me. I'm not waking you up, am I? '
'No not at all. I couldn't sleep so I'm reading a book.'
'So, I guess you're in bed. What are you wearing?'
'Nothing much – just my usual nightie.'
'But I mean under that Sandra.'
'What's with you tonight! You sound all excited!'
'Do not tease me Sandra, tell me about your panties – if you're wearing any? What colour are they?'
'Come on my lovely, it's no good talking on the phone. Get yourself over here. Forget politics and

your boring wife for the night. I know what you want, so come and get it!'

The conversation continued for a while longer and Sackenov, a true Russian, blushed slightly. Russians never joked about such things, especially on the phone. Russian men were quite prudish but paradoxically they often had another side where mistresses and prostitutes were part of everyday life. Recognising the man's voice, Juri realized that the man on the phone was none other than than theSwedishprime minister, who won't be divulging any state secrets to anybody that night apart perhaps from Sandra when he was inside her panties.

Russian presidents had significantly more class, thought Juri. They would never talk dirty on the phone because they knew that all phones were bugged. They were bugged at their request, of course. Sackenov by was now really tired so he shut down his computer and went straight home to bed.

The next evening, the same procedure repeated itself. The staff left the office and Sackenov made himself a sandwich and a cup of coffee. Hehad become a real coffee drinker during his time in Stockholm. His headphones again remained silent for hours until suddenly they burst into life.

'Hi chocolate. Hope we weren't too rough yesterday - hope I didn't hurt you? You know, you're quite something – quite a rascal when you get going?'
'Hello my darling. You'll be too late tonightto come over tonight I guess, so my little pussy will have to wait another day for another treat. So, goodnight and big hugs from me.'

For the third night in a row, on the following night, Sackenov again worked late while everyone else in the office left at the usual time. Sackenov started up his PC and sat quietly, headphones on, and waited. Five hours later, around 23:30, Sackenov sat up with a start.
'I want to be deep inside you my chocolate box!'
'Sure, you can go as deep as you want, mister prime minister!
'Why can't I get rid of my wife? Why must I have to put up with her frigidity. I can't stand her any longer. You and I must have the right to a life together. Now tell me, come on my sugar, tell me what you are wearing, and I mean under your nightie?'

This Swede is impossible, Sackenov thought. He's hornier than Bill Clinton. I don't want to listen to any more of this stuff. But I'll report it to Moscow in the usual way. They'll be delighted. Any thoughts about 'decent' Swedes, if there still are any, will fly out of the window straight away.

And with those thoughts in his mind, Sackenov

closed down, locked the office and made his way home.

The following week, I flew with SAS to Stockholm and took a taxi directly to the office still feeling irritated after the flight. These days flying with SAS had become a bore where the customers were asked to clean up after themselves; take their newspapers with them, dispose of their used coffee cups etc. What had happened to good old-fashioned SAS cabin service?

Once inside the office, I was immediately confronted by our security manager who stopped me in my tracks. Rabinstein was a fat man, and wearing his dirty, unwashed trench coatas always- the dirtiest trench coat I'd seen in many a day. He was the company's security manager who was always so stressed that he appeared to be carrying the fate of the world on his shoulders. He had not attended the police academy and had been not in the army, so the gossip was that he had only been made head of security becausesomeone with a lot of power had eased him into the job.

'MUST have been in touch,' he blurted out while staring at me with his frog eyes.
'They're a little worried about the discussions you're having with a certain Mr. Sackenov.'
'Really! Why is that? And how do they know?'

'Don't be so naive. Every single telephone call made on the mobile network is recorded and scrutinised by the authorities. All the calls and all the text messages!'

'But isn't that an invasion of an individual's privacy? Surely, it can't be legal?'

'Alexander, you shit! Politics and national security are more important than theprivacy of individual citizens. Nothing is private from the state. Let's go into your office. We can't stand here in the corridor shouting at each other. There is some more worrying information I have to tell you. So, sit down and shut up!'

I sat down in my director's chair which reflected my seniority with the back on the chair being almost 150cm high. Newcomers started off with a seat without armrests and with just a small plate as a backrest. As they were promoted, the backrests grow higher and higher. Leather was not as popular now as it used to be, as it produced shiny-ass trousers and an extra pair cost £400 at any tailor on Savile Row.

Rabinstein snorted a little before starting to speak. 'In addition to his regular diplomatic work, your Mr Sackenov has also devoted himself to eavesdropping on our prime minister when he is in the Sagerska Palace and talking on his mobile phone.'

Rabinstein made his statement in much the same official tone that is used when reading the news on TV.

I swung around in my chair and stared straight at Rabinstein's face. Christ, I thought, just look at those long, coarse hairs growing out of his nose, and I got the urge to lean forward, grab the biggest protruding hair and yank it out. I leant forward, but stopped quickly with my hand in the air, as if giving a Hitler salute, and then forced it down onto the armrest, without uttering a word.

'The Ministry of Foreign Affairs has submitted a protest. Mr Sackenov will leave the country today on the evening flight to Moscow. You must not contact him anymore.'

'What were you thinking of Rave? Why Sackenov? He has nothing to do with our business. How could he possibly be suitable for the job? If I were you, I would be much more careful in the future when hiring senior staff in the East. You know, don't you, that you must always use a security company to screen all possible candidates. Always!'

Rabinstein looked at me hard, turned around in his worn-out Boss shoes and left the room leaving the door open as he went out.

Chapter 10

A RUSSIAN WRITE-OFF AND JURI IS RECALLED

The more I discovered about the workings of The Firm in St. Petersburg and the practices of our customers, the less I liked it. The biggest difference between business activities in Sweden and those in St. Petersburg was that in Russia, the 'wrong' business decision could have direct consequences to your personal safety, such was the lawlessness in the country.

One situation I had to deal with brought the matter into focus. The largest private bus company in St. Petersburg was called Finland B Dien, which means 'Finland-for-a-day'. The company specialized in operating daily excursions to the Finnish border, ostensibly for shopping purposes, but more importantly to enable the Russian day-trippers to get a Finnish stamp in their Russian passports. Russians in St. Petersburg could easily get a Finnish EU visafrom the Finnish embassy which enabled them to enter Finland of course, but also enabled them to enter all the other EU countries like Spain. So, if and when Russians travelled to Spain or some other popular tourist destinations in the EU, they had to make a day trip to Finland to top up their Finnish stamps, without which the Finnish authorities would not renew their visas. An ingenious business solution. All Russians who succeeded in obtaining an EU visa were meticulously careful to safeguard them to ensure their continuing access to the EU.

During one of their regular board meetings, the question of financing their fleet of buses was raised on the agenda.

'As you gentlemen know, we have 20 Swedish buses on lease from Sparbanken korcina delja belja. The original amount was 100 million roubles, now the leases are down to about 50 million roubles. I'm wondering if we could renegotiate the remaining amount and get some of it written off? We have money in other accounts, of course, but the Swedish leasing company doesn't have access to them. Who knows, it might be worth a try?'

'What happens if we don't make the next repayment?'

The question came from the young lady sitting at the table. She was slim, blonde and very well dressed. She was the company lawyer, Elena Ivanova. She knewexactly how the Russian judicial system worked, but asked the question anyway because she suspected that the men around the table were not familiar with foreclosure proceedings.

'Right! So, what will happen? The Swedes will not beat the drum and play tough; partly because they really don't want the buses back, and partly because, like all true Swedes, they don't want any trouble. First, they will send out a reminder requesting payment and, after that, they'll send out a second reminder, asking for payment, but without any 'kind regards.'

'Swedes are spineless cowards.'
'Just see how they are pushed around by their women.'
'Swedish women do what they want – they dress like men and look sloppy, like and never pull a comb through their hair.'
'Swedes are weak and they will grovel before us. You mark my words.'

The men smiled at each other as the comments were uttered around the table.

Elena Ivanova, the good-looking chief legal officer, also smiledas she slowly extended her left leg showing off her light grey knee-high boots with stiletto heels. Unusual attire for a board meeting. This evoked even more general light-heartedness around the table and and the mood wasself-congratulatory and jovial.

The next to speak was the chairman of the board.

'OK, so we contact the leasing company and explain 'our position' to them. If there's a chance we can screw them, it would be stupid not to try. Elana and

Viktor, I want you to get in touch with the Swedes. You've only got one hand since Crimea Viktor, so that will be perfect. Swedes are very sensitive to invalids. They'll have a hard time knowing how to handle you!! And Elena don't forget to wear your sexy boots when you visit the bank. And look really depressed when you meet the Swedes. Who knows you might get one of their foreign aid packages?'

The sound of the men laughing reverberated around the boardroom, as it always did when the highest-ranking alpha male said something that was meant to be funny.

***

The meeting with the bank manager went very well. Elena wore a very short skirtwith her knee-high boots and sad eyes with too much mascara that had started to run a little. Viktor wore a grey suit with his right sleeve pinned in place with a safety pin bearing the regiment's emblem.They were proper, polite and quiet. However, Elena gave the manager an enticing look from time to time with the implied promise of something in the future,and tugged a little awkwardly at her skirt every so often in a show designed to attract attention to her shapely legs. Once the Swede had established a pleasant atmosphere, Viktor began to spell out the extent of company's difficult situation. They were customers of 5 years standing and had always managed their company well. They were, Victor said, an exemplary customer, especially given the country in which they were operating.

However, what the bank manager did not properly understand was Russian mentality. Russians were always waiting for an opportunity to screw their opponents. 'Free money'was always better than money that you had to work for. A Russian would take 1,000 roubles of 'free money' rather than 10,000 roubles that you had to work for, because with 1,000 roubles you could sit at home and drink beer in front of the TV and watch ice-hockey. When the money ran out, you had to find the next victim to con, or, if the worst came to the worst, get a job. Russians also had a different perception of time and could wait for years for the right opportunity to come along to make some free money.

'Thank you for coming today and informing us about your present difficult situation. Our credit analysis department will look at this and get back to you in a few days,'the bank manager said rounding off the discussion whilst knowing that he had sold half of the exposure to The Firm. He escorted the Russians back to the main entrance and as, they were leaving, Ms Ivanova stopped and faced him. Her expression become heavy and serious.
'We hope for a favourable decision after your department has completed its analysis but you should know that we will hold you and your

associate Alexander Rave responsible if you turn down our request. I hope you understand my meaning.'

$$* * *$$

Later that day, I was standing by a window gazing into the distance when the phone rang.
'It's Bengt here at Sparbanken. I'm afraid we've got a bit of aproblem with Finland B Dien. They've been here and described their situation to me, and it seems they have a lack of liquidity. Their business is not going very well anymore.'
'Wait a second,' I replied, 'Their buses are packed with young girls who want to renew their visas in Finland to be able to go to Spain and have fun. They couldn't take any more customers if they wanted to. Those bloody Russians! They are trying to screw us.'

'But Alexander, we at the bank have to assume that our customers want to do the right thing for themselves. That's what I was taught when I began in the bank 20 years ago in Stockholm as a trainee.
'Stockholm maybe,'said Rave, 'but this is something else. Many western businessmen have lost huge sums of money as well as their senses in Eastern Europe, until they finally realise that there are massive differences between doing deals in the East and the West when it comes to morals and ethics, or

121

rather the lack of them, when doing business. Deals in the East are based on total and utter, mutual distrust between those people involved.

Basically, east of Berlin and south of the Brenner Pass, the world is made up of whores and bad guys. If you have a map of Europe in front of you, you can draw a line from the Baltic Sea, across and a little east of Berlin, then straight down towards the Brenner Pass and then directly west to the Atlantic coast, and then back up to the Baltic. Outside the box, the countries are made up of people where everybody, from the little secretary to the president, lies and steals, at their own particular level. The richer regions within the EU states try to break away, hopefully to go their own way and leave the poorer parts of their countries behind in the hands of the EU. Government officials 'cook the books' to cheat other countries out of money. If you don't do it, they say, you're stupid. The 'new' EU states and the regions in the South will never ever become net contributors to the 'united Europe'.

How on earth can the bank send employees to Eastern Europe who are as naive as small babies, I thought. It'll be disastrous for them in the long run. If all the managers in the bank are as incompetent as this guy, it will be hell for them here, and in the Baltic states too.

'So, Bengt, this is what we do, I said, 'We will demand that they continue to pay according to plan or, if not, we'll take back the buses and sell them on elsewhere. Let's put some pressure on them and see what happens. Leave it with me," I said firmly.

I called Finland B Dien, got hold of Elana, the Chief Legal Officer, and let her know in no uncertain terms that I didn't accept the story that they were facing severe liquidity problems. The short phone call was of course chilly, but it was necessary to make the Russians understand that this was a serious matter that we would not tolerate.

Bengtand I together wrote a letter of demand to Finlad B Dien but, not surprisingly, nothing happened. A formal request to repossess the buses from the lessee, Finland B Dien, was submitted to court. The request was granted but Finland B Dien appealed the verdict and the decision was reversed. So, a new request to repossess the buses was submitted to the second higher instance.

***

Late one night, I was playing billiards in a hall on Petrogradsky Island with some friends when my mobile rang.
'Good evening. This is Bengt. We've just found out that Finland B Dien has connections with the new judge and it's very probable that that the court verdict will therefore go against us again. They must

have bought the judge or have some other kind of hold over him.'

'OK. So, meet me in the summer gardens at 10 o'clock tomorrow morning.'

Then I called my secretary.

'Miss Top, please call lawyer Flöjel and ask him to meet me at the summer gardens tomorrow morning at 10.'

'Of course. I'll arrange it immediately.'

In the morning, fresh snow was in the air. It was as cold, raw and dark as it can be in Helsinki, only twice as bad. Without something on your head for warmth, you would freeze to death in no time.

We met up at the main gate and Flöjel was the first to speak. 'These bastards must not come out of this with a profit at our expense. They're just playing a game to get us to write down the debt. If it's the last thing I do in this fucking country, I'll make sure that they don't succeed.'

Flöjel cast a glance at me. 'Listen. I'll pay the judge 1,000,000 roubles and bill your department 1,300,000 roubles as a consulting fee. That should sort out the problem.'

Without further discussion, all three of us turned and walkedaway in different directions.

***

Three weeks later, the case came up in court. Rather unexpectedly, the court gave Sparbanken the right to seize the buses as compensation for the non-payment. Given the verdict, Finland B Dien transferred the outstanding unpaid debt to the bank immediately and nothing more was said between parties concerned.

Thinking back to Ms Ivanova's words, I realised that I was now a marked man as far as Finland B Dien was concerned. I would be on their hit-list having challenged and beaten them in court. They would never forget and wait patiently for their revenge. Yet another reason to forever look over my shoulder and guard my back.

***

The time came when Juri Sachenov's posting in Stockholm was almost over and he was called back to Moscow for extensive final debriefing and discussions about his immediate future. Having cleared his desk for the last time and arranged for their possessions to be shipped home, Juri flew back to Moscow. After descending the steps from the plane, his feet touched the tarmac and once again he was on Russian soil. He knew someone would be there to welcome him but her feared the worst when the doors of a black SUV parked at the side of the aircraft opened, and 4 men, all built like gorillas, walked rapidly in his direction. This was not what he had expected and he instantly sensed that something was seriously wrong. They surrounded him and told him that they were taking him with them, and that he should get into the vehicle, sit down and remain silent.

When the vehicle eventually came to a halt, Juri saw exactly where they had brought him. It was the infamous Lubyanka prison in central Moscow, the headquarters of the FSB, the Federal Security Service of the Russian Federation, still with the hammer and sickle visible above the main entrance from the days of the KGB. A shudder went down his spine. Everyone knew what went on inside the prison and he immediately feared the worst.

He was marched immediately through a maze of corridors into an interrogation room down in the cellar. There were no windows. The large room was dimly light but a bright light burned over a table in the centre of the room with two chairs, one on either side. He was made to sit down on one of the chairs and handcuffed before he was left alone, in total silence.

After 30 minutes or so, he was joined by a man wearing black civilian clothes he had never seen before who introduced himself as the interrogation leader. And the interrogation began.

'Juri Sachenov. Are you an enemy of the Russian Federation?'

'Of course, I'm not. I am a servant of the Russian Federation.'

'Have your activities in Stockholm been in accordance with the oath of allegiance sworn by you upon your appointment?'

'Yes they have. I don't understand. Why are you asking me these questions?'

'I am asking you these questions, Juri Sachenov, because we have reason to believe that some doubt exists concerning the degree of loyalty you possess to Russia today after your exposure to the decadent West.'

'My loyalty to Russia is total. Never once has my loyalty wavered.'

'Why then, do your former comrades in Stockholm tell us a different story? Why do they tell us that you are infatuated with the West and its luxuries?'

'I have no idea. You will have to ask them.'

'We have done. And do you know what they tell us? They tell us that you have cultivated abnormally close relations with a number of key politicians and business leaders, and entertained them excessively and indulgently, not on one occasion, but on many.'

'They tell us that you have been engaged in developing personal ties with influential people in the business community – with a view to personal gain. You have made it clear to some of these contacts that you are sympathetic to their cause. We have recordings. You have indicated that you would be interested in discussions about your future career, in the West. We have the emails.'

'But this is ridiculous. Never once have I thought along those lines. Nothing like that has ever crossed

my mind.'

'Not according to your wife. She has reported your growing disenchantment with Russia as a place to grow up and work in. 'Russia is rotten to the core!', 'Corruption is everywhere!', 'Crime and violence is the new way of life!'

'Are these your remarks? Is this what you think about noble Russia? Do you deny these allegations? Is this the man you have become Juri Sachenov? Tell me!!!'

Juri felt helpless. He was lost for words and realised there and then that his fate was sealed. What was the point in pleading his innocence? The mind of the interrogator was already made up. Juri looked down at his hands and said nothing.

The interrogator pushed back his chair, rose to his feet and walked away from the light towards the door through which he had entered. As he opened the door, he turned to Juri.

'Later we will resume our discussions and decide your fate. But I must warn you – you know what happens to traitors and betrayers of the state. So think carefully about what you say.'

Juri was then led by a guard, still handcuffed, to a primitive cell with no heating, no water, no lights and not even a bed. Just a bare floor. And there he was left; but only for a few hours, after which he was marched back into the interrogation room and once again handcuffed to a chair.

This time when the door opened, it was a high-ranking officer in the uniform of the Federal Security Service who entered the room, and sat himself down opposite Juri.

Having made himself comfortable he turned his total focus on Juri.

'So Juri,' he said slowly, 'What have you got to say for yourself now? You've had some time to think over the allegations made against you by your former colleagues ....and your wife....so tell me, are you still a loyal servant of the state of Russia or have you crossed over the line and betrayed the trust that has been placed in you?'

The new interrogator was very detached and controlled. He didn't raise his voice or threaten Juri in any way.

Juri, however, remained silent. He looked down blankly at the table and showed no expression on his face.

The officer went on, 'Of course, you must tell me that you are still a loyal servant to the State. You have no choice, do you? To say otherwise would be an act of suicide!'

'At the same time, we have to consider the reports we have received from Stockholm concerning your actions. We have telephone recordings of the conversations you have had with prominent politicians; we have email exchanges between you and powerful business people in which you praise Sweden and their companies and express an interest in helping them in their work when your time as a diplomat is over. These, comrade, are undeniable facts are they not?'

'Even your wife has informed us of your ideas about starting a new life in the West.'

'These are not vague allegations. They are serious, specific allegations, and we in Russia have to be constantly vigilant when sending our own people to abroad to safeguard our interests. We place our trust in you completely. But we are not naïve or stupid. We expect that some will be tempted by what you see. Some may even be tempted to consider defecting. Defectors are traitors, and traitors are highly dangerous since they are in a position to seriously damage Russia on the world stage with their secrets and intelligence, if and when they turn their backs on the homeland.'

Juri looked up briefly at the officer for a second before the monologue continued, this time more threateningly as the officer leant forward towards the table, raising his voice slightly.

'You, my friend, have betrayed the trust put in you by Russia and your fate will be severe and final.

Times are changing in Russia and it is vital that those of us who uphold the beliefs and traditions of our glorious past, deal with any signs of westernisation as soon as they appear. We form the inner circle and we set the agenda. For the modernisers and westernisers we discover in our midst, there is only one outcome. You and people like you cannot be given the space in Russia to spread your degenerate ideas and pollute the minds of the population. This will only weaken the power of the state and drag Russia down. No! On the contrary, we must stay strong, be vigilant and remove the cancers wherever and whenever we see them.'

'Do I make myself clear?'

During the whole interrogation, Juri had remained silent. All he could do now was look up at his interrogator and nod. As he did so, he began to cry silently and tears ran down his cheeks.

The following day, just after dawn, an early morning dog-walker in the outskirts of Moscow called the police and reported that he had discovered the dead, naked, badly-beaten body of a man in the undergrowth. The face of the person, he said, had been more or less blown away, but he could see two bullet holes in the back of the man's head so he guessed that the man had been murdered.

Chapter 11

FINALLY, ON THE BEACH

Meanwhile in St. Petersburg, my driver parked outside my hotel in the morning at nine o'clock sharp, and we drove across the city to pick up Sophya for a day out. Today was going to be hot so we were going to the beach in Sestroretsk outside St. Petersburg.

It was a popular seaside resort a few miles northwest of the city where the beach was clean and the people there were not the type who got drunk before lunch. There was even a nudist section too which the Germans loved, but most families stuck to respectable relaxation, swimming and picnics.

When it came to the beach, Sophya was a rather conservative lady who wore her bikini with modesty. No string tops or cut-away bottoms for her; nothing vulgar in public. The design and colour of her bikini perfectly matched her pale skin and dark hair. It had probably taken her at least 5 hours to find the right bikini for our day out, and perhaps she had tried the patience of one or two shop assistants.

It was already getting hot when we arrived at the

beach. 30 degrees in the shade.

We selected a prime spot and settled down on sunbeds surrounded by our towels, cold drinks, a picnic hamper full of delicacies and a lot more besides.

Sophya was lying on her stomach, eyes closed, with her head to one side when she began to speak.

'You know, I want to live where the weather is warm and pleasant, like France or Italy.

'Yes, I can imagine. It's not unusual for women to say that, especially Russian women.'

"Well, you in the West can travel wherever you want, but it's not the same for us. We've had 73 years of captivity in the Soviet Union with poverty and dictatorship. So we take all the opportunities we can for a better way of life in the West."

From out of the blue, I came up with the idea that we should run away somewhere together. Sophya, her daughter Anna, and me. I was sure she'd say 'yes' if she got the chance. Start a new life somewhere else. She had inadvertently planted the idea into my mind and now I began to fantasise a little as I lay next to her on the beach.

Later in the day we went to the changing rooms to put some more suntan lotion onto her bare shoulders which were in danger of turning red. Once inside, she closed the door behind her and turned towards me. Then she stepped up close, very close and for the very first time, there was no doubt about what was on her mind. Her hands began to explore my body and I started to explore hers.

Within a few seconds, I had removed the little that she had been wearing. I lifted her tunic over her head and gently removed the bikini. I liked things to be out in the open, where I could see everything. And now I could. She was completely naked, and I just stood there without uttering a word - admiring her perfect female figure from top to toe. Then it was Sophya's turn to make a move. In a wink, she removed my bathing shorts, and there I was too, standing without a stitch of clothing, as naked as the day I was born.

We were both smiling at each other and Sophya was inviting me to enjoy her as she was, in all her natural beauty. She was shaved, pink, tight and fresh, as many women were on this side of the Baltic Sea. Then she started to move around me, like a naked queen on the catwalk, parading herself for my eyes only. Round and round she went trailing her finger tips against my hips as he went.

She got down onto the floor, resting on her elbows, with her ass high in the air, offering her treasure for me to enter. She opened her legs a little wider still. She wasn't playing a game with me now. This was for real.

And then we passed the point of no return, and she loved me in her own very special way, the Russian way. When we finally lay back, having reached a state of ecstasy together, there was no need for words. Our bodies said it all. This was a milestone in our relationship, I thought, and where it would take us? Nobody knew!

Emerging into the sunshine once again, we returned to our sunbeds and enjoyed the warmth of the sunshine, and the hours passed most enjoyably.

Later in the evening the day was rounded off with dinner at the restaurant in Sestroretsk. As always, it was packed with fat Russian men with their 25-year-younger wives and their tiny lap-dogs.

As we waited for the food to be served, we held hands across the table and chatted about some of the places we'd like to visit together. Paris, Rome or maybe Berlin? I wondered if you had to go somewhere else to be happy and then return to back home to your normal life? Or did you have to leave, never to return? Perhaps the latter, I thought.

'Ah, here comes my lobster! said Sophya in delight as she attacked it with her fork.

As we drove back to the city, I saw that Sophya had topped up her tan nicely without overdoing it. She was looking more attractive than ever.

Chapter 12

A STRANGE ENCOUNTER IN MOSCOW

I was constantly looking for reasons to meet Sophya privately, like dinners, theatre visits and short trips to other cities, but the situation with her daughter and the fact that her mother lived with her, and the violent death of her husband, made it hard for us to meet. Things at The Firm had become less chaotic after they had tried and failed to make me carry out their illegal transactions, and we hadn't knowingly passed any money into the system. They hadn't been in touch with us again, but we knew that something could happen at any time. In Russia, over time, you became more and more suspicious of everyone you meet. Now I was thinking more about Sophya. Who was Sophya really? I wondered. Who did she actually work for? Did she work for me - or for some other organisation?

I had employed one person after another other in the finance department to tell me what was really going on. I always trusted them in the beginning, but after a while I got the feeling that they were no longer loyal to me; that they had changed sides. Voluntarily or under coercion? I wondered.

What had Sophya's husband really worked with? Why was she 'just' sad instead of being distraught when she learned about his sudden death? Had she expected it? What sort of life was she living?

St. Petersburg was a dangerous place for me and I was playing a dangerous game. The question was, where did the biggest threat come from? If we refused to take money again, I would probably be dead within 48 hours if I wasn't able to get out in time. But, as everyone knew, the FSB sometimes worked far beyond the country's borders. Was anywhere really safe?

Gauk in Stockholm might try to ruin me, but this was one side of the story that he had no idea about. Luckily enough. However, it could turn into a major scandal and destroy The Firm.

Flogel was quite upbeat the next time we met at the Charlotte café in centre of St. Petersburg.

'Rave, I've a lot to tell you about Anton, your driver.'
'Good Flogel. Tell me what you have.'
'Well, I can tell you that Anton is definitely not involved in money laundering, neither is he connected to the security police. He's just a regular Russian. We've run a full check on him, so we're sure.'

'We have traced him to his apartment in the suburb of Kubschina, south of Polkova airport. His nerves have gone, and he's scared stiff because his life was threatened by the thugs who attacked you and because he almost witnessed your death. It was Anton who got you an ambulance as soon as the gang had fled the scene, and it was thanks to him that you came quickly under treatment in the American hospital and that you still alive today.'

I stared at him in disbelief. Was Flogel trying to save Anton or was he speaking the truth? Anton had clearly changed his normal route that night. Why had he done that? Was it a coincidence? Hardly. The men were waiting to ambush us as we drove along the road.

Flogel looked tired. I wondered how his law firm was actually doing? Foreign companies were leaving Russia every week now. It had to be bad for his business, I thought.

'The men ordered Anton to stop the car as you were being dragged along. Then they cut the rope with a knife, jumped into a vehicle and disappeared. They probably had orders not to kill you but just to hurt you a lot as an example to other directors who didn't want to play their game. The market had to know what it cost to go against these guys.'

'OK, I guess what you're saying is true, because you're the one who has looked into it. But – I'll get rid of Anton, whatever you say, and get myself a new driver.'

We sat quietly for a while. I didn't believe Flogel. There must have been a connection between the men and Anton. Anton was forced into this, but the question is when did he get his orders? Possibly when we left the Maximus.

'Has anyone gone through Anton's phone and text messages?'
'No, we couldn't find his phone when we were there.'
'Yeah, I can understand that. Because, I'm sure he got a text message during the evening with instructions.'

I looked accusingly at Flogel who didn't bother to look at me.

It was very difficult, if not impossible, to know what Flogel was up to. He would say so much, but then no more. That would be it. I wondered what he had done here all these years. Why had he stayed so long in Russia without his family? Twenty years was a long time and it extended over the childhood and adolescence of his sons. But he seemed to have a good relationship with them and seemed to be pretty satisfied with life all things considered. He was probably paid extremely well to keep the law firm in business in a country like this.

'I think we're done here, so time to me to go home to catch up on some work', I said with a friendly smile.

'OK, but I think I'll go to the gym and train for an hour or so.'

Flogel was very fit for his age. He probably worked out at the gym three times a week at least. We left the Charlotte café and went in different directions.

That evening, my thoughts were taken up by to two questions. One was what would happen if and when we were told to cooperate with more money transactions? Panic would probably break out and we'd have to get out of the country as quickly as possible. It was more about 'when' than 'if' and I realised my days in St. Petersburg were almost certainly numbered. And maybe Sophya too was also thinking about leaving the country in a hurry, with me or without me?

The second issue was how to persuade Sophya to let her mother take care of Anna and to spend a night with me once in a while. Sophya was a widow. Her mother was a woman with traditional values. Of course, she would not look kindly upon it if her daughter spent the night with a foreign businessman who also happened to be her boss. We needed a watertight story to reassure her mother that every was totally respectable and proper.

A week or so later, I was sitting studying the menu in the Mansarda restaurant. I had invited Sophya to join me for dinner and was waiting for her to arrive having arrived early myself. The Mansarda was probably one of the better restaurants in which to spend an evening in St. Petersburg. The food and service were of a very high standard.

Half an hour after the agreed time, the lift doors opened and out stepped Sophya, dressed for the evening in a simple straight dress in what had to be called 'moss green'. She wore no jewellery, and her heels were low. A very presentable lady – possibly a diplomat's wife in the eyes of the world?

Once we were seated and the drinks had arrived, I looked at her and said, 'Sophya, you know I want you, don't you?'

She looked innocently at me and said nothing as she sipped her drink.

'Let's fly out of the country together, build a new life in a new place. I can apply for a job at UN Habitat in Nairobi or somewhere. Anywhere, as long as we are together.'

'It's hard for me, Rave. You have to understand. I'm a widow. My mother is my mother. She would be unhappy if she knew what we were doing. Anna must go to a Russian school, and have Russian as her native tongue. You know that it's hard for me.'

The conversation during dinner was 'difficult' and it felt like something had come between us. The reality of everyday life, I guessed. I looked across the table, and into Sophya's eyes. Who was Sophya? Was she with me or working on the other side? When would 'they' come to The Firm and demand that we did what they said? Maybe tomorrow, or perhaps in two years?

Russians, I knew, used young women to turn men's loyalties or to trap them into becoming tools of the state. I knew I had to look at Sophya in a sober fashion and decide what sort of a person she really was. The difficult thing was to be rational when emotions were involved.

At the same time, I knew I was caught in her grip. I knew it, if I was honest with myself – I was completely hooked on her and all her charms. And I was happy with that. But, for how long?

The Dubajedova canal was dark, cold and dirty and the traffic on the streets had virtually disappeared when we came out of the Mansarda into the cold night. I sent Sophya home by car and walked back to my hotel by myself. I didn't feel that we could be intimate that night. Something was dividing us.

***

By the next morning, I'd come up with a plan. I knew how to create a good cover story that would satisfy Sophya's mother. Sophya and I would then go to Moscow for two days of business meetings. I asked my secretary to book the flights and a hotel for the two of us in Moscow. She booked us into the Hotel Savoy. I would take room 11, the only room with a balcony that overlooked Petrovka. Petrovka was a parallel street with Tverskaja, Moscow's main boulevard.

Naturally, room 11 was next to room 12, which was to be Sophya's room. Room 11 also had an inner door between the two rooms which could be opened, thereby creating a suite. It was ingenious and typically Russian. All 'right and proper' as far as observers were concerned, but the arrangement allowed for passionate 'encounters' behind closed doors.

We were booked on a morning flight and landed in glorious weather. Moscow in the summer was wonderful, at least during the first part. Then it became too hot and, on recent occasions, forest fires had actually threatened to ravage the city. One summer, we had actually closed the Moscow office due to nearby forest fires and the smoke and heat.

But still, Moscow was a fascinating city, full of interesting places and sights, even more so if you knew your way around. It helped a lot if you knew how the traffic flowed and in what direction. If, for example, you were staying at the Savoy and had arranged dinner with a client in Puskin Square and didn't walk, you could end up in a two-hour traffic jam around the Kremlin. Instead, you should reserve a table at, say, the Scandinavia, which was just a 15-minute walk from the Savoy.

After a half-busy day, we had only 20 minutes in which to shower and get ready for dinner with a small delegation from the famous company Astro Knogo. Dinner was booked at one of the best seafood restaurants in Moscow; 'Not far from the East', on Pushkin Boulevard just south of McDonald's.

Sophya entered the foyer in her green dress with a simple gold chain around her neck and, from there, we walked slowly up the hill to Pushkin Square and then down to the restaurant.

The place was buzzing – full of life and busy activity.

The businessmen and their teams were streaming in, shaking hands, and exchanging banal greetings with each other. They were a bunch of monkeys, all working in the same boring business; all wearing slim-fit jackets from Hugo Boss, with Alcantara elbow patches. My God, I thought, this looks like a Christmas lunch in a company director's private dining room. No doubt they'd all come from the backwoods and worked themselves up to become assistant finance managers.

Sitting later with our business guests, the somewhat stilted conversation alternated between courteous remarks, meaningless jokes and tittle-tattle. Luckily, for me, I had invited a 'professional diner' from The Firm to join us - a man by the name of Carl de Beer. Carl could only count to 10 but he could talk the back legs off a donkey, a skill he'd picked up from his father. Carl glared rather dismissively when he clapped eyes on the bunch we'd invited to dinner. Nevertheless, we ordered Komchatka crabs, prawns from Grebbestad, and white wine from Slovenia, in fact everything imaginable and unusual that we found on the menu.

During dinner, the one female in their number, who actually looked like a streetwalker from Irkutsk, must have been struck with a bad conscience because she told me, out of the blue, that they had put their entire business into the hands of our biggest competitor. She wondered if we were still prepared to foot the bill.

I was momentarily lost for words; torn between killing her boss with my bare hands and standing up and pissing all over him. He just stared across at me the whole time with an inane expression on his stupid face.

Once out on Petrovka, we thanked our guests for having the great kindness to spend such a delightful evening with us.

Sophya and I set off at a brisk pace, heading back to the Savoy. We didn't intend to offer these ass-holes 'one for the road'.

Suddenly, out of nowhere, two clown-dressed dwarfs appeared right in front of us. One of them, a man it looked like, was pointing a revolver straight at me. We stopped. I pulled Sophya in behind me and she held her hand up against her mouth in horror. We said nothing. We stood there, about three meters from the dwarves for a few seconds which felt like an eternity. Then, without warning, they turned around in unison, and started shuffling slowly up towards the Kremlin, heads close together in animated conversation. I could hear one of them, the man, laughing to himself is response to something his partner must have said. And then they were gone.

It was all rather surreal.

Sophya and I continued our walk back to the hotel without saying a word. What was that all about? I wondered. Someone wanted to scare us, and they had succeeded. But why? We knew it wasn't the FSB; they didn't usually dress up as clowns. They didn't need to, people said ironically.

At the bar at the Savoy, I spoke to the bartender.

'We bumped into two dwarfs on our walk home tonight who threatened us with a revolver. They didn't say anything, but after a few seconds they just turned around and walked away. What do you think that was all about?'

'Aha! You too! It seems there are two Danish dwarfs roaming around the city, trying to discredit Russia and to scare tourists. I know the police would like to know where they are tonight and what they are up to. They're trying to track them down.'

'But why are the dwarfs doing what they're doing?'

'Nobody really knows but we think it's an act of revenge after the Danes weren't allowed to unload a shipment of pork in St. Petersburg last month because it was too old. They tried to say that it was perfectly safe for human consumption but the authorities said 'no'. So, 2,000 tonnes of pork had to be destroyed and the Danes were furious. Everyone knows that you don't take money from a Dane, or else.'

'Yes,' I joked, 'but aren't there already too many pigs in this country without importing more?'

The bartender didn't think that my joke was funny and he began to surreptitiously angle his wristwatch towards me to take some sneak photos for security police. I knew what he was up to. I was a foreigner making fun of mother Russia. All foreigners were the enemies of Russia!

I turned my back on him and looked around the bar which was otherwise half full of older men who were travelling with 'their daughters'. The background music was mostly disco covers. In

Russia, clandestine meetings like this were done quietly.

Sophya glanced at me, put her hand on my arm and told me that she was tired and ready to go up to our room. I stood up, gave the bartender a nod, and sailed out of the bar with the mainsail up and my beautiful woman in tow.

The night was intense, but not long. The door between our two rooms was duly opened and our rendezvous began – and by the time the clock struck midnight, the mammoth had roared and the hooves had pounded on the gravel, then – silence. A caress and a hand on my shoulder. A sweet goodnight. Pure bliss.

Chapter 13

A FORGED SIGNATURE

My time with Sophya since that day in Sestraretsk had been wonderful. Even though we didn't meet all that often, each time we did see each other it felt great. Business procedures were working smoothly in the office, although there were still times when I thought we were doing things weren't supposed to be doing. If anything, the feeling was getting stronger, even though I couldn't see anything irregular in the documentation or the transactions.

One day, I woke up with a nasty feeling that the day would be not turn out well, although I didn't know how or why. A few strange things had been happening and I didn't know how to deal with them. I got to the office at the usual time and signed the letters and documents placed there by my secretary despite the fact that the translations into English were not very good and I didn't really know what I was signing. Later in the morning, I decided to go out for lunch. I wanted to have to time by myself to think, so I told my driver just to drive around for a while. When we stopped at some traffic lights, my cell phone rang.

It was Ost from the Swedish consulate on the line. His whisky voice made him instantly recognisable.

'Hi, Rave, how are you? We're a little concerned about an application that we've just received from your office regarding a certain Miss Sophya Sachenova. It's her visa application. She's applying for a company visa with her daughter, and the application, it seems, has been signed by you.'

Mr. Ost was a civil servant who had worked for over 30 years for the Foreign Office in Sweden, at the Ministry of Foreign Affairs, but he'd never had a career to speak of. That was because he had three fundamental flaws: firstly, he stuck to the truth and wasn't a hypocrite, secondly, he wasn't a socialist or a feminist, and thirdly, he was honest, too kind and wanted to "do good".

All of these had effectively put a stop to his career.

Nevertheless, Ost was head of visa applications. He was a typical white, heterosexual, middle-aged man who had worked all his life and could do his job without having to think. Mr. Ost was slightly overweight despite playing indoor bandy, occasional tennis and going to the gym twice a week. He was going bald and liked a good whisky. He used to smoke but had given it up a couple of years ago for health reasons. He had a daughter in Stockholm whom he loved dearly and wanted to meet more often, but his ex-wife prevented him from meeting her. This was the worst thing that had ever happened to him and, of course, he missed his daughter bitterly. Ost owned an old sports jacket which he wore at the Swedish Club where he went to meet his fellow countrymen. He had made some good friends over the years at the British and Finnish consulates who had given him invaluable advice on how to deal with stubborn Russian bureaucrats without paying them the bribes they always expected.

He met many interesting people who visited St. Petersburg on business, but most of all, he wanted to meet his daughter once again and soon. Not being able to meet her brought tears to his eyes. How could his ex-wife be so cruel? Why did they have all rights in respect of custody of children in Sweden? Under the law, he was entitled to meet her, but if the mother said 'no' or just took the daughter away when he was going to meet her, then he was powerless. Several times, when he'd planned a visit to Sweden to meet his daughter in accordance with the court's decision, she'd taken daughter out of the country to foil his plans. The Swedish authorities did nothing about it when he complained to them.

'Rave, are you listening to me, because this is important!' Ost said, raising his voice at me down the phone. 'Are you listening?'

Clearly something was wrong, very wrong.

'Yes, I'm listening,' I said, trying to recall the documents I might have signed.

"First of all, it is quite unusual to apply for a visa for your daughter, like Sophya has done, and secondly, and this is where it gets serious, we think your signature has been forged, not only on this application, but on a number of other documents besides.'
'Really? That does surprise me because I can't actually remember signing the application you're talking about.'
'Look, I suggest you come over to the Consulate immediately and I'll show you the application.'

So we drove straight to the Swedish Consulate, parked the car and I made my way up to Ost's office

'Thanks for coming so quickly. How's business by the way?' Ost asked me, with a wry smile on his face which showed he knew something about the problems facing companies operating in Russia.
'Well, things are a bit complicated here in St. Petersburg at the moment, to say the least,' I said trying to avoid the question.
'Rave, as I told you on the phone, we're worried that your signature may have been faked on a number of occasions.'
'But who could have done that? It's not possible?'
'Well, we know that these little Russian cheats try to forge our signatures,' Ost said as he produced the application forms and slid them across his desk. He

had one eye on me and the other on the forms. 'See for yourself'!

He pointed at the signatures.

'Yes, you are right!' I said. 'Those are not my signatures! They're not. Someone has tried to forge them! But they are clearly not mine!'
'We see lots of forgeries, Rave, from Russian girls who use their relationships with Western businessmen as a way out.' When he said the word 'relationships', he paused slightly and pronounced the word as if it was a disease.
I felt both guilty, stupid and fooled.

'I'm afraid you'll have to take action in this case Rave – you don't have a choice.'
'I understand what you are saying,' I said, realising that maybe I'd had my last friendly conversation with Sophya.

'Rave, it will only get worse if you don't face up to the facts here and now. I've seen so many Western businessmen cheated by beautiful, smart Russian women. Taken to the cleaners. Many of these guys didn't even have their pants left when they returned home. And if the women didn't steal from them, they turned them into alcoholics or drove them out of their wits both physically and mentally. Very few marriages or so-called 'relationships' with Russian women last long, believe me! Honey traps are the worst. Then we're talking about women working for the FSB – in which case, you're in bed with the KGB 24/7. Every day and every night. Your home's bugged and there are listening devices everywhere. The girls report every move you make. And if you return home to Sweden to a good position, they stick with you and report your every move. It's even worse if you work for an interesting company or get a good position in the defence industry.'

'Really! So, it's as bad as that, is it? I had no idea.'

'No, it's not as bad is that, Rave, it's worse. The Mafia in St. Petersburg often need to send their people out of the country but they're blacklisted. Perhaps you've heard the rumours that the Consulate has delivered visas to some of these criminals. People with heavy criminal records and hired killers, sent out to kill people in Europe and the United States! All I'll say is that I've had to clean up so much shit here at the Consulate, you wouldn't believe it.'

'On one occasion, one of the senior officials here at the Consulate, a gay, found that St. Petersburg was 'heaven-sent' for gays. Actually, it was heaven and hell. It was heaven to begin with but hell later on. He met some young homosexuals who looked like adults, even though they were only 16. They had fun together and, of course, they filmed him in action. According to Russian law, he was a paedophile and naturally they blackmailed him. He had to give them the visas they wanted.'

'Another time, a guy from the NevskiDvor Mafia met the woman who was responsible for visas at the Consulate and coerced her into working for them. She and her partner got a nice car each for their services; a BMW and a Mercedes. She started issuing visas to extremely dangerous criminals.

But then, following a newspaper article in one of the business newspapers, the Foreign Ministry found out what was happening and clamped down on the issuing of illegal visas immediately. The woman and her partner were threatened by the Mafia and he had a nervous breakdown in the elevator at the Consulate. He shouted over and over again that the NevskiDvor Mafia were going to kill him. The next day he got a severe beating-up. Not by the Mafia, but by his wife. That's when I was called in. I came here to clean up this rat hole.'

'What a country we're living in! Can we trust anyone here?'

'No, we can't. Not at the moment. You can't trust a soul. So, try again to think if you have signed any other documents in the past few weeks.'

'Maybe, maybe not. I don't think so. Nothing I can remember - even though, as I said, I sign lots of documents in the office every day without knowing exactly what I'm signing.'

'That's not good Rave, not good at all, is it? We can do so much, but we can't take care of everything.'

'So what do you think I should do?' I asked. I felt that my secretary may have fooled me good and proper and I knew that there were those who wanted to push me out.

'Return to Sweden. Review the case with your boss and The Firm's management. Let someone else from the company come here and take over for a while. Then they'll have to find a way of controlling the situation, and that will take time.'

'Well, thanks for the advice, Ost. You've given me plenty to think about. Sometimes a person can be lulled into thinking that everything's fine but the calm can be very deceptive.'

"Actually, everyone who's here in Russia on business should go through a course with us so they understand the rules of the game, but there's nothing we can do to make them do it.'

I realized, on my way to the car that I ought to travel back to Sweden as soon as possible and report back to Gauk. So, two hours later, I was about to board a plane at Pulkovo Airport when my phone rang. It was Igor, my Russian CEO, with a question.

'What are you planning to do with Sophya?', he wanted to know. 'Give her three month's salary and six weeks holiday! No way! We've got to fire her now, Rave, immediately, today!'

He was clearly very angry.

I realized I had to dismiss Sophya with immediate effect. It would look suspicious otherwise to the people in Stockholm if I didn't. And it would also send out the wrong signals in the company. The signal would be that 'the boss protects his lover'. That would never do for me.

So, she had to go.

Later that night, after landing at Arlanda, I sat down in my apartment in Stockholm and I immediately called Sophya in St. Petersburg. I carefully explained the situation to her and the decision I had been forced to take. She burst into tears straight away and begged me over and over again to let her keep her job.

'Sophya!'I said, 'It's over. We don't have a choice. You must see that. You can't keep your job – not after what's happened. I can't protect you after what you've done – forging my signature on official documents.'

The following morning, when I met Gauk, I informed him that I had fired Sophya. He made fun of me as usual in front of his fan club, showing off his power, with his entourage appreciating the show. He went on and on, mocking me over what had happened.

'The only people who would dare to do such a thing against me are my wife and perhaps my mistress.' Chimney and Mushroom laughed on cue, which was what they were paid to do. Gauk did not have a mistress. We all knew that. However, of course the joke was aimed at me and I knew that my days in charge of the business in Russia were hanging on a very thin thread.

'OK,' I said to myself. 'From now on I'm working only for myself. Fuck you Gauk and The Firm! I'm going to take what I can get, and you won't know what's happening until it's too late.'

Chapter 14

FISHING IN IMATRA

I realized that The Firm needed to be reconstructed. A smaller number of different business areas had to be phased out, sold or simply wound up. It had become pretty clear that private loans, private sales and money transfers had to go immediately.

In Stockholm, everyone was gathered. Gauk, Garbage, Poisonous Spider, Chimney and Mushroom accepted my proposals unconditionally. Gauk said, rather surprisingly for once, that he thought I was right; that I don't have to convince him, and all the others nodded in unison as usual.

Back in St. Petersburg, I called my management team in and we decided to get rid of all the company's private business. It would all be terminated with immediate effect.

But I could feel an icy wind sweeping through the office. People were scared and it was clear that impromptu meetings were taking place behind closed doors to which I was not welcome. The atmosphere was tense and heavy. An unpleasant cloud of worry was spreading through the office and everyone was nervous.

The next morning, when he arrived at work, Igor my CEO, bulldozed his way along the corridor, pushing and knocking into people, until he tore open the door of my office door and stood there facing me and looked me hard in the eye. He was clearly frightened of something. His face was bright red and, in his English-Russian dialect, he told me that he had decided to leave The Firm. He wanted to be relieved of his duties immediately, he said.

'Why Igor? Why do you want to give up your job?' I asked. I was really taken aback. 'This is your dream job, so why now?'
'Rave, don't you understand? You must have considered the risks when you decided to enter the Russian market. Why do you think the authorities gave you a license?' said Igor getting really cross. I'd never seen him like this before.
'Rave, what you're doing is very dangerous. You can't close the channels for money laundering. Don't you know who you're dealing with?'

After a few more words of warnings, he was gone.

He was right. I knew that. From now on, we would be facing more major problems, as if we didn't have enough already. I felt a sense of fear creeping into my body and shivered at the thought. The people we were up against were extremely dangerous and we'd issued them a challenge. Again, I thought I would have to think very carefully about my future actions.

After leaving the office for the last time, Igor seemed relieved as he walked away even though he took a couple of quick looks over his shoulder as he walked towards his car. His driver pulled up beside him and, as a final gesture, drove him home to his apartment in the central part of the city.

***

Early next morning, Igor and his family left St. Petersburg and set off for Imatra. He was looking forward to a total break from The Firm and St Petersburg and, even more, to a week with his family and some good fishing in their dacha on the Finnish side of the border.

He was no longer responsible what happened at The Firm, but he knew that Rave and the other foreigners didn't understand how dangerous everything would soon get.

'Let's put this behind all us and just think about enjoying ourselves for the next week, shall we?' said Sonja as they drove out of St. Petersburg.

The children's voices piped up in the back seat. 'Papa, papa, do we really have to go out fishing? We want stay inside by the open fire and play computer games instead. It is more fun. It'll be really cold outside!'

The dark blue Pajero approached the border control,

the first of four, two of them being on the Russian side and two on the Finnish side. The queues were quite long as usual; a mix of commercial vehicles and private motorists in one single, disorganised mess.

'For Christ's sake! Can't the bloody bureaucrats do something about this?' Igor grumbled away to himself. 'Last time it took us four hours to cross. When you see the border controls and the military everywhere, you'd think we were still living in 1946. Nothing has changed,100% distrust from both sides, 100% bureaucracy.'

Finally, they reached the first checkpoint and Igor got out of the car with the family's passports. He entered a small office manned by two fat customs officials who seemed to have been squeezed into the tiny space so that they could sweat properly in their woollen uniforms.

Back in the car again 15 minutes later, Igor drove forward in the queue of cars at a snail's pace to the next station. Here there was another tiny office, manned by another two fat customs officers in their own overheated cage with the smell of dust, coffee, sweat, and files stuffed with kilos of typed reports hanging in the air. More questions, suspicious looks and Russian bureaucracy. Igor felt angry over his own nation's inability to modernise. However, he would never express any of his views to his friends and definitely never to a foreigner.

'At least the air flights operate reasonably well,' he muttered to himself, 'otherwise this country would still be stuck in the Middle Ages.'

It was spring in Karelia, with snow still on the ground. But it was sunny, and the sun was getting stronger by the day. Igor drove on and Sonja and the children all seemed to be in good spirits after the delays at the border controls. Good food, some 'real' drinking, visiting friends, pimple fishing and vodka on the ice were what lay ahead.

'We don't want to go fishing! Sitting still, waiting for ever and freezing to death. We don't like fishing!'

The children laughed and played around in the back seat, sure that they'd be able to skip the outdoor activities in order to focus on computer games and TV programmes. Finnish TV broadcast Russian channels too, which was good since it made them all feel at home.

Igor and Sonja spent the first day settling in, playing with the kids and having a long, relaxing evening dinner. Taking care of one another. Sonya could see that her husband was starting to feel more at ease, and his comments about the company, Rave, and recent events were becoming fewer.

Morning, Day two. After a heavy overnight frost, the sun rose on a spring-like Karelia. The family was still asleep when Igor, after enjoying a substantial breakfast, took his fishing equipment and walked out onto the frozen lake. He drilled a hole in the ice, set his hooks on the line on and sat down on his backpack which, with its smart construction, also functioned as a chair. Nothing happened in the icy hole. Igor took out his hip flask and took a large swig of Russian vodka, Standard, which was his favourite.

The day continued in the same way. No life in the ice holes, but Igor could feel the warmth of the sun on his back and the glow of the vodka inside. He sat leaning slightly forward, elbows on knees, concentrating on the hole between his feet.

At lunchtime, Sonja took the children with her and went out onto the ice in the warm sunshine to Igor who had been fishing all morning. She though it was time for lunch and that Igor should spend some time now with his family and not just sit and drink like a typical Russian on holiday.

As they approached Igor from behind, Sonja saw Igor still leaning forward, but uncannily still. He was motionless. Then she saw the hole in the back of his head. Igor was slumped forward with his head almost down on his stomach. Sonja understood straight away what had happened and didn't want to turn Igor around to look at him. Neither did she want the children to see what was left of his face, and the pieces of his brain which were splattered around the open hole in the ice. Sonja knew instinctively that a shot had come from far away without it being heard. And for all she knew, whoever had shot Igor might very well be aiming at her and her children that very second, so she rapidly gathered the children together and they all returned to the dacha.

'Is Papa was going to have lunch with us or not?' the children asked innocently.

The local Finnish police did their usual job but with no involvement; they went through the motions, but they knew. They'd seen it before and they knew that no one would investigate what had happened. They would receive orders to send the corpse home to Russia and close the investigation for 'special reasons', and the investigation would be taken over by the federal police in Helsinki who would simply throw the folder into the bin. They didn't want to have any trouble; they didn't want to be involved in Russian internal affairs. The fact that the deceased man was the Russian CEO of a Swedish firm in St. Petersburg didn't make any difference.

Sonja was informed about what would happen to the body of her deceased husband, and the police offered to help her pack and return home to Russia immediately. Obviously, she wouldn't want to stay there any longer and, besides, no-one knew if the perpetrators were still in the area or what their orders were.

Sonja and the policemen packed everything while the children sat on the couch, holding each other and crying. With the children and all the luggage in the car, Sonja drove away from Imatra on the winter road towards the border crossing.

One of the policemen stood and watched them as the car's rear lights disappeared over the hill. Another officer cordoned off the house and the small fishing hole that Igor had made with tape, to show that they were crime scenes. They looked at each other, feeling sorry for the beautiful, young Russian woman who was now returning back to a completely different life in Russia. Without a husband, without an income, without protection.

At a bar in the small town of Imatra, two men sat and ate dinner. They spoke Russian. Brown beans and fried pork, Karelian strong beer. Nice to have a really good meal after a day like theirs.

'Good thing I didn't have to cut off his cock. It's sad when the kids need to see something like that. But still, it was a nice job, if there are such things in our business. We don't want to be brutal pigs, do we?'

'By the way,' said his partner, 'what are you doing this weekend? Come over and have some drinks with me and my wife, why don't you? Mother-in-law comes to visit and always nags me a lot that I don't treat Vera and the kids well enough, and that I don't give Vera enough money for food and clothes for the family. It would be great if you could come so I wouldn't have to listen to all that shit.'

The two men looked at each other and laughed out loud. Everyone had a mother-in-law in Russia.

After finishing their meal, the two men stood up and threw some euro banknotes onto the table. They gave the waiter a cold look, and then left the bar, letting the door slam behind them as they left. Outside, it was empty and dark, no-one could be seen and it had started to snow.

Chapter 15

SPYBABES

During the Soviet times, Russian women, or 'spybabes' as they became known, were trained to work as spies in a school near the Bulgarian capital of Sofia. The women were trained in a way that could be likened to military training, with additional emphasis on social skills, language skills and sex and eroticism. They were young; they were beautiful and were taught how to use their female guiles in the bedroom to get what they wanted. The women moved around within the Soviet Union, got married, had children and usually had civilian jobs while being on standby for special assignments. These varied from having dinner with a target in a restaurant, to moving to somewhere new and getting a job in an organisation with a view to establishing contact with a specific person over a longer period of time. A kind of mole you could say.

Judith Lownds was recruited as a young girl in St. Petersburg and attended the school in Sofia. After graduating, she was placed in Stockholm where she made contact with her Controller, whom she then met at regular intervals at pre-arranged places, for briefings and debriefings. Long before her Stockholm posting, Judith had established contact with the Church and especially with the priests who had been active in East Germany's feared security system, STASI. These priests reported the East Germans who tried to escape and their accomplices to Stasi. Many of those reported were on the receiving end of life-long prison sentences in terrible conditions. Others were summarily executed.

Some of the priests worked in Stockholm for the Russian intelligence service and were very helpful when it came to producing the requisite ID documents needed for Sweden to accept a particular person into the country.

Judith had one of her regular meetings with her Controller. She spent two hours shaking off any possible 'tail' from the Swedish secret police before the meeting in a park in a Stockholm suburb.

After the customary small talk, Judith was given her new assignment.

'We want you to arrange a Swedish visa and citizenship for a woman.'

'OK, and who is she?'

Judith was shown of a photo of Sophya.

'This is the woman. You might even know her. She's worked for us before.'

'Yes, I've met her,' said Judith. 'And I should be able

to arrange this. It may take some time but I'm sure I can do it. I have a contact that has connections in the Migration Board. It will cost, but it can be done.'

The Controller stuck his hand into his pocket and pulled out a thick wad of Swedish banknotes which he quickly handed over to Judith. 'Tell me if you need any more,' he said, before turning around and walking away.

To be eligible for Swedish citizenship, a person must have lived in the country for a minimum of five years. You also needed a residence permit and be able to show that you were a law-abiding citizen. And, first and foremost, you had to be able to prove your identity. This was where the STASI priests came into the picture. They could forge the required documents, such as birth certificates.

When everything was in place, Judith could then contact her source at the Migration Board's office and obtain the visa and passport. So far, it had worked perfectly and a number of Russian agents had been able to enter Sweden to live and work successfully in Sweden under cover as Swedish citizens.

Sophya would soon get a new identity, a new life, and become a Swedish citizen citizen.

What that would mean for her, she had no idea!

Judith Lownds' father was a Russian citizen and her mother was from Moldova. They were a well-established Jewish couple in St. Petersburg and members of the Communist Party. Judith was a very attractive young, blonde, Jewish girl. She was also intelligent and quickly learned to speak a number of different languages at school. Despite the fact that she was born into a relatively poor family, Judith had climbed the social ladder in St. Petersburg and when the Soviet empire collapsed, she was quickly and easily installed into Stockholm with a visa and work permit and soon became established among the Jewish elite in Stockholm.

Judith enjoyed life in Stockholm. She worked as a piano teacher, and as a qualified translator and interpreter. She didn't work very much but money didn't seem to be a problem for her. It came to her anyway, as if by magic. Perhaps someone was supporting her? She had a good life and met many interesting people. Needless to say, she was frequently invited out by love-besotted young men.

So, life was good and she loved it. 160 cm tall, thin with a high bosom, a slavish face with witty eyes and the demeanour of an angel, a well-sculpted nose and a mouth made for kissing.

***

Benny lived in a small run-down town not far from Stockholm. His German parents had survived the

172

Holocaust during the war and had lived in transit camps on the continent before they were allowed to move north.

They arrived in Sweden without a penny to their name and started a new life from scratch. Benny's father repaired shoes and his mother cleaned in a cheap hotel near the Stockholm Central Station.

Life was hard for the family but things improved over the years, and with help from other immigrants their situation became increasingly comfortable.

During Benny's upbringing, the family members were regular visitors to the synagogue where Benny met boys and girls of the same age with similar interests to him. Benny decided to do everything possible to become part of the inner circle at the synagogue and the other Jewish circles in order to climb socially and economically. It would be his way to access money and achieve success.

He made sure that he attended all the events that he possibly could at the synagogue and became a member of the Jewish association of art and culture.

One evening in August, there was a classical music concert, performed by the young talented members of the congregation. Of course, Benny was there; dressed up in his best suit and tie and ready for anything that might happen and any beautiful women who could possibly come his way.

Sitting behind the grand piano was the most adorable blonde beauty that Benny had ever set eyes on. A really attractive, Jewish family girl. He had never seen anyone more beautiful, and not surprisingly, she was surrounded by an entourage of smartly-dressed young men. They all saw her as the potential mother of their children. A young Jewish girl like her, they thought, would marry a conservatively educated Jewish boy from the congregation and they all thought they were made for the role.

There and then, Benny made a promise. 'That beautiful young girl will be my wife.'

Not only did he admire her beauty, but he believed that she would also be his ticket into the Jewish community he had been looking for.

After introducing himself to her that night, he walked Judith home. So, now he knew her address. He started bombarding her with roses and presents, invitations for dinners and the theatre. His interest in her became stronger and more intense as the weeks went by. At first, she was quite cool, assuming he was just a gold digger who wanted to climb, but he didn't give up. He continued to pursue her. After a while, Judith began to enjoy some of his approaches and his apparent sincerity. Was it love? Real love after all?

After six months, she invited him to her apartment

and, lo and behold, before long they were married.

Benny was happy. Everything he had dreamt of had come true. Although he had an ordinary job as a postman, as Judith's husband he was invited to meet with the inner circle of the Jewish community.

They lived together in Judith's apartment and the years came and went. Judith became pregnant but had a miscarriage and it seemed like theirs would be a childless marriage. Then, to make matters worse, some of Judith's 'finer friends' started to see Benny as a boring, mundane person, and they started to fall by the wayside. Invitations to parties and trips dried up and, within a relatively short space of time, Judith and Benny became socially isolated, with only each other for company. Almost inevitably, the basis on which their marriage was built began to crumble.

Love changed to hate for Judith. She now hated him. She had her own money, and nobody, including Benny, knew where it came from. Someone was supporting her, but Benny didn't know who. He had no idea what her other profession was.

He accused her of being greedy and not spending enough money on the parties they still had with the few friends that were left. According to him, their friends felt that she was snobby, mean and arrogant and it was her fault that they were alone.

One evening, Judith was sitting alone on the couch,

looking at old photos of parties and trips with friends they no longer had. Dinners, laughter, playing cards and having fun together. She started to cry.

The door opened and Benny entered the room wearing his postman's shirt with sweat rings around his armpits. He had worked the late shift and sorted mail all evening. She looked at him and thought to herself; he's 40, he's bald, he wears cheap working clothes and he's boring. He's ruined my life and that's the simple truth.

'Get out of my apartment, Benny. Now. Just leave!'

Judith looked at him with hatred in her eyes.

'Then, come back tomorrow and pick up your stuff. After that, I never want to see you again.'

Benny just stood there speechless.

He could tell that the battle was lost even before it had begun. There was nothing he could say or do change Judith's mind. So, he turned around, walked out into the hall and closed the door quietly behind him as he left. Whether he liked it or not, his days with Judith were over and there was nothing he could do about it.

Benny knew that Judith had always been the strong one in their marriage. The money she'd received had given her the upper-hand and he had suspected more recently that someone had been supporting her. Someone in St. Petersburg perhaps? Someone with power? It scared him a little.

And now he was on his own again - just another immigrant with a shit job and no contacts. The only thing he still had was his old mother who lived in a one-room flat on the outskirts of the city.

He made his way to the subway station and headed in her direction.

Chapter 16

A RAPID EXIT

Now, after Igor's resignation and execution, I had been left completely on my own at The Firm. Everyone seemed to be taking a step back. It was chaotic in Stockholm and the atmosphere was like a funeral in the St. Petersburg office. Sophya was still in St. Petersburg but didn't speak to me anymore. How much worse could it get? Someone was using The Firm for shady business – I had known it since the day I walked through the door, but I couldn't put my finger on it. Still couldn't.

This was what Russians were good at. Manipulating operations without foreigners knowing what they were up to. So far, I hadn't really been able to find out what our business actually was. That was probably why I was still alive. Igor and our CFO had always excluded me by using Russian as a shield. Despite trying to hire some loyal allies, I had not been able to find out anything of interest.

Everyone was involved, I thought. They all knew what was happening. The driver, the secretary, the hotel staff. Probably even Sophya? Everyone was getting a piece of the cake. How big was the scam and how did it work? The Russians constantly updated the management routines with too much detailed information: a proven way to hide the true facts by 'over-informing'.

Garbage and his men ran around like rats in a wheel. They didn't understand that they would not be able to change anything here. Every time you found one doll and opened it, there is a new smaller doll inside. The Russian dilemma. I was completely unprotected and the last one to know what was going on. I was responsible for Igor's death because I forced him to reconstruct the company against his wishes in a way that 'strong influential forces' didn't think was a good idea. I had no one to talk to. Stockholm would never understand what the situation really was.

I also saw that my smart little secretary now had a look in her eye that she hadn't had before. The look you see when Russians think they are on top. They may have crawled and kissed your ass, but now they had the upper hand it was time for revenge and they liked it. I could see in her eyes that I would soon find out how it was to fear for my life in Russia without any back-up.

I was on my way to a lunch meeting with my art agent. We'd had many interesting meetings in the past and I always enjoyed her company. She was a Russian Ukrainian woman in her forties, slim, well-dressed and she spoke good English. She was always very understanding, like all Russians when they could smell money.

Lunch with her in the city centre was a way for me to get a view of the world outside the office walls.

She was waiting for me outside the restaurant but behaved rather stiffly. Where was the warm greeting and smile that I usually got? In Russia, it works like this. Russians are Russians and foreigners are the enemies of the Russians. She, like everyone else around me, was well informed and knew what the police were watching me and soon she began to preach the Russian nationalist mantra to me.

'As long as you foreigners come with your cheap money, it is good for Russia.'

'But you can't grow too much and become important to the infrastructure without attracting attention and eventually becoming 'state-owned' in some way.'

'We can take back your business whenever we want. Nothing is more important than Mother Russia and the prosperity we build for our citizens.'

She went on and on with her propaganda and her hatred of the West. Gone were the discussions about art, friendship, wine, travel, family and so on. Her tone was hard.

***

That night I dreamt that Sophya came to me with a little box in her hand. I was eager to take the box and remove the lid.

'Take it easy my friend,' she said, 'I'd like to give you a present.'

She slowly began to open the box herself. Must be a valuable gift, I thought. The scent was wonderful.

'Take it, take it now!' She held the box high in the air and I tried to reach it.

Then she lowered it in front of my eyes. It was a heart, cut out of a body, full of blood and still beating. I wanted to take it and hold it. But she held it high above my head again.

Then she started sucking the blood; sucking it out of the heart, the blood running from her mouth until the heart was dry and had stopped beating.

'Now my little friend, we will go home and lie down in bed. Everything will be fine,' she said to me before laughing like a witch.

- HA HA HA HA HA...!

I woke up with a start, covered in sweat and shaking like an animal. My sheets were wet through. I tried to push the nightmare away, out of my mind, but the memory of her drinking the blood stayed with me and I lay there waiting for the dawn.

Later the following day, just after lunch, my secretary came into my office with a small note in her hand on which she had noted a name and two phone numbers. She gave me the note then looked down at the floor and took a half step backwards.

'A policeman has called. He wants a meeting with you. He didn't say what it was about.'

She looked frightened and I understood why. No Russian wanted to get involved in police matters. Without a foreign passport, and with no embassy or company to back you up, you could disappear without anyone asking what had happened. The little man in Russia was completely defenceless.

Flogel was quite clear when he spoke. 'You're not going to any police station. We'll send one of our Russian employees in your place. It's out of the question! A police officer isn't always a police officer. It could easily be a trap. This could be the work of the FSB. Everyone knows what they are, and that's why people are afraid of them. And then again, it could also be the FSB working for someone else with a different agenda.'

We sent a female colleague to the police station in my place, but she was not able to find the policeman who wanted to talk to me. He was not at the police station and she couldn't trace him to any station in St. Petersburg either. She was convinced it was the security police who wanted a meeting but, in that case, who were they working for, who was behind it, and what did they want to discuss?

They more we speculated, the more uncertain we became. One theory was that perhaps someone was trying to kidnap me in order to squeeze The Firm for money. That was a distinct possibility, but then again it could be something completely different. No one wanted to stay around to find out.

'You have to leave Russia today.' The order came from Gauk and as such was non-negotiable. There was nothing more to say. Two tickets were immediately booked for the evening flight to Stockholm. One for me and one for Flogel.

On our way to the airport, Flogel asked me who I thought might be involved in the threat against me.

'Maybe Sophya and her friends - or people close to Igor?' I continued, 'and then again it could be a set-up from Stockholm, masterminded by none other than Gauk himself. A ploy to make me scarred, to humiliate me before firing me on a fake accusation?'

'I'm sure the sole purpose is to get me fired. Sophya, or others close to me, have possibly leaked information about my activities. Who knows?'

'I think you may be right Rave. There could be a threat from inside The Firm,' said Flogel. 'Could be

Gauk and his boys trying to make it look as if the Russian security police are involved. Could very likely be something thought up by one of those ass-lickers who wants to break into Gauk's inner circle.'

At the airport, my driver parked the car and turned to face me. 'One way or other, Mr. Alexander, I do not think you will be allowed to leave Russia.' He wasn't smiling.

He had the same expression on his face as my secretary; a look that testified to control and revenge. You come here with too much money, take advantage of our young girls, drink our vodka. All foreigners are Russia's enemies.

I said nothing, but quickly took my luggage from the car and gave him his usual 1,000 roubles. Then I started elbowing my way through the Departure Hall with Flogel in tow. As usual, the queues were long and it was slow going through passport control. What happens if I get a red light? I thought. How deep are the pockets of the so-called officers? If it's Gauk and his boys behind all of this, then it'll be OK, but if it's the Russians and there's a price on my head, then I could be in real danger!

As I came closer to the front of the queue, I became more and more convinced that I would be stopped and my mind raced away thinking about the possible outcomes, all worse that the one before. I could feel my heart beating faster and faster as my breathing became shallower. All I could do was keep my eyes on the floor and hope that it was my lucky day. And finally, when my turn came, I got a greenlight at the passport control, thank God, and we pushed on with a huge sense of relief through the crowd to our gate where our flight was boarding.

When we were flying at 30,000 feet and had left Russian airspace, Flogel turned around a few seats in front of me and raised his glass of champagne. He made the 'V for victory' sign and we both smiled in the knowledge that we had made it out of the country with our lives intact.

Chapter 17

GAUK'S WRATH

I felt much better after having landed at Arlanda Airport, 60 kilometres north of Stockholm. Both Flogel and I felt quite tired but relieved to be back in a civilized country. We took the airport bus to town.

'I must say, Rave, it's nice to be home again, even if we don't know what tomorrow will bring.'

'Yes, absolutely. It's good to be back in Stockholm again.'

'Actually Rave, I don't feel completely safe in Stockholm either these days. There are so many strange things going on here too. The FSB has agents here, you know. They could easily arrange something against us here in Stockholm if they wanted to.'

This was definitely not what I wanted to hear now that we were finally back home, so I stayed quiet.

'No matter what you might think Rave, that's how it is. I heard about a businessman who returned to Sweden after doing some suspect business in Russia. The Russians here in Sweden shadowed him, harassed him and threatened him and his family until he finally committed suicide. If you've once been in their claws, they don't let go. They want more all the time.'

'Let's get together somewhere in a few days and catch up on things,' Flogel suggested and I nodded.

We shook hands and I watched him disappear in his taxi. I flagged down a taxi to take me back to my apartment. Even by Swedish standards it was rather spacious, very modern and tastefully furnished. A great place to live in other words. It also overlooked a park and, as the taxi drew up outside the main entrance, I admitted to myself that I had missed that view for a long time.

Having eaten and tidied away, I poured myself a drink and start browsing through the newspapers to catch up on the latest news.

Typically, the lead story was the latest government report on overweight men and women and how they needed to be supported nationally with the creation of a new department employing hundreds of specialists. I curled up on the sofa and fell asleep. Nothing much had changed in Sweden.

***

In the office the next day, Gauk wanted a meeting with me. I wasn't sure what the meeting was about although I had a pretty good idea, and I was feeling somewhat apprehensive. Probably the whole death squad would be in attendance. Chimney, Ash, Mushroom, Garbage and little Poisonous Spider from the treasury department would all want to cut me to pieces in the boardroom. 'I'd ruined our business in Russia.' 'It was my fault.' I would try to explain, but would they believe me? No way. And I had to hold back some of the information- I couldn't tell them everything.

'Rave, Gauk wants to see you in the boardroom! Now, so make it snappy!' Garbage barked in his unsavoury voice.

'I'm on my way'.

'Well hurry up! We don't have all day.'

Entering the boardroom, I felt like a lamb being led to the slaughter. Almost the entire company has a grandstand view to witness today's event. I felt extremely small; an insignificant, meaningless person that could be dispensed with at the drop of a hat even though I knew that I held a number of aces.

A large chair was placed in the middle of the room and Gauk settled himself into it whilst his team of supporters lined up behind him to give their backing, as always, to their lord and master. The Nuremberg trials were probably a walk in the park compared to this.

Pointing towards a smaller chair opposite his, Gauk

began. 'Sit down Rave. We have to speak. To begin with, tell me what the hell is happening in St. Petersburg? Igor has been murdered for fuck's sake. Murdered!'

Gauk was breathing heavily due in part to his asthma. He was convinced that one day he'd die of asphyxiation and perhaps he was right.

He looked around the room with his blood-stained, swollen eyes, which looked as if they were about to pop out of his head at any second. Then he stood up and surveyed the supporting cast behind him. One by one, from left to right. Ash, Chimney, Garbage, Mushroom and little Poisonous Spider from the finance department. Gauk was a big man. He physically dominated everything and everyone in the room with his whole body. As always, he was the absolute centre of attention. And his brain was the sharpest of the sharp.

The five of them looked down at the floor to avoid eye contact with Gauk and waited for his next utterance, but it was Garbage who spoke first.

'Something is completely wrong here,' said Garbage. 'We should never have sent Rave to Russia in the first place. He couldn't handle the responsibility. His focus was all wrong and he was too horny to keep his mind on the job.'

Garbage looked around to see if anyone was

nodding, but apparently no-one was ready to agree with him.

Then Gauk began. 'According to you all, Rave was the one who was supposed to understood the Russian market best. It is too late now to say it but, he couldn't handle the job. You should all have spoken up much sooner. So, I'm hanging you all out to dry for this, do you understand! All of you!'

Garbage visibly shrank in his baggy pin-striped suit and tried to make himself as small as possible.

I sat silently opposite Gauk listening. Everyone was talking about me in the third person.

Gauk was extremely angry and continued with his 'show' without actually looking at me directly.

'Well yes, the murder is front-page news now in all the newspapers, but it's not such a big deal, is it?' said Mushroom meekly.

'Not yet maybe, but we in Stockholm will have to take all the shit because Rave in St. Petersburg couldn't handle his job,' said Garbage.

Poisonous Spider nodded; everyone was silent.

Garbage had always hated Rave. Rave had been successful with women which he had never been.

Garbage honestly thought that Rave had spent all his time screwing whores and drinking whisky at the company's expense. He, Garbage, should have been sent there instead of Rave. He would have solved all the problems and built the business into a profit-making enterprise. We'd have made profits in the first year – St. Petersburg would have been the most profitable country in the Group. Yes, Garbage thought, I would have steered the ship well. Rave is a bastard! Just an incompetent, disloyal bastard!

'But this this whole business must not, under any circumstances, harm The Firm's good reputation. We must show the world that we have taken the problem seriously and that we are taking the necessary steps to correct things. Have any of the journalists called?

'One journalist has called and wants to know what our strategy is for dealing with St. Petersburg.' Mushroom replied, sweating profusely.

'Say that we have nothing more to add other than what is on our website, and that we do not, I repeat not, launder money to Sweden. We work with real financing and create business opportunities for our customers in Russia.

'What is this shit? What has Rave done? What's he involved in? The Firm's good name is in danger and why don't any of you know anything about this? You're all just a bunch of wankers. You are fucking useless. All of you. You can't make money for the company and you haven't got a clue about what's really going on. It's totally unacceptable. Not good at all. You're a bunch of losers, that's what you are. Gentlemen. You suck!

And once again, everyone looked down at the floor, diverting their eyes away from Gauk.

'Chimney, it was your goddam job to keep an eye on Rave. Why didn't you do just that, you dick-head idiot?
'I tried, but Russia's too far away, and they only speak Russian so it's impossible to understand reports and stuff like that,' Chimney pleaded, getting smaller by the minute.
'But have you even been there?'

He was becoming even more nervous now, his body curling up as he listened to Gauk. He nodded.

'How many times?'
'Twice.'
'Just twice, in all this time? You can't do business sitting on your ass. Haven't you understood that yet?'
'Yes, but it was really complicated with the visas and everything. You've no idea of all the problems that come up!'
'What!' bellowed Gauk as he seemed about to explode. He looked around the room at all the

hangers-on standing silently with their heads down, and then announced his verdict.

Gauk's voice boomed across the room.

'Rave must go! It's that simple. As of this second, you no longer work for The Firm. So, get out of my sight! Now!'

At which point, I followed Gauk's instruction and left the boardroom.

He meanwhile continued to rant and rave.

'Somebody fix the papers and make sure that Rave signs them straight away. This smells to me like a money-laundering scandal. And do you all get it? Do you understand? If we've laundered money for the Russians then we're all finished. Dead.'

'If you want to keep your jobs here – if you want to receive your pensions, then we've got to act NOW! Do I make myself perfectly clear?'

'Rave's name must be removed from all The Firm's

Russian documentation and the authorities with whom he's been in contact.'

'And finally, 'Gauk continued, 'Why was Igor murdered? We have to arrange a meeting with the Russians.'

'Chimney, arrange a meeting with the Russian trade delegation at their earliest possible convenience.'

'And the rest of your idiots, go through all the transactions between Russia and Sweden in the last six months and hide or erase everything that looks like an irregular payment.'

Ash was the next to speak. 'But since Igor has been murdered, everyone has to understand that it is the Mafia who are behind it. And then it is a job for the police and we can avoid any liability.'

Ash thought he'd been so smart but decided not to make any further comments. Garbage left the room quickly. When he had gone, Gauk turned to Poisonous Spider.

'Talk to HR. Make sure we fire Garbage too along with Rave.'

Poisonous Spider from Treasury smiled almost imperceptibly.

Gauk went on talking.

'We need to find out everything. What has Rave done and how deeply are we involved? What will it cost us to get out of it? We must to get to the bottom of this now while we can still have a chance to control it.'

Gauk signalled to Poisonous Spider with a dismissive wave of the hand that the meeting was over.

Chapter 18

A VISIT TO THE DENTIST

Stockholm was the home to a Nigerian dentist by the name of Yusuf Bello. Bello, a magnificent physical specimen in his prime. In addition to being a highly competent dentist, he also serviced his patients/customers by doubling up as a fertility guru. He had developed a service for the containment and cure of 'an itching condition' experienced by both his male and female clients from time to time in their genital regions. He referred to the condition as Golitis; something which could never be completely cured but could be kept under control through Bello's interventions. He had built up a long list of loyal customers who returned for treatment at regular intervals, and the thrust of his business in the elegant clinic on Birger Jarlsgatan, in central Stockholm, had slowly shifted from dentistry to the treatment of Golitis.

The service was not exactly announced in neon lights outside his clinic but rather it had become known through the best marketing channel in the word — by word of mouth, which was both highly discreet and highly confidential.

For 'educational purposes', and as 'insurance' against any of his clients who might for some reason want to turn the tables on him, he always documented his intervention treatments with the aid of hidden video cameras. His clients were naturally blissfully ignorant of the covert filming, as too was his assistant Ken, a well-trained, slim, young man who was very much 'hands on' during treatments. The considerable volume of his entire filmed material was stored on Bello's hard disk.

Bello had a number of bank accounts, but amortising his loans on time was not one of his strengths. Paperwork and red tape. He didn't take them very seriously.

Every morning, bank manager Sven Thorn, one of Bello's Golitis clients incidentally, went through the day's overdraft reports, and invariably, the same name, the dentist's, would appear on the listed accounts. 'He really must do better,' Sven thought as he stared out through the window on a very grey morning, 'even though he has a fine pair of hands,' and something stirred within him.

The bank's head office had sent out a directive to all its branch offices to draw up a list of their customers with payment difficulties and to specify, in concrete terms, the measures to be taken to ensure that these people were 'encouraged' to take their business elsewhere.

'Hannu, come here please, would you?'

Sven's right-hand man, Hannu Uupne, was an Estonian like Sven, who had arrived in his mother arms on a boat 30 years earlier. They were like blood brothers.

Hannu's family had received financial support from Russia to 'start their new life in Sweden'. Hannu and his parents were still deeply loyal to the Russians. He still didn't really understand why they'd had to flee a country that had supported them financially, and still did. It was a bit strange to him, but he knew that if he saw or heard something, or came across pictures, documents or anything in fact which could be of value to Russia, then it was his absolute duty to pass it on to them, even if it was about someone close like Sven, or even his own parents. Hannu had his own contact person in Stockholm. It was a woman called Judith Lownds.

'Hannu, you're driving your taxi tonight, aren't you?' said Thorn. 'We've got to get our dear friend, the dentist from Nigeria, sorted out one of these days. So tonight, I want you to stop by his clinic at about midnight and pick up his day's takings, and then bring the money here in the morning. We'll count it here in my office and then deposit it into his account.'

'No worries. I'm go to Randolf's at three thirty to collect their cash so I can visit Yusuf beforehand.'

'Bello will like the service we're offering and won't mind paying a small fee for it,' Sven continued, 'unlike all those who hate paying, no matter how small they are. But Bello needs our help and we need him.'

'I'll call him and make the arrangements. He'll understand. He trusts us.'

Both men look pleased although Hannu, some 20 years younger than Sven, didn't yet fully know the extent of Bello's 'other business' or that many of the dentist's clients attended the clinic in the evening.

Everything went according to plan. Hannu collected cash first from the nightclub and then from the dentist. In the morning, he and Sven counted the money, set aside their own personal service fees, and handed over the banknotes to the cashier to be deposited into the respective accounts. No one asked about the origin of the money.

Two months later, Hannu was making an end-of-month Friday night collection. Randolf's was packed with people and the place was rocking. Hannu decided to have a mineral water in the bar and to see what was happening. He stood at the bar with his bag, now stuffed with bank notes from the dentist, beside two ladies of 'mature age' who had clearly forced down a few too many tequilas already.

'And listen to me Sara; If you have problems with your itching, now that your husband has gone to Japan, then I can give you a really good tip,' the taller one of the two said giggling.

Sara turned towards her friend and showed Hannu a flash of her magnificent cleavage which was as big as the Grand Canyon. Hannu feasted his eyes on the spectacular view, leant closer, and listened more carefully to the conversation.

'What did you say about a good tip?'

'I said that there's a dentist I've heard of. He's called 'the stallion from Lagos'- a magnificent specimen of manhood, they say. His clients are diplomats, businessmen and women, bankers, politicians, you name it, and he has an assistant who is very tender who serves both men and women.'

'What the hell are you talking about? Fuck, there goes a hole in my tights. I'll take them off.'

Sara stood on one leg and began to pull at her tights but only managed to fall backwards over the bag full of money, and into Hannu's arms.

Accidently, Hannu's hands were all over her breasts as he sat her up at the bar and apologized.

'It doesn't matter pretty boy! If you want to be friends just write your number here.'

Sara pulled up her skirt to expose her panties and turned to offer him her lipstick to write with. But when she looked up, he's was making a rapid exit with the bag safely in his grasp and she stumbled over her tights and fell back onto the floor again, at which point, two security guards moved in and did their best to help the two women to recover their dignity.

Hannu, by now sitting in his taxi, took out a piece of paper and started to write down what he had heard. Elite prostitution perhaps with customers from the establishment, politics, the business world, the military, the mafia. Both men and women. Judith might very well be interested in digging into this a little? There may be photos as evidence; everyone took photos these days.

When he'd finished writing an account of what he'd overheard, he started his taxi and drove to Sigtunagatan.

He rang Mrs. Lownds buzzer and she admitted him into the building. He walked up the staircase to her door and posted his report into her letter box before beating a hasty retreat and driving home.

Having read Hannu's report, Judith called Kovalchuk the following morning to brief him about this interesting piece of information. They agreed to meet up at one of their usual contact points. Judith waited at the corner of the street dressed for jogging. She saw Kovalchuk get out of his car and walk past her at a leisurely pace. She followed him and soon caught him up. They walked and talked around the block without actually making eye contact.

'One of my informants tells me there is dentist on Birger Jarlsgatan with a high number of prominent clients who enjoy the extra services which on offer to the right people. People from different walks of life, like politicians, senior military officers, bankers, civil servants, diplomats, you name it.'

'So,' said Kovalchuk, 'Book a time with the dentist and say you're worried about your old fillings from Russia. Then try to get him to deliver his "other" service. He must be called 'the stallion from Lagos' for a reason. Brush your teeth properly before you go.'
Kovalchuk turned around smartly and stepped out into the middle of the street where a cruising black Mercedes stopped for a second. He jumped in and was gone.

'The stallion from Lagos. Hmmm I'll book a time tomorrow morning.'

When Judith called, Ken offered her a time at 8 pm on a Tuesday evening. 'Mr Bello only has evening hours at present,' he told her.

'Then I'll take it, thank you.'
Tuesday night arrived. Judith had rehearsed her story which was that she felt lonely and depressed and thought that I could be something to do with her old fillings.

When she arrived, Ken was sitting behind the counter like a little boy, blinking with his long eyelashes. The clinic was ultra-chic and the magazines were for the super-rich. Judith saw no signs of cameras or microphones, but she didn't expect to – professional installations were always invisible.

Bello was punctual. On the dot at 8 p.m. the door to his treatment room opened. An unexpectedly, refined, super-trained man stood in front of her, his arms outstretched in a warm, welcoming gesture. Judith bowed her head slightly, not because she thought he was an African king, but because she'd spotted the large bump on the front of his tight, white trousers.

'Well, well, well!' she thought, 'he really is hung like a stallion! This is going to be good.'

The examination began. Yusuf commanded respect as he worked systematically around her mouth while Ken assisted. He was very thorough. He took photographs and X-rays, and described Judith's dental status to Ken who took notes.

Finally, Bella concluded his examination and told Judith that as far as he could see there was nothing wrong with her teeth, but that she should come back if and when she felt she needed a further consultation.

Leaving the clinic, Judith made her way to where she would meet up with Kovalchuk, taking the usual precautions against being tailed. They started to walk and talk without actually appearing to be doing so.

'Nothing happened to indicate that Bello offers more than dental care. So, I would guess that he has an exclusive circle of clients based on personal introductions who avail themselves of his more intimate services and that would not include drop-ins like me tonight. In which case, they must be very important people. Pity really – I'd have ridden to heaven on the stallion tonight, if I'd had the chance!' Judith added. Then amazed by her own words, she blushed a little and Kovalchuk gave Judith a cold look.

'What is this!' he thought! 'Working with sugarbabes who can't distinguish between business and pleasure. I'm tired of all women who can't think rationally and do their job professionally. If she gets it wrong this time, she'll get it right between her eyes.

The following evening, Kovalchuk, Judith and a younger colleague called Vlad went along to the clinic again. It was 9 pm, pitch black and raining outside but the lights were still on in the dentist's surgery which faced onto the street. They turned up their coat collars and Judith showed them the way in.

Through the main entrance, they made their way upstairs to the second floor and then through another locked door. Vlad was a locksmith and he picked the locks as they went further into the building. They entered the reception area. It was empty. They approached the treatment room. It was anything but empty.

To their disbelief, none other than the Russian ambassador's wife, Mrs Kryganova, was riding for her life, legs straddled over Mr. Yusuf Bello, and both of them were going at it for all they are worth.

'Aaaah! Yusuf! You fill me up completely. Deep inside. You're so big. Come on, come on! More, and harder.'

Mrs Kryganova's whole body shook and rose into the air as she gave out a mighty cry when she reached her climax, only then to deflate like a balloon that someone had shot with a gun.

'Out everyone, out now!' ordered Kovalchuk.

Once out on the street, Kovalchuk stared hard at the other two.

'No-one has seen anything. Right? No-one has heard anything. OK? If this leaks out, then I won't spare either of you! Understood? So, go!'

Vlad and Judith walked away, while Kovalchuk went back inside and up to the second floor. He stood in a dark corner of the staircase and waited. Twenty minutes later, the Ambassador's wife emerged looking clearly quite happy with life. After walking down the stairs, she stepped out into the cold evening air, turned left and starting walking towards the Dramatic Theatre for a taxi.

He'd take care of her later, but now the important thing now for Kovalchuk was to find out whether there was any video-recorded material in the clinic.

He sneaked back into the clinic. The lights in the surgery were still on and Bello was sitting hunched over his PC. When Kovalchuk reach Bello, he placed his Uzzi firmly against the back of the dentist's head. He didn't move a muscle but sat perfectly still as if made of stone. Neither of them said anything. Bello was petrified and slowly, very slowly, he turned his head to face Kovalchuk. Kovalchuk spoke in a whisper.

'You will now give me all your video films and every voice recording of every single client you ever had in this clinic. You and your giant fucking cock have humiliated our entire country and I would gladly put a bullet through your skull, so do exactly as I say or I just might.'

Bello understand that one false move from him and the Russian would pull the trigger, so he turned slowly back to face his PC and gave Kovalchuk the password.

Kovalchuk scrolled through the images as the appeared on the screen. Jesus Christ, he said under his breath as he recognised high-ranking politicians, women as well as men, businessmen, mafia bosses, an East German priest he had worked with before…. And could this be a Swedish minister? These images were a goldmine. He could do so much with them. Bello had done him such a favour he must be rewarded properly, Kovalchuk thought.

The silencer had been on the Uzzi all the time, so when Kovalchuk pulled the trigger, it just sounded like a tennis ball hitting a wall. 'Nothing personal,' said Kovalchuk before placing the PC under his arm and hurriedly making his way out of the building into the night.

***

A couple of days later, Kovalchuk was sitting at the FSB's headquarters in Moscow with his boss. They went through the video material.

'We don't need to watch the footage of the ambassador's wife. It just needs filing away. They were taken over a period of three years, so there's a lot.'

'So, let's focus on the bankers, the politicians, the mafia, the diplomats, the prime minister of course, and all the rest of them. Only the royal family isn't represented. Otherwise, they could all be among the guests invited to a Nobel banquet.'

'Some of these faces will take time to identify but at least we can see that this face belongs to the Swedish prime minister. Let's look for more politicians and bankers. We need to bring in a Swede or someone who knows Sweden well to identify all these people. But then the material must be cleaned from any Russian connections, like the ambassador's wife. There may be more wives. I hope not, but we can clean it later, just the two of us.'

***

It was a big day in Kiruna, the northern-most city in the Swedish provinvce of Lapland. The local Social Democratic chairman, Mrs. Lena Sundh, a fast-paced political upstart, was giving a speech in the main square to an audience of about 20 wind-battered, snow-covered people.

'We are currently engaged in in-depth discussions with Chernemetova, the Russian airport organization, to finalise the construction of a large international airport here in Kiruna. The airport must have the capacity to enable the largest cargo and passenger aircraft such as the B747 Antonov and the like, to land here. The whole idea is based on the aircraft industry saving time and money by flying over the North Pole and stopping here at Kiruna for refuelling and service. If we get the permits required, we will become a large, stable employer for at least 100 people for decades to come here in Kiruna. We are primarily aiming for cargo flights, but we know that more and more tourists want to see the northern lights and visit Santaland. With the large airport in place, a lot will happen that will be good for the region. Any questions?'

An older man stepped forward. 'Is it not dangerous to let the Russians build this airport. They could later use it for military uses, or deploy troops on land here and say they are protecting their assets?'

'No, oh no. Look, I think we have to forget all about Bond films and the old view of Russia. We have a modern partner to deal with in Russia today. If you want to be successful in business, you have to believe that everyone wants to do the right thing. That is how it is here in Sweden and, of course, how it is out there in the rest of the world. And the fact is tha twe women think a little bigger and are more forward-looking in cases like this. I myself have been invited to the Black Sea for a holiday with our Russian party comrades. It's great when the winds of history blow us all forward. Today we all have to think big. We've had Russian men and women studying here in Kiruna at our university for a number of years. The entire programme has been paid for by the Swedish state and the results have been very good. well. Today there are many connections between Russians and Swedes who live here in the north. So, if there are no more questions, I would like to thank you all for listening. Thank you very much.'

* * *

Bello's coffin was sparsely adorned with only two flowers. The parish priest for Hedwig Eleonora held a short speech about better understanding between people of different ethnic backgrounds across national borders. Bank manager Sven and Ken were the only two who attended. Sven would dispose of the estate which was considerable although there were no known relatives. Ken cried all through the service. For him, Bello was his guiding light and his beloved friend.

No-one in the world was as sensitive or as caring as Yusuf.

'Goodbye my friend. I should not have left you alone that night with clients. I will never forgive myself.'

'I will miss your company and your warm hands. May you rest in peace,' Sven said to himself.

The small group walked around the coffin, down the aisle and out into the open air. The said nothing to each other and dispersed onto Storgatan, Sven with tears in his eyes.

It must have been a case of jealousy, thought Sven. If only I could find out who the client was that night, it might be easy to see who the jealous person was. Then I would use an old friend of mine from Estonia to put matters right. Sven was really upset over Bello's murder.

The newspapers described it as a gangland murder. Maybe the victim had gambling debts?
However, the story quickly disappeared from the front pages, being replaced by the debate over the possible Russian participation in the new Kiruna airport.

The Swedish Commander-in-Chief, together with the other centre-right and conservative political parties engaged in campaigning against Russia, pointed out how incompetent the Russians were.
The prime minister, on the other hand, talked on television about the need to think outside the box and try new methods to stimulate trade and employment. Especially in the north. But, he added, perhaps this project was going a bit too far, given how the situation in the world looked. The debate hotted up!

On the one hand, there were the northern feminists who who accused the " old men " in the capital of being narrow-minded and old-fashioned, and on the other, the Commander-in-Chief and the right-wing parties warning that war might break out at any time.

'Why do you think we have reintroduced conscription and are busy training 4,000 man?' they asked.

***

One month later. Christmas was approaching – an occasion when the Russian ambassador traditionally held his annual banquet for 200 or so guests at the embassy on Kungsholmen. The prime minister and his partner were there together with 4 other ministers.

Other guests ranged from a representative of the Swedish royal family to the year's winner of the Eurovision Song Competition, Ahmed, who sang Sweden's entry entitled 'You mustn't touch me'.

Every guest was given a present when they left the banquet –this time, a Russia doll which could be opened into seven parts. The prime minister looked amused back in his official residence when he stood the women up, one by one in a line, above the fireplace.

■■■

In the morning after the party at the Russian embassy, the PM received a telephone call from MUST. It was Jan.

'Prime minister, someone cut the Russian Cultural Attaché's throat late last night. We have put all the resources we have at our disposal into the investigation. The Russians have gone completely crazy and it's important that we solve this quickly if we are to limit the damage.

I would highly recommend that you speak straight away to the Russian President. Then, we have to look again atlast night in microscopic detail. The killer was almost certainly one of the invited guests, possibly someone who hid and stayed behind when all the others left.'

Within 10 minutes, the PM was with Jan at Must's HQ.

'This is much too big for the police. They are not smart enough for this kind of investigation,' argued Jan. 'Think about how they handled the Palme murder. So, we've taken over the investigation. This is not a terror act. It's not that easy,' he went on. 'Drugs and extramarital sex maybe? What has the Cultural Attaché been up to since he arrived in Stockholm? Was he unfaithful to his wife? Were they swingers? We need to start mapping out their lives, and the people around them. We'll need additional resources of course and measures have already been taken to bring us up to strength. We're now gathering all the intelligence we can.'

***

Up in Kiruna, Anna Sundh received an early morning call from one of associates in Moscow. 'Mrs. Sundh, we will do everything we can to carry through this deal, if only to honour the memory of our Ambassador Kvaganov who was a true friend of Sweden and a peace activist. You will not have to convince your principal of the excellence of the business. The Russian bear has done that for you.'

***

The Russian Ambassador's wife was called back to Moscow to face the music for her adventures in the dentist's chair. The chief interrogator, Irina Kataskova, stared coldly at Mrs Kryganova and there was total silence in the room despite it being full of people. Russia was using the situation to show what happened if someone became too Westernized.

'Do you understand that you have betrayed your husband, your family and mother Russia?'
'Do you understand what I'm saying?'
Mrs. Kataskova maintained a strictly neutral but determined tone of voice.

'He was wonderful,' Mrs. Kryganova answered almost inaudibly.
'I cannot hear you. Repeat what you said so that the jury and the whole room can hear you. Your husband and children are present.'

Mrs. Lyobov Kryganova slowly turned to her
husband.
'He was wonderful. You…..,' she said looking him in
the eye, 'can never ever be a man like him.'

BANG! The interrogator's gavel crashed down onto
the wooden desk.
'Section B Kopryc 18. Siberia. The trial is closed'.

With a stern face and with gavel in hand, chief
interrogator Kataskova, walked past the accused
without giving her a look, swept past all the
journalists and disappeared out of the courtroom.

***

Kataskova's verdict meant that Kryganova would
have to fly right across Russia to reach her final
destination in Siberia.
'We ask you all kindly to take your seats as quickly
as possible and make yourselves ready for takeoff as
quickly as possible. We will then board a convicted
prisoner who will be transported to our final
destination Magadan. Service on board will
commence once we are in the air.'

Two policemen boarded the plane with Mrs.
Kryganova between them in a foot shackle and
handcuffs, wearing only a light red prison uniform.

Once in the air, the plane circled around Moscow
and flew off east towards Magadan on what would

be a 9-hour flight. Viktor and Luba from the penal institution were waiting for Kryganova when the aircraft landed.

'Welcome Mrs. Lyobov Kryganova. We are from the prison and we will take care of you in the best possible way. First, we have clothes for you for the cold Siberian winter.

In fact, they give her an old worn-our coat which was much too big, a pair of carpenter's trousers and two sweaters that smelt of sweat and tobacco. Lyobov realized that this was not the time to quarrel and that she needed all the clothes she could get. Out here, no-one could expect any special privileges. She put on the clothes in the arrival hall and the whole party marched out into the cold Siberian night.

'My name is Irina Detsomskerdetskernova. I am in charge of this facility. I welcome you here and I am convinced that we will get along well with each other if you do exactly what is expected of you and think positively. I know all about you and I understand that you like scrubbing floors and stairs, which is at least a clean job. Now, let's go to your sleeping quarters and visit your comrades there.

The group moved along. The long corridors were empty and looked like military barracks. Perhaps they were originally old military barracks. Today though the facilty was grey, cold, intimidating and extremely depressing.

Lyobov criedsilently to herself. Her husband and children were still in Stockholm. How would she ever recover from the humiliation she was now meeting? She hadn't received a fair trail, not that she had expected one, and the proceedings were turned into a propoganda exercise against modern Western women. The verdict itself was handed down by a furious female judge in words that no-one understood and for reasons that no-one was given.

'Kryganova. You can polish the stair rails as well!'

 Lyobov's story was a national talking point and vicious comments about her behaviour in Stockholm were presented all the time in the Russian state media. Russia had condemned her as a traitor and she was a figure of ridicule in the eyes of ordinary Russians.

Day in, day out, the drudgery began and continued relentlessly. She was soon mentally and physically exhausted and subject to verbal abuse both from the other inmates as well as from the prison guards. However, she worked in silence and never complained. There was no point in answering back. No point in getting into slanging matches.

No one can take my memories of Yusuf away from me, she thought. He lit up my life, he gave my life a meaning and made me feel like a real woman.

If this is actually just a cooling off period and a symbolic act rather than a real prison sentence, she thought, and if I can be of as little inconvenience to the guards as possible, then I might be able to get out of here when all the publicity has died down and move back to Moscow. You never know. At least now she could half believe in some sort of life-after-prison. The thought gave her some comfort, but not a lot.

Chapter 19

ESCAPE TO PANAMA

I had now prepared a plan for me and my daughter Anna to get away from St. Petersburg and requested permission from Kovalchuk to move to Panama which he had approved. My mother would be well taken care of by my employer and she had given her blessing to our move to Panama.

Panama was now a highly attractive alternative compared to other tax havens. The Russians, with the help of Western banks and the tax experts in Panama, had created a 'product' for private individuals which had grown into a mass market commodity. It was available to anyone wishing to avail themselves of the services. As always, the EU authorities were lost and three steps behind and the number of immigrants into Panama was steadily increasing.

Panama was not a cheap place to live in but there were many benefits besides the tax situation and the good weather. Poor immigrants from other Latin American countries working in Panama meant that labour was cheap. A car wash cost virtually nothing.

The Russian colony had grown considerably with

newly arrived wealthy Russians with expensive tastes who demanded the full range of the latest products and services. There was a Russian church, a Russian school, Russian doctors and dentists and so on, all to unite and provide for the Russian community in Panama.

Unfortunately for some, Russian women outnumbered Russian men in Panama by a ratio of 4 to 1 so there was a great need for those women with a healthy sexual appetite to buy their sex. The doctors recommended their women patients to have sex at least twice a week, which for some was out of the question unless they had a fat purse, which many did.

On Kovalchuk's instructions, I contacted Svetlana. He saw that I needed to take a break. He didn't want to wear his girls out unnecessarily. A well-trained spybabe cost a lost to train and had to survive the real-life situations they encountered. It was then they became good at their work; not by sitting on a school bench. He assigned Svetlana, his No.1 in Panama, to give me all the help I needed and support me in every possible way.

I emptied all my accounts and the insurance money from my deceased husband and moved it all to the West-European bank Merida which had an office in Panama. Svetlana arranged an apartment for us and, of course, a school for Anna.

Everything worked smoothly and went very fast. My 'employer' arranged an exit permit from Russia in 10 minutes instead of the usual 10 months. It took only 2 weeks from the time I had decided to move to Panama until Anna and I were sitting on the plane on our way to Panama.

I packed my bags with a sense of excitement and anticipation. This would be perfect. Men were stupid, dumb and easy to deceive. Women, at least the smart ones, knew exactly what to do. I took my mink coat out of the wardrobe and laid it in a large suitcase. I had already packed 3 suitcases and a large container with things which Juri and I had bought. Now he was dead but I was alive. I had had enough of Rave too, but felt secure with my Swedish passport in my handbag. I was in full control. I had taken command.

When Anna was ready, we'd be on our way and leave St. Petersburg behind us, I thought.

When the driver had helped with the luggage, Anna and I got into the car and, as we pulled away, I looked back for the last time at what we were leaving. There were no regrets. I had bought Anna the very latest smart phone to keep her occupied, so she hardly noticed what was happening.

Now, I thought, we're on our way. I've bought an apartment in Panama City near to the beach which overlooks the sea. It's in a gated residential area and it's big; 300 square metres. It's perfectly located, has an enormous pool, and security guards who can protect me if Rave or anyone else comes to call.

We flew first to London and then on to Panama and disembarked in Panama City, tired but happy after the long flight. The tropical heat hit us in the face when we stepped onto the tarmac. No more winter clothes from now on. The airport was lively but efficient, and after the usual questions from the passport control officer, we began our new life in our new country.

Svetlana had arranged to pick us up with a driver and as we emerged from the terminal building, she welcomed us with massive Russian hugs and off we went to the apartment where a warm shower would be perfect after the long journey across the Atlantic.

"Buenos Dias!" beamed the driver José when he opened the car doors and placed the luggage into the car boot.
"Hola!" I said, not relishing the idea that I would have to speak a lot of Spanish from now on. What a pain! Why couldn't they talk to me in my own language?
'Do you like Panama City?" I asked Anna who was still completely absorbed by her new smartphone. 'Hmmm, yeah, mum, mmm,' which wasn't an answer. She wasn't interested in talking to anyone. She was totally focused on her smartphone.

We drove through the city and finally arrived at our protected community with its beautiful gardens and flowers in full bloom. It was situated in the very best part of Panama City and all the apartments were owned by the "super rich". I wanted to be a part of the jet set here; a 'normal' life just wasn't for me. José carried the suitcases up to the apartment on the fifth floor where I unlocked the door and we entered.

'Look mummy. What a view! I can see the whole ocean from here. It's wonderful. And the balcony is so big. I can see the mountains from here as well.' Anna walked around the balcony which was actually big enough to be called a terrace.

'I'm so happy you like it. This is where we'll be living, and we've found you a school.'
'Will we be living here? Mummy, why didn't you tell me?' Anna said, suddenly getting very cross.
'Honey, I didn't want to worry you,' I said sympathetically.
'What do I tell all my friends in St. Petersburg?' she said with a touch of sadness in her voice.
'You will soon make new friends here Anna, I'm sure. But now we have to unpack. And by the way, there's an IT specialist here called Pedro, and he's promised to help you install your computer.'
When Anna walked into her room and saw her furniture from St. Petersburg, she felt much happier

straight away so she came back to me and gave me a big hug.

I unpacked. I hung my mink furs in the big closet and wondered when I would use them in this hot climate. But I loved them and couldn't be without them.

I left Anna to unpack in her room and took the elevator down to the garden. I loved the smell of the wonderful flowers and I strolled down though the gardens to the bar where I ordered my first mojito from the bartender in my new country. It tasted delicious. When I got back to the apartment, Anna was happily chatting away to her friends in St. Petersburg on Skype.

After wishing her 'goodnight', I walked into my new large bedroom and looked through the window out over the sea. I loved the view. In fact, I had bought the apartment very much because of the fantastic view. I put my cell phone on the bedside table, connected the charging cable and closed my eyes. When I fell asleep, I felt extremely satisfied with myself.

Chapter 20

SVETLANA THE FIXER

Svetlana told me about Alfons and I checked him out on the internet. His name was Alfons Azteka and he was the estate agent for the apartment I had bought. Alfons had his fingers in every pie you could imagine. He had helped many Russians to channel their money into bank accounts in Panama. His mother had moved to Panama from Iraq forty years earlier and his father had travelled from Nicaragua in the 1980's to take part in a manifestation in honour of Sweden's former prime minister. Alfons was born shortly afterwards; nine months afterwards to be precise.

He was a Latino with a typical Latino moustache who spoke loudly and fast. Alfons met Gudrun Tyeman, a Swedish woman, who had been active in the Vietnam War and had gone down to Nicaragua to work as a volunteer to help the Communists gain power. That was when she met and fell in love with Alfons who was a real character; a man born out of the political left wing, but also a fiery guerrilla man. Later, Gudrun learned that he was more of a businessman than a guerrilla fighter, and that his communist leanings did not stop him from making money...and picking up the ladies. He was intrusive, but not aggressive. He did things his way. Inevitably, however, after a passionate start, their relationship cooled down and eventually the warm feelings they had had for each no longer existed. She was unhappy with her choice of husband and wanted to go back to Sweden to start again. But she was married here in Panama. She had a little daughter she had to take care of, and she knew that Alfons wouldn't let them leave. So, she was stuck in Panama. She had daydreams about living in a red little cottage in Sweden with a husband she could trust. A man who did what he was told. Someone she had control over. But she couldn't control Alfons and was resigned to her fate although it still caused her pain.

Alfons was almost always out and never at home. Gudrun had no idea what he did when he left in the morning. These days, he seemed to work mainly as a broker and lawyer. In Panama's heat, his white shirt was always stuck to his sweaty body and being overweight didn't help either. Not here, in this climate.

'Alfons, good to see you,' I said when we met for the first time. We had talked several times on Skype and the internet about how to channel money, black money and white, to Panama. According to Alfons, some of the black money he handled came from drugs and some from the slave labour done by North Korean prisoners who 'worked' for Russian companies in Vladivostok and other Russian cities near the Chinese border.

'Senora, como esta usted? Good to see you here in Panama,' was Alfons greeting to me.
'Yes, everything has gone very well. When we arrived, I got the keys to the apartment without any problems,' I told him.
'We still have some papers to sign, and some keys and access cards to collect, so we'll have to go to the head office,' Alfons said sweating profusely.
'I think I may have some new customers for you, by the way,' I said.

I wanted him on my side, so I turned on my female charms with a broad smile that few men could resist.
'I like new customers! They mean more money for me and bonuses for you too,'' said Alfons. 'Now, shall we go to the office.'
We jumped into the car and drove away.

After lunch, Svetlana dropped in to meet Anna and me, and we sat on the balcony and again admired the view.

'It's great to see you here Sophya. I'll show you the

best hair salon in Panama City and I have such a good nail salon too that will be just perfect for you.'

After having broken the ice, we started talking about the social life in Panama.

'I will introduce to some really famous, wealthy people who have moved to Panama, Sophya. You can make some serious money if you want to. Easy pickings. Some of millionaires are actually pretty good looking as well,' she joked.

As she talked, I understood that Svetlana was clearly interested in getting her hands on even more money. She was hungry for more and wanted to fool a new man into parting with his cash.

That's not for me, I thought. I won't do that again. I've been there, done that! Why take any more risks? I'm here now and I want to stay firmly in charge of my own life.

'By the way, there's a big party tomorrow at the home of a former Prime Minister, my friend Hector. There will plenty of rich, famous guests there, like the oil oligarch Sergey and the rock legend Brander.

'And also, Sophya, I've arranged someone for you to play with! Your very own 'toy boy'. He's really awesome. He's 26 and you'll just love his muscles. Tell him to grease himself with sun oil, and then sit back and let him keep you happy.' Svetlana said with a broad grin.

'What's his name?' I asked.

'I call him Pepito,' said Svetlana, sending a text message.

'Svetlana, you're amazing!' I said with a mixture of disgust and joy.

'And as I said, with your appearance you can make a lot of money down here. A girl like you can always do with a little pocket money. You'll meet some very influential celebrities tomorrow. But don't ask them any personal questions about their money, at least not to start with. In any case, usually you don't want to know. Remember, ignorance is bliss, a virtue! So Sophya, I'll pick you up tomorrow. Be sure to wear your best dress. By the way, Pepito will be here within about thirty minutes. Time to make yourself ready.'

After 30 minutes my cell phone came to life with a ring signal.
'Sophya?' asked Pepito.
'Yes, I answered slowly, taking control of the situation.
'I'm on my way to meet you and trying to get in through the main entrance. Can you get someone to open the gates?' Pepito continued.
'Yes, I can. Just stay where you are,' I answered.
I contacted the security officer who let Pepito enter through the gates.
'Hola Amiga. You live 'muyrico' here,' Pepito said with a dazzling smile.
He pushed back his light brown hair with his nicely tanned hand and posed for a second or two. He was very good looking and had quite a body. And he knew it.
'Please come in Pepito. I suppose Svetlana has told you what this is about?'

"Si, I know." was Pepito's answer.
'Good. So go into the bedroom and wait for me there.'
I checked through the apartment and made sure Anna was asleep, and then I went back into the bedroom and locked the door behind me.

***

The next day was the day of the big party and I woke up alone in bed still feeling the effects of yesterday's 'fun and games' with Pepito.
I went into the kitchen and had breakfast with Anna. The sun was shining and I was happy. And then, right out of the blue, I suddenly wondered what Rave was doing, and who was he with? It wasn't the first time either. And I asked myself why I kept thinking about Rave like this? Did I still have feelings for him perhaps? I shook my head a little.

In the evening before the party, Anna and I had dinner on the balcony. The babysitter appeared at 8.00 pm as agreed. I was already wearing my best outfit consisting of a very stylish, long, red gown, with high-heeled crocodile leather shoes from Gucci.

When my mobile rang, it was Svetlana.

'Sophya are you ready to leave?'

'Yes Svetlana, I'm ready.'

'O.K. - time to come down. I'm waiting outside.'

The chauffeur opened the door to the black Range Rover for me and I settled back into the cream-coloured leather upholstery beside Svetlana.

'Welcome to Panama,' said Svetlana moistening her lips. I pressed the button that raised the glass between us and the driver to avoid him overhearing our conversation.

'You learn quickly, for someone who's just arrived in Panama. Now we are going to the most famous palace in Panama, namely the Palace of the Herons, or Palacio de la Garzas.'

'I'm really looking forward to it. But tell me Svetlana, how have you managed to get so close to absolute power here in Panama?'

'Aha! That's one of my well-kept secrets.'

After driving through the magnificent archway, we got out of the car, made our way up the five steps and entered into the main reception hall, from where we were escorted into the impressive Yellow Hall. The champagne was flowing and we started to mingle with the celebrity guests.

'Dearest Hector, this is Sophya,' announced Svetlana. 'She has just arrived in Panama from St. Petersburg, and she's a Swedish citizen as well as being a Russian one.'

'How interesting and what a delight to meet you Sophya. As a matter of fact, we are very good friends with the Prime Minister of Sweden. He comes here with his wife quite often - as do many representatives from Affordia, the Swedish bank – the biggest in Sweden, if I'm not mistaken?'

After a fantastic evening where we met many interesting people, we moved on to Hector's huge villa just outside Panama City, with its illuminated gardens, fountains and pools.

'Hector, your house is amazing,' I told him. 'I love heart-shaped pools.'

'They're good for romance and for business,' Hector said rather suggestively.

The enormous villa was full of people who danced right through the night as the champagne kept on flowing. When, finally, we were driven home, the sun was already up.

After a short nap, I woke up feeling uneasy with myself. My thoughts were jumping around and I found myself thinking back to St. Petersburg, to my deceased husband Juri, to Anna, Sweden and Rave. What had I done? Sacrificed everything for the Panamanian sun and these opulent foreign males who probably weren't worth getting involved with!

Suddenly I was full of regret over my 'hasty decision'.

I sat down and wrote an email to Rave, with tears welling up inside.

Dear Rave,

I hope you miss me. Things are good here in Panama. But I miss you. I feel guilty and no joy. I regret that I was mean, false and greedy. I want nothing more than for us to be together again. Please forgive me.

Always,
Your beloved Sophya.

Chapter 21

VISITORS OF THE WORST KIND

'She is a bitch above everything else. If I ever meet another woman like her in my life, I'll walk away instead of letting her humiliate me. Her idea of an 'escort service' is more than wild- it's more like perverted. Sexual innovation really turns her on. This morning I couldn't help seeing everything she had. She flaunted her body and she gave me the lot!'

Pepito was so angry with what Sophya had done in front of him.

'Sophya wanted help,' she said, 'with a leaking toilet. After a few minutes she had taken off everything; and I mean everything – all her clothes. So there she was, strolling around from the bathroom to the bedroom and back again, parading her breasts and pussy as if I didn't exist. She was naked, and apparently feeling quite safe – almost unaware that her theatrical posing was arousing me. But she knew! She fucking knew, the bitch!'

'I looked at her in the bathroom. She was teasing, she must have been – standing there, in front of the mirror, playing with her towel until she knew for sure that I had the complete picture of her, her breasts, her stomach, her ass ...the full catastrophe!'

'Right there and then I would have given so much to fuck that woman until she couldn't take it anymore. But she was the one who decided when, where and how. She was the piper who call the tune. And she's a taker and not a giver. She takes me when she wants me but never gives herself. Bitch!'

Pepito left the apartment feeling anger and frustration. He wanted to screw Sophya on the spot but knew that it was she who decided, not him, and today was not the day.

One evening, a few days later, Pepito, Santos and their new-found friend Michael sat drinking in a bar. The drinks were flowing and they were all becoming louder and more aggressive. Pepito told them about Sophya and how she had humiliated him. Santos laughed, showing his yellow teeth and came up with an idea.

'Why don't we simply go around to Sophya, knock on her door, and ask her if she'd like to be peacefully and quietly fucked by all three of us. There's not a chance she'll say no if there is one of her against three of us. When she says yes, we'll fuck her nicely, and if not, we'll rape the bitch and teach her a lesson.'

Pepito, already drunk on cheap tequila, was all for it. He thought it was a great idea.

'Yeah,' he said, 'Let's skip dinner, steal a car and get over there right now. The risk that she'll go to the police is zero. She'd probably get raped by them too, if she did.'

When there was a knock at her door, Sophie wondered, 'What on earth? Who could that be? I have things to do – like a dinner to arrange.' She was still wearing only her negligee but when she saw it was Pepito and two others, she decided, albeit reluctantly, to open the door and in they came. Pepito and his two cronies.

What do they want at this time of night? Pepito has been tricky lately. He complained when I whipped him a couple of times. But why has Pepito dragged along these idiots with him? What do they want? Sophya asked herself.

'Hola amigos, como estan?' Sophya said as they entered the apartment.

'Sophita! Senorita! Muy guapa.' Santos smiled.

'Come in. But not for too long. I'm going out to a party soon.'

Sophya pretended to be happy to have visitors.

'But can I at least offer you a drink before you leave?'

They all nodded and Santos, the 'giant' from San Juan, winked at the other two. This would be an easy match. She was bound to say yes. She might even like it!

I have to get rid of these pricks, Sophya said to herself. She'd make some small talk to start with but then they'd have to leave.

The conversation was slow to begin with. They chatted about everything from the political situation in the country to the approaching autumn storms that always came at this time of the year. Pepito didn't participate in the conversation but kept his eye on Sophya and her body language. She's giving Michael an eye-full, he thought, as a leg emerged from the negligee she was wearing. Then she let him pat her knee and rub her thigh a little higher up. Michael was waiting for Sophya to open up completely, but she's probably wearing panties, he thought, and has every intention of keeping them on.

Santos, having had two drinks, then moved over to the sofa where Michael and Sophya were sitting. The heat suddenly increased in the room, and Pepito and Michael pretended to have a discussion about something important which developed into a bit of a shouting match. At the same time, Santos was trying hard, rather roughly,

237

to get more intimate with Sophya, but with no success.

'I like a little fun and games like the next girl, but Santos, this isn't the time or the place, so can you cut it out!

Sophya got up and moved away into the bedroom.

Santos leaned towards Pepito and said, 'She's ready to die for it, you know. Anyone can see that. If you can't, then you're fucking blind! So, let's get on with it! What are we waiting for?'

At which point, Sophia shouted from her bedroom. 'There's something wrong with the shutters in here. Can one of you come and help me fix them? I'm afraid I'll pull everything down if I do it myself.'

Santos had not been in the bedroom for more than a minute when Sophya screamed, came rushing out with her negligee more off than on, and threw herself into Pepito's arms.

'You have to go Pepito. All of you. This is getting out of hand!' she shouted, now with frightened eyes.

'So, what do you say to a good serious fuck, a fuck for fun of course?' Pepito was joking no more. This was serious.

The men were suddenly silent and watched her like hawks, while she stared at Pepito for help.

Then Santos moved forward, grabbed Sophya, put a towel in her mouth and tied it behind her head. She kicked and tried to hit him but she couldn't.

What are they going to do? Kill me? Where's my phone? I must find my phone, Sophya thought.

'Now you little Russian whore, we'll teach you what a fuck really is. I have never raped anyone before, but today's the day! Throw her on the bed in the bedroom!'

Fucking Pepito. I'll get him. He's been paid for his sex but now he's dangerous. They might knock out my teeth. They can kill me. South Americans! They're disgusting. I must kick them. I must fight.

Michael squeezed her breast and told her to be a nice girl but the more she kicked and hit out, the more excited he became.

'Boys,' Pepito spoke again, 'it's not the plan that Michael alone should have all the fun here. We're here to screw her together. So, let's fuck her in the order we know her. That's me first, then Santos and then Michael. OK? Is that alright?'

Santos and Michael nodded without taking their eyes off Sophya.

Pepito did everything methodically. He had played with her body on several occasions when it had pleased her ladyship so he knew exactly how and where to move around her body. Sophya realised again that the men were deadly serious and dangerous. She was just trying to survive the situation. She tried to get in a kick from time to time but it was no good. She didn't have the strength.

'Now just you listen,' said Pepito, 'there are three of us. We're going have you all through night, again and again - so many times you'll lose count.'

'I CAN DO WHAT I WANT, I CAN DO WHATEVER I WANT!' shouted Pepito in a state of euphoria. In fact, all three of them were now completely out of their senses.

Out in the corridor, a small person sneaked away from the bedroom door to her own room on small, silent feet. The tears trickled down her cheeks and she hugged her dolly hard. She lay under the bed and held her hands to her ears to close out all the sound.

A few hours later, early in the morning, Sophya's daughter entered the bedroom, and saw her mother asleep on the bed. She was not wearing any clothes and looked as if she'd been in a fight which of course she had. The bedroom looked like a battlefield. Anna began to sob at the sight of her mother.

'Mummy, mummy, wake up! Wake up please mummy! What's wrong with you? Why do you look like you do? Who were those men here last night, and why did they hurt you?' Anna helped her mother to the bathroom and into the bath without another word. Then she turned on the taps. The sores, the blood, the bruises and the smell – it was all incomprehensible for a 7-year-old girl. The only thing she understood was that it is not good for them to stay in Panama. If Daddy had still been alive, he would have protected them against these nasty men.

***

Five months later, the situation in Panama changed drastically. The TV and newspapers were full of articles about the deteriorating situation in the country. The world community decided that Panama should immediately change its laws to close the favourable tax loopholes that many international companies and individuals had exploited in recent years. Overnight the value of apartments and houses fell, there was an exodus of foreigners, and the night life and the sex trade all but disappeared. Even the trade in organs was badly affected, unfortunately for the police, who in collaboration with the local surgeons had turned the illegal business into a gold mine.

The Panama Government passed a new law which stated that all citizens with Eastern European passports (including those with dual nationality) would have to leave the country within 24 hours. Obviously, the law applied to citizens from Russia, Belarus, the Baltics, Ukraine and a number of 'stan' countries to the extent that they were present in Panama. Chaos broke out particularly among the Russian contingent in Panama who, for several years, had created a small calm corner of Russia for themselves with genuine Russian piroshky buns, a Russian church, Russian traditions and Russian schools all in a warm, pleasant climate. Many had invested not only in their own homes but also in Panama-based companies which would now also be seized under the new laws. All of their assets had to remain in the country, as did their capital in the Panamanian banks. These funds were to be used to pay back the tax revenues fraudulently withheld from their home countries. They would also be used to pay fines and administrative fees. In practice, this meant, at best, that these tax exiles would just about have enough money to buy a ticket home, or to another country still open to them.

'I have to get out of here,' Sophia realised. 'I must get away. This is not what I planned. Why did it all have to go wrong like this? After just six months. Who would have thought it? At least I have my escape route option. I'll return to Sweden and create a new life there again. Sweden is a good country for me. So many gullible people who do what you tell them to do. The idiots! I know that Kovalchuk will be able to find new assignments for me there.'

Sophya made her mind up there and then that it was time to make a move. She started packing the few possessions they would take with them in two small bags. She guessed that the airport would be so chaotic that anyone with too much luggage would never be able to get onto a flight. Better to leave everything behind and just carry hand luggage. When she'd managed to buy a ticket to Stockholm on the internet for herself and Anna, she called Judith and asked for her support in Sweden which was immediately forthcoming. Judith had already taken care of several of her spybabe colleagues from Panama in recent days. Judith and the people she worked for were well aware of the situation in Panama and knew how badly it had damaged Russian interests in the country.

When Sophya and Anna arrived at the airport it was packed to bursting point with people wanting to get out of the country as quickly as possible. The mood was similar to that of Saigon's last days, 40 years earlier. The irony here was that the people who were fleeing for economic reasons were well-dressed, multilingual, and accustomed to the best service at all times. Now other laws applied. No holds were barred in the fight for the last seats on the flights up to Mexico City, Houston and the other major hubs on the routes out of Panama. Sophya, however, was able to put her Russian skills to work and be generally unpleasant, verbally abusive, pushy, brazen and insolent. She quickly elbowed her way through to the check-in counter and completed the usual procedures in record time.

Having reached their cruising altitude after take-off, the passengers quietened down into their own relaxed flight modes. Sophya turned to look at her daughter who appeared to have fallen asleep with her doll in her arms with her head leaning against the aircraft's window.

'Anna. Anna, are you awake?'

The only sound which came from the little girl was the sound of gentle sobbing. Sophya realized that the memories from Panama would scar Anna for the rest of her life.

'Why does everyone hate Russian's mother? We haven't done anything to them? If only Daddy were here,' she said quietly to herself.

Chapter 22

MRS. RAPP'S GODS

In Houston, the police checks were extensive, as always at American airports. Everyone knew that the plane was carrying economic criminals and fraudsters. Public opinion in America and the rest of the Western world had turned against these groups to such an extent that they were beginning to fear for their lives. The attitude of airport officials and customs officers spoke for itself. Passengers were redirected within the Arrivals Hall with sour looks from hostile faces. Sophya and Anna were flying on to New York and from there to Stockholm. Eventually after many hours in the air, they landed in Sweden.

Judith was waiting for them at Arlanda Airport; as always punctual, well-dressed and very presentable. Sophya finally appeared in the Arrivals Hall feeling tired and worn-out, holding Anna by the hand.

'We only have hand luggage with us. That's all we decided to bring.'

Judith knew what had happened. She knew about the rape, and she knew that their savings had been frozen.

'Our staff in Miami will go down to Panama and sort things out as much as they can regarding your apartment and belongings. We'll be notified later in the week,' Judith added.

'I've managed to fix you up with a job as a home help. You and Anna will be staying in an apartment in Stockholm owned by an old lady who's a bit of an alcoholic. She's quite harmless but she talks nonsense a lot of the time. You'll be taking care of her, preparing her food, and looking after her hygiene for the time being while you wait for your new orders. I'll take you to the apartment immediately. It's in the centre of Stockholm, quite near to where I live actually.'

'Very good. That's fantastic. You've thought of everything Judith at such short notice. Thank you so much'

'So then, shall we go?'

Actually, Judith was quietly pleased that things had not gone so well for Sophya. She had always disliked Sophya deep down but now, meeting Sophya and Anna face to face, she felt rather sorry for both of them.

They were soon in the city after the drive in from the airport. After entering the main entrance, they took they lift up to the 5th floor and knocked on the highly decorated door. There were only two apartments on the 5th floor, both presumably they were quite spacious.

Having been admitted by a little old lady, Mrs Ekman Rapp, Judith presented Sophya and Anna to her.

'Sophya and Anna,' said the old lady. 'So very nice. Come in, come in and tell me your story and let's listen to it with a small drink.'

Anna and Judith went into the bedroom that would be Annas, and Sophya was left sitting in the drawing room with the old lady who now had a glass of liqueur in her hand.

Looking around at the state of the apartment and the state of the old lady, Sophya wondered how long she would manage to live like this?

Sophya didn't tell Mrs Ekman Rapp 'her story', and within minutes the old lady had forgotten all about her question anyway and started babbling away about herself and her meaningless life.

'Rum and Martini are my Gods. In order to buy them, you must have money and money you get by working. This is a fact I learned long ago even though, today, the whole city lives on state hand-outs and is crawling with incompetent, work-shy parasites. Admittedly, I have inherited my money and never had to work, but there are huge differences between people and people. I, to my total satisfaction, am a member of the ruling upper class.'

What she did not say was that she had married into the upper classes and has literally 'screwed around' for years to avoid working. In actual fact, she was a communist before she married. Cleverly, she had kept quiet about it and said nothing to her husband, so she could play her 'role' and become a real upper-class lady who complained about everything which even included the communists. But today's communists weren't communists in the real sense anymore. They were all namby-pambies. It suited her to talk disparagingly about the communists without for one second feeling like a hypocrite.

'Of course, they are,' said Sophya. 'I totally agree with everything you say. You're quite right.'

'Do you think so? What was your name again?' asked Mrs. Ekman Rapp.

'You can see, can't you, that it's considerably finer and much cleaner here in my home than it is in the homes of the lower classes,' Mrs Ekman Rapp continued without waiting for Sophya's answer.

'Going back to my Gods, there are many ways of enjoying them but I have one speciality. All you need is a shaker, some ice cubes, tonic, lemon and gin. When this is mixed together, you get something very drinkable indeed. But young lady, you look like you're being interrogated by the KGB, or whatever they are called? So would you like to join me in a drink?'

'Well yes, thank you. That would be very nice. But … KGB, what does that mean? I have no idea. And I hope you will teach me how to make your special drinks. I don't know how,' Sophya concluded, with her hypocritical smile which Mrs Ekman Rapp wrongly took as a proof of Sophya's ignorance and kindness.

'My dear girl, we shall get along very well together. I can hear that. It will be great fun. What was your name, again? And yes, of course you will learn how to mix drinks. It's all a part of a good upbringing and general knowledge. Yes exactly, general knowledge. That's how it was before, in the good old days, when people were educated differently. But now, it seems, there are fewer and fewer people who know anything at all in this country. What was your name my dear?'

'My name is Sophya and my …'

'It is terrible what is happening,' Mrs Ekman Rapp interrupted as she turned on the TV news.

Sophya realized, sitting there opposite the lady who smelt of pee and looked like a skeleton, that Mrs. Ekman Rapp just had to die. She had to. The only question was 'How'. When she was gone then the apartment would be hers. The old witch was a disgusting relic of the old, rotten, upper-classes and should have been dealt with a long time ago. Secondly Sophya need a place of her own for dinners and meetings with friends and acquaintances.

Mrs. Ekman Rapp, who had now turned the TV off, turned to Sophya again and pointed to the bottle and the glasses.

'Of course, one glass can't hurt,' Sophya said smiling, 'Shall I try to mix the drinks?'

'Mmm,' nodded Mrs Ekman Rapp in approval as she took a sip of Sophya's concoction. 'It tastes very good indeed. One feels so sophisticated with a drink like this, don't you think?'

'When I go for a walk, which I do every afternoon, I always have my little hip flask with me. One shouldn't go out naked, should one?' Mrs Ekman Rapp laughed. 'It's so nice to walk around and occasionally take a small sip of the Lord.'

'Yes, you heard right. I called him the Lord, my God, though my friends don't like it. They try to play tricks on me and take him away. If they could, they would stamp on me, see me bleed and then jerk him out of my hands. Then I'd be finished,' the old lady went on becoming more and more deluded. 'Everything seems to have become muddled for me as I've got older, and it goes without saying that all the sacrifices I have made over the years have taken their toll. Poor me.'

'Yes, Mrs. Ekman Rapp. I'm sure you are right. You have worked hard in your days. You've lived a hard life. There aren't many who would have survived,' Sophya said sympathetically, putting her head on one side.

'By the way we're having afternoon tea here today, or was it tomorrow,' Mrs Ekman Rapp continued.

It was time for the old lady to take a bath, so Sophya filled the bathtub and helped her out of the chair.

'Now it's time for a quick bath before dinner, Mrs. Ekman Rapp. That will be nice, won't it? Let me help you to undress. Shall we go into your bedroom, and let me take your glass.'

Judith had installed Anna in Sophya's room and came out into the drawing room to talk to Mrs Ekman Rapp and Sophya. She approached the old lady to say goodbye.

'Mrs. Ekman Rapp, I'm so pleased that you have become good friends with Sophya and Anna. This arrangement is going to work very well. Sophya is so kind and friendly. She's quick and good with her hands, and she's reliable. Anna is very good at school and will be able to help you a lot.'

'Well, well, how very nice. Is that what you think? In that case, I'll just have to believe you then,' replied Mrs. Ekman Rapp looking at Judith somewhat sarcastically.

'Goodbye then Mrs Ekman Rapp.'

'Goodbye Judith,' said Mrs. Ekman Rapp. 'Come back soon.'

'So many invitations, so many dinner parties I have given and so many receptions I have attended. Queen Sibylla, Queen Sibylla ... There is no one here in the neighbourhood who can remotely come to near to matching my list of official engagements. Queen Sibylla ...'

Mrs. Ekman Rapp's bedroom was not very clean or fresh. Sophya began to remove her old-fashioned undergarments and her urine-impregnated pantaloons.

'Now please remember, Mrs. Ekman Rapp, you have to tell me if you need to go to the toilet. You can't just let your water flow in this uncontrolled way. We'll put you into diapers from tomorrow.'

'Imagine if they think I'm an imposter; think if they don't come to the afternoon tea party, just because I want Him to be mine, that I try to make Him mine.'

The old lady was still ranting on as Sophya lowered her carefully into the bath, one leg at a time, then took the showerhead and rinsed warm water over her.

Anna was now standing in the doorway and looked at the old lady in the bath.

'What an ugly old lady,' she said in Russian. 'What are we going to do here? I want to go to school, I want to play.'

'One thing at a time Anna. Now go and make yourself a sandwich and I'll come out when I've finished bathing her.'

 The afternoon's proceedings, short and intense as they were, could have been taken from the repertoire of a left-wing theatre group, Sophya thought. Unfortunately, they weren't. This is my reality until I receive new orders. How did I end up here, she thought? How come I lost everything in Panama? It was all so well arranged. And, despite everything, strangely enough, I still somehow miss some of those good times with Pepito.

Sopyha was awakened from her daydreams when Mrs Ekman Rapp splashed water onto her. Sophya took her by the hand and helped her to shuffle into the bedroom. The alcohol, the hot water, the evening and the new guests had finally exhausted her.

Then it struck Sophya that she might just have found

a solution to the problem of the old lady, and went through the plan in her mind over and over again, refining it until it felt watertight. She rolled onto the bed and fell fast asleep immediately.

Chapter 23

REMOTE REVENGE

The following morning, Judith popped in again to see that everything was alright with Sophya, Anna and the old lady. Mrs. Ekman Rapp had already had her 'morning prayer' when Sophya admitted Judith into the apartment. As the two ladies chatted, they heard a 'pling' from the bedroom which they knew was an alert on Sophya's PC.
It was a greeting from Kovalchuk who had promised to clean up in Panama after Sophya's beating and rape. He'd ordered Vladimir to solve the problem.

Sophya sat down in front of the screen and clicked up the screen. It was Skype video. Live.

She saw everything in real time and was eagerly curious to see what would happen.

When she studied the image on the screen, she saw a badly lit room which looked like an old potato cellar. In the middle of the room, there was a man, sitting on a chair, with his back to the camera, tied securely in place with his hands behind his back. He was gagged. Something had been stuffed into his mouth. Maybe a potato. Whatever it was, it meant that the man wasn't able to speak.

Then the picture switched to a face-on view, and she saw that the man sitting there lashed to the chair was Pepito. His eyes were wide open and he just stared straight ahead at the wall in front of him.

'Do you know this man? 'Vladimir asked Pepito as he gave Santos a push forward. His hands too were tied behind his back and he was gagged with a potato in his mouth. His trousers were wet around his crotch.

Vladimir's voice could be heard very clearly, despite the small echo in the basement. His gun was clearly visible too, pushed hard into the side of Pepito's head

 'This man is a criminal. He's a rapist. He's a vile, disgusting animal. Don't you agree, Pepito.'

Pepito continued to stare blankly ahead, eyes bulging.

Sophya watched the screen in silence.

The atmosphere in the basement was tense, to say the least. No one said a word. Then Vladimir leaned forward, close to Pepito's face, smiled and spoke.

'So Pepito – time for you do you what you have to do! Do what a real man would do, and then you will be free to go.'

Vladimir removed the ropes and the potato from

Pepito's mouth, handed him a large sharp knife, and nodded towards Santos.

'A vile, evil rapist, right? It's either you or him! So do it now and you will be a free man.'

Pepito looked at Santos, with sweat running down his face and shaking with fear. He stood still for a while, gaining his balance, while the room vibrated with the heat and the fear.

First, Pepito loosened Santos' trousers which fell down around his ankles. Santos' eyes were wide open, as big as goose eggs. Pepito then grabbed his penis and with a single slash, he severed it from Santos' body. Blood spurted everywhere. Santos fell down on his knees and screamed out his agonising pain in a never-ending cry. His face was the colour of a dead corpse.

Without waiting a second, Vladimir then walked up to Santos from behind, put his revolver to the back of his head and pulled the trigger splattering Pepito's face with Santos' blood.

'Now turn him towards the camera.'

Sophya saw a half blown-out head with the eyes still staring into space. Pepito let Santos' body fall heavily down onto the floor.

Sophya turned away and rushed to the toilet where she vomited cascades, emptying everything she had in her stomach. She stood up, rinsed her mouth out and went back to follow the live pictures from Panama on the screen.

'Well done, Pepito, you're a winner. Now, roll him up in this net, carry him outside and put him in the back of the truck. We're going for a ride.' Vladimir was calling all the shots.

The truck was a well-used Dodge Dakota pick-up truck with a tarpaulin ready to use to conceal the body. There was no traffic to speak of as they drove out onto the streets and away from the scene. No police officers were in sight either. They drove up onto a major highway and travelled six or seven miles until they came to a section where the road was being extended.

It was blocked with a boom gate but someone raised it as they approached, and the truck made its way into the road construction area. Vladimir drove on, down towards a bridge under construction, where concrete mixer trucks were lined up waiting to tip their concrete into the foundations.

'Get him off the truck and throw him in the hole over there,' Vladimir ordered.

Pepito climbed out of the truck, walked around to rear, and dragged Santos' body out from under the tarpaulin, onto the ground and then towards the hole for the foundations. Once there, he dropped

Santos' body into the hole where it slid down on the wet concrete like an enchilada to the bottom.

Pepito stood shaking with exhaustion and fear, as he looked down at Santos' body.

'You can go now Pepito,' said Vladimir as he slowly walked up behind Pepito. 'You can go.'

The shot entered through Pepito's neck and exited through his mouth. His throat appeared to explode with blood which then gushed out through his mouth.

Vladimir took a step forward and gave him a gentle push. Pepito fell into the hole and, right on cue, the next concrete mixer rolled forward and began to fill the hole with concrete.

Vladimir looked into the camera with a broad grin and waved to Sophya.

'Mission accomplished, Sophya. We're leaving Panama tonight. End of broadcast.'

Sophya closed down Skype and the screen went black. Again, she made her way to the toilet sobbing. The room smelt of vomit.

Chapter 24

IN LONDON

I sat there with a piece of paper in my hand that I had discovered in my wallet. It was the slip of paper on which the pool player from Belarus had written her phone number. She'd also written 'Next time we'll play for your virility'. She was a very attractive, I remembered, and I quite explosive in her own way I imagined. Maybe she was dynamite in bed? Why not? So why not take a chance to have a fun weekend in London with the 'pool pro', Irina from Minsk?

I twisted the little piece of paper a few times in my hand debating the pros and cons of the idea, and then, having decided, I dialled her number.

'Hi Irina, Remember me, Rave, from the pool hall in St. Petersburg? Well, I'm going to London next week and I was wondering if you'd like to tag along with me? We could even play some pool for old time's sake!'

A burst of laughter hit me from Irina at the other end of the line. She had probably never received an invitation like this before. But I was chancing my arm, I knew. Russian women despised cowardly men, but they adored the cheeky ones, the mischievous ones, the reckless ones, those who challenged you to get what they wanted. They wanted men to kill to conquer their bodies. It turned them on.

'Well sure! London! That would be fun.'

I heard the words coming from somebody far away, inside a prison, isolated from the world outside. Far away inside Belarus. A country controlled by a despotic ice hockey player. A country that was bankrupt and which survived only through its friendship with Russia.

'If you can fix a visa, of course, and that may not be so easy.' I was smiling into the phone and she noticed it and cut in, 'You fucking snob. I'll come and I'll.....well, just you wait and see,' she laughed, and then she hung up.

***

Compared to Moscow, driving through London on a weekday evening was like driving through a small Swedish town. And tonight, London was relatively quiet, a little rainy and 14 degrees.

The taxi took me from Heathrow terminal 3 to my favourite hotel, the Egerton Place Hotel near Harrods.

Irina was already there. Her Aeroflot flight had landed earlier than my flight. When I approached the reception desk, Irina, who was nicely dressed up but a little nervous, threw herself in my arms for a big hug before I could speak to the receptionist and check in. I'd stayed there quite a few times before so she knew exactly who I was.

'How nice it is to see you again, Mr. Alexander. Welcome to our hotel.'

'I'm travelling with my daughter on this occasion.'

'Of course, you are, Mr Alexander. How very nice.'

After we'd washed off the travel dust upstairs, we looked at each other. A little cautiously. She was so slim, so wiry. It suited her temperament. She was a real livewire and people like that never put on extra pounds unnecessarily. She was a little shy too, and went away to dress and start the makeup process that would probably take at least an hour. I sat down and watched as she lined up her small jars in front of the mirror on the dressing table. She handled everything with a speed that showed she had been doing it for many years. She worked in silence. Maybe she was a quiet type after all?

'Would you like me to have a light lipstick?'

'I like everything about you – light lipstick included.'

She laughed in a little girlish way and finished her makeup. Then we left the hotel to go out for dinner.

As we were leaving, we met the hotel receptionist again in the foyer. I stopped and smiled at her.

'She's not really my daughter you know?'

'But Mr Alexander, they never are, are they?'

You were always treated so professionally here in London. The hotel staff had seen everything. There was no doubt about that. London was the world's largest tourist city. Nowhere in the world did as many people come every year as tourists as they did in London. But London also had a world-class escort service business. You could see it everywhere; in the hotels the restaurants and the night clubs, all over town.

A short 10-minute walk took us to the corner of Draycott Avenue and Brompton Road. There we found an absolutely delightful little seafood restaurant that was only half full. Irina was wearing a simple dress, not too challenging but pretty, and heels, not too high but high enough to show her legs off nicely.

'I've never been to London before so thanks for inviting me. You're a generous person. I knew that I'd hear from you sooner or later. You're the type. When you pick up the scent, you go for it with all you've got, like a hunting dog, with your nose to the ground and your tail in the air until you reach your prey. Then you bring it to the ground. And that is where we are now.'

'Imagine that! I didn't know you were the poet too. Have you ever had anything published?' I teased her, and she seemed to enjoy it, judging by her smile.

Then she became more serious.

'It's not difficult to get a visa in my country as long as you can pay. You were so kind and sent me 100 euros and that made all the difference for me. But I'm not a call girl even though it might seem so from my behaviour. You're a very attractive man and it's not often you get the chance to meet someone top-notch like you!' she explained. 'But I want a family; it's as simple as that'.

She looked up at me with her green-grey, slanting eyes, and that steady, experienced look which said 'you don't push this girl around anyway you like'. I had to be very clear and careful about how I expressed myself to her. Otherwise, she'd eat me alive, with her sharp canine teeth.
As the evening wore on, I realised I was getting tired. I wasn't tired of Irina, just tired, so I paid the bill and we prepared to leave.

'You deserve a serious man who can provide you with a family,' I said. 'In the East or in the West. It doesn't really matter.'

'Have you got tired of me now that you know I'm not going to be one of your quick lays?'

'No. not at all. I like an evening with an intellectual woman who stimulates me – intellectually that is.'

I spun the ice around in my glass which she saw and took as a sign of irritation.

'That's crap! I can see it on you. I can suck you off at the hotel if you want me to. It's no big deal. I have to pay for the dinner and the fine hotel somehow, don't I?'

'That's quite enough,' I said crossly. 'Now let's go back to the hotel for a night-cap in the bar.'

Out on Brompton Road, Irina took my hand and walked happily along to the hotel. Neither of us spoke.

'Good evening, Mr Alexander. How was your evening?'

'It was great thanks. We had dinner at the seafood restaurant not far away. The food was excellent.'

After the drink in the bar, we took the lift up to our room and made ourselves ready for bed. I was already in bed when Irina came back into the room from the bathroom in a pair of pyjamas that would have looked great on a 10-year-old.

She looked adorable.

I took her in my arms and savoured the smell of her body and the touch of her soft skin, and then fell fast asleep with her in my arms.

***

Lovely girl, lovely weekend. It was raining a little as it so often did in London and we were out at Heathrow, Terminal 2. I felt rather sad that the weekend was coming to an end, and Irina did too, but I think we were both relieved that we didn't go any further with our relationship than we did.

In fact, I was longing for Sophya. She was the woman for me. It was all quite clear to me now. That's what I'd found out over the weekend. I waved off Irina who was risking her life by flying with Belavia to Minsk.

'I'll ring you tomorrow.'

'OK Rave Alexander. And thanks again for a wonderful weekend.'

She blew me a kiss and then walked away to catch her plane.

I disappeared underground and finally, after all the lifts and escalators, found myself in Terminal 3, ready to board the SAS flight home to Stockholm.

On board the plane, I sat next to a fat woman who looked as if she might work in public relations or something. She tried to strike up a conversation but I showed her my back and looked out of the window as we took off. I closed my eyes. How many times had I taken off from Heathrow? I fell asleep and began to dream.

In the dream, I saw all the people working at The Firm in Stockholm. They had all become rams and were eating grass outside in a field. They had sheep eyes. It looked as if they were somewhere in northern Italy. At the same time, in a bar in Berlin, Gauk sat drinking beer in large drinking stein. He was naked and grossly obese. One of the heavily-breasted waitresses walked up to him with more beer which she proceeded to pour over his head. Greedy as he was, Gauk tried to drink the beer as it ran down his face which was soon wet from the beer and red from the alcohol.

A whole roasted piglet was brought in and placed on his table. Gauk looked at the piglet with great glee, and asked for some extra pig fat which he used to lubricate the pig's mouth before taking out the apple. Then, with the help of the pig fat, he forced his own head into the pig's mouth and started to eat the pig from the inside. Gauk filled his mouth and chewed on the fatty pork, belching loudly, and then he asked for more beer. The buxom waitress lifted the pig by its tail and poured beer into the pig's anus which Gauk then duly quaffed as it ran from the piglet's mouth. Quenching a thirst by the back door, one might say.

Thereafter followed much gorging and guzzling that would have been impossible to beat anywhere other than Berlin. Herman Göring himself would have been proud if he'd seen Gauk scoffing the roast pig and then, finally, trying to mount the buxom waitress.

Gauk lifted her up by the waist, raised her skirt and pulled down her old-fashioned underwear, which revealed her nether regions and considerable amounts of black pubic hair. It was almost possible to imagine Osama bin Laden hiding in there.

'Now scream,' ordered Gauk, 'scream like a pig.'

Gauk took a firm hold of the waitress's ears and twisted them until they almost separated from her head.

Then he launched himself onto her - filled with the anger of someone who really didn't like what he was doing.

The waitress lady by now was completely blue in the face. Her ears had become swollen and looked like cauliflowers.

Gauk turned away looking traumatised because he couldn't get it up despite his efforts to stir himself, and he let go of the woman's ears and then sat down. His trousers were on the floor and his underpants were around his knees. He both felt and looked like a pathetic failed fool. He just sat there without uttering a word.

The buxom waitress stood up, straightened her clothes, puffed up her hair and rubbed her swollen ears. She turned around, slowly at first and then more purposefully. They looked at each other.

Suddenly she threw herself at Gauk and took a bite out of his face. She bit and chewed before swallowing pieces of his nose and lips. There was blood everywhere. Gauk ended up on the floor in a pool of blood, and everything was in upside down. The restaurant owner came running out with a small wet wipe in his hand to clean up the mess.

And then, the SAS pilot landed the 25-year-old 737 onto the runway at Arlanda Airport with the traditional heavy bump that was one of the well-known SAS trademarks. I woke up with a start, soaked in sweat, remembered my dream, and realized that it is just that – a bad dream. I wondered what on earth I'd eaten to give me a dream like that.

Chapter 25

DIE UGLY LADY

Sophya had taken care of the alcoholic old lady for quite a long time, she thought. Far too long actually. She'd grown tired of keeping her clean and generally taking care of her. But as things stood, she had no other choice. Sophya had nowhere else to go, so she felt almost trapped and was getting very frustrated with the arrangement. However, she had recently started giving much more thought to how she could get her hands on the old lady's apartment. Right now, she just had to sit tight, play the good Samaritan, and bide her time. The question was, how long would she have to endure it?

During one of her meetings with Judith, she raised the question of the apartment once more.

'Things are getting rather desperate there, Judith. How do you think I can take over Mrs Ekman Rapp's apartment?'

Well, Sophya, I understand your predicament and I've been doing some research. I think there may be a way. The thing is, it's like this. Mrs Ekman Rapp's apartment is a condominium. She owns it, she doesn't rent it. And as such, she's in a position to leave it to you in her will if she so wishes. What you need to do is get her to write her will in which she leaves all her estate, all her assets to you. There may be a problem if she has any distant relatives because they would probably like to take over the apartment if they could, but I haven't tracked down any relatives yet in my research, so I don't think there are any.'

'OK. I understand. So, I'll start by talking to the old dear about it and see if it's possible to persuade her.'

'My guess is that it'll be impossible but sure, give it a try and we'll see what she says. She may be only too pleased to leave the apartment to you. And even if she has any relatives, she may hate them.'

'I'm just wondering Judith. Do you think we could forge a will?'

'No, I don't think so. It would be too complicated.'

'OK, so I'll just have to think of another way, and actually I may already have one.'

In the days that followed, Sophya became more and more impatient over the apartment.

Why is it always me stuck in these difficult situations? The old bitch does nothing but drink her way through every day and she expects me to sacrifice myself for her welfare and comfort. She can't expect me to wait on her hand and foot all the time. I'm not her personal nurse. The time has come now to do something about her. I've got to come up with a way of getting rid of her in order to take over the apartment.

The angrier Sophya became, the better she was able to think of ways of dealing with the old witch. Finally, the idea came to her in a moment of clarity. She'd thought about it before, but couldn't get all the details to fall into place. Now, however, she knew straight way that her idea would work. It was perfect and, most importantly, no one would suspect anything at all.

On the following Saturday, Sophya woke up feeling tired. She had been out partying with Judith on Friday night at one of the best places in town. There had been a lot of drinks, perhaps a few too many, which of course were bought by the different men they'd met during the evening. They had danced all night long and had laughed a lot. They'd had a really good night out.

She had fallen asleep immediately when she came home in the early hours. But now it was 6.30 in the morning and the demanding Mrs Rapp was shouting over and over again for her breakfast.

'Sophya, I want my breakfast. Is it too much for an old lady to ask for her breakfast? I'm hungry. Please Sophya, come and give me my breakfast.'

Sophya dragged herself out of bed although she felt badly hungover and almost ready to throw up at any moment. Good job that Anna was sleeping over at friend's apartment and wouldn't be back until late that afternoon, she thought.

It took quite a time for Sophya to fix something for them to eat, but after half an hour she was able to serve the old lady a nice breakfast.

'Thank you, Sophya. That was delicious,' said the old lady. 'Now you can help me to the toilet.'

Sophya walked around the apartment thinking how nice it would be when she finally owned it. She knew she'd thought of a smart way of getting her hands the place and now it was time to talk it through with Judith. Judith was good at finding workable solutions and she'd know if Sophya's plan would work or not. So, time to contact Judith and tell her the plan.

Judith and Sophya met in a coffee shop near the old lady's residence. They each ordered coffee and a cinnamon bun.

'You know I just have to have the apartment, Judith. It must be mine and it would feel so good to fool the old bitch into giving it to me. It is certainly very valuable too and I need money.'

'But as I said, Sophya, you must get her to leave the

apartment to you in her will. It must be in her will, otherwise you won't have a chance of acquiring it. And that's the problem, because I don't think she'll leave it to you of her own free will, do you?

'No, I don't think so either. But - maybe it can be arranged. I have an idea about how to do it. To make it work. I have to trick her into signing a document, something else, something completely different. Can you help me with it, do you think?'

'Yes, I can. I can draw up a will for her to sign, but then you'll have to get her to sign it without her knowing what she's actually signing. You'll need to be very cunning.'

'Good. Great, we'll do it. If you can provide me with the will, then I'll fix the rest. And then the apartment will be mine.'

***

A few days later, Sophya received a document from Judith that would be used as the will. Now it was only a matter of getting the old lady to sign it. Sophya had her plan and now was the time to implement it.

Three weeks had passed since Judith had supplied Sophya with the printed testament before the right opportunity presented.

Mrs Ekman Rapp called for Sophya.

'Sophya, I wonder if you could possibly go to the bank and withdraw some money for me? I've almost run out of cash.'

'Yes of course I can,' Sophya said, 'but then I'll need you to give me power of attorney. Give me a few minutes and I'll write one out.'

She waited for a couple of minutes and then entered the drawing room holding a document in her hand.

'So, would you like to sign this?' Sophya said.

Without reading the document, the old lady put her signature on the bottom right-hand corner, and handed it back to Sophya. In doing so, she had just signed the will which gave the apartment and all her other assets to Sophya on the day she died.

A minute or two later, Sophya came back into the room with a new document. She'd now written out a real power of attorney that she would use at the bank in order to withdraw the old lady's money.

'Sorry, but you'll have to sign it again, I'm afraid. There was a small mistake on the first document.'

'But of course. That's not a problem,' said the old lady as she wrote her signature for a second time.

'Thank you, and now all I need is your ID. Then I can go to the bank and take out your money.'

Sophya had no problems withdrawing the money at the bank, even though she thought the cashier looked at her a little suspiciously.

She now waited for the right opportunity to put the final part of her plan into action. She had to be sure that the old lady was sufficiently drunk to get her to do what she wanted. The opportunity finally arrived one afternoon when the old lady had had a great many sips of the Lord; considerably more than usual. Sophya poured her a very strong gin grog and handed it to the old lady, whilst pouring herself a very weak one.

'So, my friend, here's to you. Let's enjoy ourselves. Skål!' said Sophya.

'Well, thank you, my dear. I'm so pleased that you're taking the time to keep me company and join me with a drink. It feels very lonely to sit and toast with oneself,' the old lady said slurring her words.

'I can quite understand. So, let's share a toast together. To your very good health!'

As soon as their glasses were empty, Sophya filled them up and the old lady emptied her glass in one long sweep with the next toast.

After a number of gin grogs, Sophya decided it was time to proceed to the final step of her plan. The old woman was finally sufficiently drunk.

'Now it's time for your bath, so I'll go and prepare everything.'

'Yes, please do. A hot bath would be very nice.' The old lady slurred her words even more.

Sophya had to almost drag her to the bathtub and only after struggling strenuously with the old lady, was she able to sit her down in the bathtub. Sophya offered Mrs. Ekman Rapp yet another very strong gin grog which the old lady gladly downed in one.

When she was about to fall asleep, Sophya took hold of the old lady's head, dragged it forward quite a way and then smashed the back of her head very heavily against the bathtub with all the power she could muster. It made a sickening thud. The old lady was knocked out by the impact and lay there unconscious. Slowly but firmly, Sophya pressed her deeper into the water and held her there for several minutes until eventually she had stopped breathing. She was dead. The plan had worked perfectly and Sophya would now stand to inherit the whole of the old woman's estate.

She waited for half an hour or so, clearing away all signs that she had been drinking with the old lady and then she called for an ambulance.

She told the ambulance staff that she had come home and found the old lady lying in the bathtub and immediately called for help. The ambulance staff quickly confirmed that the old lady was dead and that she must have fallen while getting into the bath probably due to the amount of alcohol she had consumed, and had received a severe blow to the back of her head in the fall, then fallen unconscious and then drowned. When the police arrived, they made the same assessment. The official cause of death was 'accidental death through drowning.'

The apartment would now belong to Sophya. It would be hers.

Chapter 26

MY DOUBLE

In the tobacconist's shop, the owner was looking somewhat nervous when I walked in to buy my newspaper, as I always did, every day of the week. I was one of his regulars. His name was Samir. He was always very cheerful to all his customers including me of course. Today though, when I entered, he diverted his eyes and tried to avoid contact by pretending to have a lot do arranging the sweets and newspapers. It felt a bit odd, but it didn't have to mean anything special. Everyone has their off days.

I handed him the money and Samir gave me the paper with a nervous 'Thank you Mr. Alexander', then he looked away. I started to flick through the pages, turning them quickly to glance at the headlines, and as I did so, a slip of paper fell from the newspaper and sailed down onto the floor. I bent down and picked it up.

There was a message on it, hand-written in capital letters, which stated that I was not, under any circumstances, to tell a living soul about the money-laundering operations between Sweden and Russia. The message was not signed and there were no clues as to where the message had come from.

There was no-one else in the shop. Just me and Samir. Samir didn't know where to look to avoid eye contact with me and he'd lost his ability to speak, but then Samir knew from his own experiences in his home country that the rule was to look elsewhere and not know anything. This was the second time this had happened in a short time; in the same shop, in the same way, with the same message, when I bought my newspaper.

I could see that Samir was scared. I didn't think for a moment that he was involved in any way. He didn't know who they were. But I could see that he knew that the best thing for him was not to know anything. Maybe I should have a quiet word with Samir quietly to see what he might be willing tell me, and if that produced nothing then perhaps, I would have to resort to some heavier interrogation methods. In the end, however, I decided to say nothing.

'Not much of interest in today's newspaper, Samir, but I suppose I can always use it to wrap up the herring with!'

'Haha.' Samir laughed nervously at the joke which he didn't really understand.

I left the tobacconist's and walked out into the sunshine on the street. When I glanced back over my shoulder, I saw Samir looking at me through the window. I could see anxiety in his gaze and a look that said 'be careful'.

By the time I got home, I had decided to contact MUST, the Swedish Intelligence and Security Service. I had a private contact there that I had used for other purposes, and was able to set up an informal meeting with one of their officers, and the following morning the taxi made its way through rainy streets in the heavy morning traffic on its way to MUST's headquarters opposite the Royal Palace. The name of the MUST officer I met was Jan who turned out to be a normal looking man without any unusual physical features; a man of average age, average weight, normal hair and normal everything else as well. It wouldn't be easy to trace him because he looked like everyone else. He wouldn't stand out in a crowd.

Jan listened to my story, his head on one side like a dog listening to his master, and he clearly became more and more interested in what I had to tell him as I told him what had happened.

After a while, Jan interrupted the session and said that he wanted us to go into a safe room and continue the conversation there. He looked quite concerned and tense.

We went into a room which contained a table and two chairs which were facing each other. There was a microphone on the table. As we made our way to the safe room, I saw a man I thought I recognised in an adjoining room. I knew his face but I couldn't place him. The elderly gentleman sat listening to something through headphones. Perhaps he was going to listen to our conversation? Jan ignored him completely and we sat down together and the questioning continued once the microphone was activated.

'Given your background and the way they have approached you, Rave, we believe that the FSB or the Stasi priests in Stockholm are behind the threat,' Jan said.

He continued, 'The priests have been in Stockholm for over 30 years. They established themselves here in Sweden with the help of a wealthy family, who for many years were highly influential within the Socialist party. For a few years, one of them occupied the Prime Minister's post in Sweden.'

'The priests specialized in money laundering, drugs, protection rackets and prostitution. During East Germany's heyday the priests were also informers and passed on the names of any East Germans who tried to get in touch with them looking for help in escaping the dictatorship in East Germany.'

'We've been working for a long time to try to get those of them still left out of the country despite their valid permits, but we still haven't completed the job. It's taking time to clean them out and we think that now we have to resort to unconventional methods in order to get the job done. Without any doubt, we will never be allowed to expel them legally. Sometimes you have to resort to Stalinist methods to remove Stalinism.'

Jan allowed himself a small smile, but behind the smile I could detect a very determined man who had dedicated his working life to dealing with the priests. Jan's hatred of socialism dominated his entire life and gave him his energy and motivation. As we sat talking, it seemed to me that he had seen an opportunity – a way of completing his mission.

'But we also know that the Russians always try to take back their own. We'd like to make a proposal to you shortly where you can work for us in order to remove these men. Twisting the old cliché, we think it's an offer you won't refuse. We can't solve the problem legally, but we can certainly fix it if we stay under the radar and carry out our plan with your participation. Let's talk again soon when you've been able to think things through. We'll be in touch.'

With that, the meeting was over as fast as it began. Jan stood up, we shook hands and he left the room.

I realized that Jan was right. I couldn't say no to their proposal. I had to step up to the mark and do as I was instructed. I left the building, crossed the street and looked for a taxi with the uncanny feeling that someone was watching me.

Back inside MUST headquarters, the man in 'the room next door' walked to the window, opened the curtain a little and looked down at me on the street. He turned to Jan and asked, 'Who is he, really, and what's his game, I wonder? You never know, he could be very useful to us?'

It was still pouring with rain from the dark, heavy sky. Not a good day if you were looking for a taxi. I stepped out into the road in front of the traffic and waved to all the taxis as they approached but of course they were all taken.

As the next taxi approached, I could see that it too was taken, but it slowed down anyway and the rear window rolled down. I heard a voice from the back seat say, 'We are going to the airport, but, if you want a lift, hop in.'

So, I jumped into the back seat to get out of the rain and looked out through the side window at people scampering along the pavement to find some shelter.

'Thanks for giving me a lift. It's quite a sky fall.' I said to my generous fellow-traveller.

'My pleasure. I know how difficult it is to get a taxi in weather like this.'

I wasn't looking at the man when he spoke, but I thought I recognized his voice.

Neither of us spoke for a few minutes as we drove through the city traffic. Then the man beside me turned and spoke in a deep, well-educated voice.

'It is important to stay on top of every single fact when you're in a situation like yours. Forget one detail and you can finish up dead. You know who you're up against and it scares you. That's why you ran straight into the arms of MUST today. I understand you. I would have done the same if I were in your shoes. You should act quickly and spontaneously. Carry out your mission with MUST and then take yourself down to the Alps, to your little hideaway, with your second identity. The old man with the beard is the key to your cover. Go and see him the next time you are with your family.'

Then he fell silent. I had listened to him carefully as I watched the traffic through the car window, but

now it was time for me to get out of the taxi.

'I'll get out here now. Thanks for your wise words and your hospitality.'

As I closed the taxi door, I looked at the face of the man who had been sitting beside me. He was in the far corner of the back seat; a man of my age, wearing the same suit as mine, the same overcoat and with the same hairstyle. He smiled at me as the taxi driver drew away.

It was me sitting in the taxi. I had met my own double by some strange coincidence, or was it something else? Was it some kind of a brain reaction? Some sort of stress hallucination? Or a ghost? Had I been sitting there talking to myself?

Back in the apartment, I changed out of my wet clothes, leaving them in a pile on the floor, and sat down in front of the TV without a thought in my head.

Chapter 27

SOPHYA GOES TO WORK

Kovalchuk contacted Sophya when he had a new assignment for her in Sweden – a 'tidying up operation' he called it. The FSB wanted to eliminate a Swede who had used sophisticated financial instruments to enable his Russian client's subsidiary company to move very large sums of money out of Russia invisibly into Sweden. Money that should have been taxed in Russia; disappeared without trace. So, he was engaged in criminal activities against two countries; Russia and Sweden. He had to be made an example of, to deter other like-minded fraudsters.

They walked at speed through one of the city parks and Kovalchuk described what Sophya's role in the operation would be. The target she was to meet was the representative of a Russian oil company interested in buying a chain of petrol stations in Sweden owned by DIPEX. They had been on sale for some time. A deal like this required the help of a smart tax expert to ensure that the taxation payments would be minimised or, even better, avoided completely. Eugen Storskalle was that expert. Sophya was to contact him and, having established a friendly relationship, she was to use her female charms once again to lure the target

Storskalle into the hands of Kovalchuk who would then complete the assignment. A simple job for Sophya which wouldn't take longer than 24 hours.

She began by flying down to the town of Lenhult – a 30-minute flight. Lenhult was a small idyllic town in the south of Sweden which could have been taken straight out of a children's book from the 1950's. Even though it was a small town, it was well-known as the town in which one of Europe's largest companies was founded. Having checked in at the City Hotel, she strolled around the town and planned a 'romantic walk' with the target planned for later that evening.

Eugen Storskalle, a former accountant, a male-chauvinist pig and a complete ass-hole in every possible way, was the chairman of Lenhult's City Council. He still ran his 'small' but world-renowned consulting firm where he helped his wealthy clients to minimize their tax liabilities in return for a very handsome fee.

Not only was he a corrupt businessman and politician, he also preyed on women to satisfy his own sexual needs, and like many others like him who had 'got away with it' for such a long time, he thought he was untouchable. Invincible. The longer he survived, the greater were the risks he took in life, both with the deals he masterminded and the women he abused.

Sophya had an appointment with Storskalle for dinner. Once they had made the initial introductions, she got straight down to business.

'As you know, my name is Sophya Sackenova. I represent an oil company based in Moscow. We have been interested in the small petrol chain, DIPEX, that has been for sale for a long time and we now believe that the seller is starting to soften.'

It wasn't just the seller who was softening. Eugen Storskalle both softened and hardened at the same time. In front of him sat an extremely attractive, sharp, young Russian woman, for the day dressed in a dark blue straight dress with a high, simple neckline, half sleeves, discrete nylon stockings and well-polished high-heeled shoes - high but not vulgar, at least not by Russian standards.

'Of course, my company has a finger in every transaction of a reasonably large size in this part of the world. There are always some lucrative loopholes to exploit, especially with regard to Russia and Sweden. For instance, you can make money with a company here if you have a Russian mother, even if the company isn't profitable.'

The waiter came over with the menus and then moved on. Virtually the entire Lenhult elite who were assembled that night in the restaurant sat and admired Sophie with gaping mouths like people who suffered from vertigo looking over a precipice.

Storskalle basked in Sophya's glory and lapped it all up.

They ordered a fish dish each, pike-perch, which looked delicious, but Sophya left hers basically untouched. It was only 6 o'clock and she wasn't hungry. She was thinking about what was to come. Storskalle ate his food quickly, chatted incessantly like a canary, and drank most of the bottle of wine himself. Over coffee they chatted about families, summer cottages in Sweden and in Russia. The time passed quickly and Storskalle was by now feeling pleasantly relaxed and somewhat horny, and curious to know what Sophya's plans were for the rest of the evening. He reached across the table and covered her hand in an intimate gesture that Sophya had been waiting for and she responded with an affectionate smile.

Eugen wanted more time with Sophya, much more. Sophya was so beautiful and he was now seriously thinking about what his chances were of seducing her later on.

Sophya had been ordered by Kavulchok to propose a walk to 'shake down the dinner', so 'Let's take a stroll around the moat near the city prison, shall we?' Sophya suggested. The old city prison looked like a museum with its illuminated walls and moat. You wouldn't think from the outside that it was still an operating criminal institution but behind the medieval facade there was a state-of-the-art closed facility with a security class 2 rating.

Eugen agreed immediately. He would have agreed to anything. They prepared to leave. He was being excessively polite and he held Sophya's coat for her to show what 'a man of the world' he was, but it all fell flat when she saw that he was wearing the wrong trousers for his suit jacket.

Jesus, thought Sophya, what a jerk... I'm surprised he didn't turn up tonight wearing a Hawaiian beach shirt.

The two walked out of the hotel, Sophya staying close to Eugen, and made their way towards the prison in the evening darkness. As they approached the moat, Sophya sensed that it was very quiet. There were no security guards to be seen anywhere. She was a little surprised, but obviously, she thought, there's a difference between prisons in Russia and Sweden. Here everyone liked to be 'pals' with each other. But nevertheless. This was class 2 closed facility!

Kovalchuk was waiting with some men, concealed and ready to move. Eugen wasn't a difficult target. He was middle-aged and overweight, poorly trained, unused to physical fighting and somewhat intoxicated. He'd be easy prey for Kovalchuk's boys and, sure enough, they took him out without him uttering a word.

***

In the morning, Storskalle's dead body was found floating upside down in two metres of water with a heavy lump of concrete tied around his legs. His body moved a little in the water as the water lapped against the bank. A crowd of people on their way to work had gathered at the scene when the police arrived. No one said anything, but everyone knew who was dead in the water.

No one had seen anything. There were no witnesses.

The FSB had shown that they could do what they wanted to do. Their reach extended beyond their own national borders.

Journalists from across the country flooded into Lenhult during the day with many questions, but there were no answers. According to police, Eugen had apparently taken his life by drowning in the moat. They had no more comments to make at that time.

'What happened to the beautiful woman after dinner? Who was she? Where was she now?'

'He, Storskalle, hardly seemed depressed during the evening,' according to one of the witnesses who saw him in the hotel. 'On the contrary, he was clearly in a good mood when the couple left the restaurant after dinner.'

'Did she dump him? And if so, would it have affected him so much that he had decided to take his life? Hardly!'

'He was a womaniser who loved to conquer and was quite happy if it ended after a one-night stand.'

'How could it happen without the security guards seeing it?'

'Has MUST made a tacit agreement for the FSB to eliminate Storskalle? He was everyone's enemy.'

'Are any of those involved double agents for the FSB and MUST?'

'Has Storskalle had a relationship with the Russian security service before, perhaps even worked for them, and maybe has had to be silenced?'

'Maybe there is another deal that Storskalle has been involved in; one that went wrong in some way, and now he's paid for it?'

The speculation in the media came thick and fast and, as always, the sky was the limit in terms of conspiracy theories.

Sophya, back in Stockholm the morning after her assignment in Lenhult, had dinner with Anna and Judith and was listening to Anna.

'I'm going to Gröna Lund with the school next week,' Anna announced. 'There are live animals and pigs. The teacher's said we can feed the animals if we want to.'

It seemed as if she'd mixed up Gröna Lund, the amusement park, with Skansen, the outdoor zoo, but it didn't matter. The important thing was that Anna thought it would be fun to go. Judith thanked Sophya for the dinner and made a final comment before leaving.

'You did really well Sophya. A great job.'

Sophya felt satisfied with life and fell asleep in front of the TV with Anna in her arms.

The TV news announced that the death of a prominent local politician in the Social Democratic party in a small town in southern Sweden was the result of a tragic suicide. The police now officially confirmed that Eugen Storskalle had committed suicide late the previous night. No one knew why. The Prime Minister was interviewed and said the usual things about his thoughts going out to Storskalle's family at the time of their tragic loss.

The following day, interest in the case had completely vanished from the news. The media had moved on and were writing about a ship's cat that had run away and was lost and starving somewhere in the harbour of Slite, a small port town on the island of Gotland. The whole country had become totally focused on the fate of the cat and angry too that the municipality had not done more to help it.

Chapter 28

WE MEET AGAIN

I contacted Sophya. I knew I needed to work with her in order to fulfil my assignment. But in actual fact I rather wanted to see her again anyway and to be in her company for a while. Perhaps I was still love with her? Perhaps not? But the prospect of talking to her again excited me.

I wrote a brief letter to Sophya and sent it by courier to the address given to me by Judith.

Sophya,

I know you're back in Stockholm. Please come to the bar in the Grand Hotel tonight. We need to talk about something of major importance. Plus, so much has happened to us both privately - I'd really like to see you again.

Yours,
Rave

Later that evening I made my way to the Grand Hotel. It was a chilly, damp spring evening in Stockholm. 7 degrees, raining, and wind blowing off the Baltic. The streets were almost deserted because people had either decided to take the subway home or were caught in heavy traffic.

I made myself comfortable in the bar and looked

around. Further into the dining room I spotted Chimney sitting and dining most probably with a customer. He laughed his empty, nervous laugh before the customer said anything funny. Everything was as usual. I looked away and ordered a cup of tea and biscuits. I knew Sophya hated men who smelt of spirits. Russian men still drank a lot, even though it was less now than before. Sophya didn't like it because when they drank, it wasn't possible to control them. That was when they beat up their women and behaved violently in public at the least provocation.

When Sophya appeared, she was as graceful as always; with the gait of a panther as she made her way up the stairs up to the reception, before turning right and entering the bar. She walked over to me and, standing very close, she smiled the smile of a long-lost friend.

Her dark blonde straight hair sat like a ball around her head. Her fringe, her round face, those blue Siberian husky eyes, her lean shoulders, and small breasts, flat stomach and flared trousers from her strong hips were Sophya exactly as I remembered her – but even better.

We looked at each other without a word. It had been two years but Sophya didn't look a day older, I thought, apart from a slight bruise beside her right ear. It looked like she'd got a bang or bumped into something. Maybe a car accident, maybe she'd slipped on the street, or maybe it was another man?

I said nothing but gestured to Sophya to join me at the table.

When the waiter arrived, Sophya also ordered tea and biscuits, then we sat and looked at each other. There was a great deal of tension in the air and my head was full of flashbacks: the first time we made love, the betrayal, her murdered husband Juri. I wondered whether I should kill her there and then, or love her for everything that had happened between us. Was it worth going into the details of the past? Where would that lead? Sophya was probably still struggling to recover after returning from Panama, but she was still the women she has always had been and she still worked for the FSB as she always had done. I was no longer naive. I had learned my lesson. I knew exactly who I had sitting in front of me. And in spite of everything, I still loved what I saw.

'You know I want you,' I said looking her in the eyes. 'There's no need to start digging into the past, we are two of a kind.'

Sophya at first was silent. She looked down at the teacup and moved it slightly.

'My job is to source information that is of particular

importance to my country. I am a spybabe with all that means. I cannot and must not give up that role. I have only one employer and my loyalty is to my country. You might not like to hear it, but that's the way it is. So there. Now you know exactly how things really are.'

Sophya put on her special smile and saw that I was softening up. She felt good sitting there with too.

'I love you and I want you,' I repeated. This time, Sophya took my hand and gave it a squeeze.

Without further ado, we stood up, paid the bill and made our way out into the wet spring evening. We walked towards my apartment, Sophya holding my hand, head down against the wind and choosing her steps between the puddles. Passers-by looked at 'the loving couple' and nodded at us with a knowing smiling.

Inside the hall, I took off her coat, unbuttoned her blouse and cupped my hands around her firm breasts. Her trousers fell with a silent golden swish around her feet, and I bent down and kissed her through her panties. Then, naked on the floor, our bodies were possessed in an orgy of kissing and passion which had no limits. We were two planets orbiting around one another, never still for a second, and moaning with pleasure as our hands explored each other like never before.

Joined as one, we moved like synchronised dancers,

rhythmically, together, in time with some unheard
music - picking up speed and heading towards
the great crescendo, which, when it came, left the
two of us totally exhausted and supremely
contented.

'It's cold here on the floor,' said Sophya.

I had fallen asleep, but now I opened my eyes. I'd
probably dozed for half an hour. I looked at Sophya
and smiled.

Let's go and lie down,' I said, as I picked her up and
carried her through to the bedroom.

I took an extra blanket and wrapped it around her
lean body as we settled on the bed. I opened the
window slightly as the church clock struck
midnight. It was deserted out there and we both fall
asleep in a pile on the bed.

When we woke up in the morning, a yellow light
filled the room. The sun was shining in and a new
day had begun.

 Sophya sat in my dressing gown at the breakfast
table where she was eating a lightly boiled egg and
two slices of toast.

'You know, don't you Rave, that I'm not on the pill
or anything, and I don't do abortions. Women in

Russia don't. What happens, happens!'

I knew Sophya had to be lying because she must have had several abortions earlier as an inevitable consequence of her work. On top of that, she liked the feeling of being pregnant. It made her glow.

'Who's taking care of Anna? Judith?' I asked.

Sophya nodded.

'I want you to be with me Sophya. There's no one else for me.'

I rummaged in the table drawer and triumphantly brought out a toothbrush head for an electric toothbrush. It had a small pink ring on the lower part to distinguish it from other toothbrush heads. I handed it to her a little ceremoniously as I bowed my head slightly.

'For you.'

'How many colours are there? More than there are women in your life?' Sophya joked.

I looked at her with a slightly hurt expression.

'Don't look like that Rave. It's very sweet of you,' she said with a playful smile.

She looked rather pleased with herself and was

radiant in the morning sun. Maybe she was pregnant after last night's love-making?

She wanted to do this. After all that had happened, and perhaps because of it, she wanted to be serious about our relationship.

Had Sophya fallen in love with me for real? Despite everything that had happened? Despite the harsh environment we both lived in?

She may have fallen in love with me seriously for the very first time, I thought.

Chapter 29

THE GERMAN 'KING'

The bar was empty, apart from an apparently important person who sat alone, with a drink in his hand, surrounded at a distance by five men dressed in black and wired up with communication devices to make sure 'their man' was not disturbed by journalists or anyone else who got it into their head to have a 'chat' with him.

The German 'King' was visiting Stockholm.

Sophya and Judith got out of the elevator, directly opposite their 'workroom' on the third floor. They were regular customers at the hotel and, of course, everyone's favourites!

Security allowed them through to the bar. 'The German stallion', as he was called behind his back, looked up, and nodded to Sophya in a flash of hope. He perked up immediately at the sight of the two ladies and sat there looking like a cat staring at a canary sitting on the ground, unable to fly. He knew now it would be a nice evening.

It didn't take more than a couple more drinks for the German to tell them his life story, to pour out his sorrows, and tell them how miserable and lonely he was.

'I lived in Bremen as a child, without any parents,

but with my old aunt who tried to take care of me. I fought a lot and used to bite people I didn't like, and they were lots of them. My adult life has been one long success story- straight ahead like an express train. I've been healthy and active for over 40 years and accomplished enough for three men by working so hard. But all I've known has been the sound of my own voice as I have pushed forward, clearing everything and everybody out of my way. Yes, I've been ruthless in my success. But, over the years, I've paid a high price. I've became emotionally and spiritually dead.'

'But not anymore! Some time ago, I met an Eastern European woman who's very close to me today and now, with her by my side, I have 'woken up' and I can see today what I couldn't see before. The only important things in life for me now are money, power and, most of all, sex. It's all so clear to me now.'

'My first fling was with a woman who lived in Karlskrona in the south-east of Sweden. Sleeping with her was like eating a freshly-baked slice of bread after a long fast; even the crust tasted good. I rolled the bread around in my mouth for a long time before swallowing. Then I swallowed and swallowed again, taking many pieces of bread into my mouth and every mouthful made me feel younger and more alive.'

'But girls, you don't know how beautiful you are. I'm

so lucky to be here with you. I don't deserve you but, you know, you can make an old man who's far away from home very happy

The German started to well up inside, and it looked from his eyes as if he was about to cry. Judith suspected, cynically perhaps, from his play-acting, that he was now beginning to make his move.

Isn't there anything these men can come up with that we haven't heard before, Judith thought to herself. What a bastard. I'll ask Kovalchuk to have this fucking German taken out. No wonder the West has problems when people like him are their business leaders, Judith thought.

'Poor little German businessman,' Sophya said sympathetically. 'You haven't had your way with women, but now you can have your way with me and feel safe because I'm an honest, sincere woman. I work as a nurse in Stockholm, and tonight I can be just for you, just yours. And this is my friend Judith, she's as gentle as a lamb, and she also wants to be yours, just for tonight.'

The German looked around at the girls with his big tearful eyes. He liked what he saw, and he was getting pretty drunk, but sufficiently alert to understand that Christmas Eve would come early this year.

'I'm so lonely,' he repeated to himself as he walked

out of the bar almost hanging from Judith's and Sophya's shoulders. They were heading for the lift to take them up to his room.

The staff working in the reception saw what was happening, smiled at each other and then carried on with their work.

Having entered his room, the German fell onto his bed, flat on his back, and was snoring within 30 seconds. Judith and Sophya sat down on the couch and turned on the TV. Sophya was relaxed, quite happy to have a TV evening, no need to hurry. After a while though, she too had a hard time keeping awake.

'Let him sleep for a couple of hours,' said Sophya. 'We've got the whole night in front of us. Let's just wait and see what happens.'

At five o'clock, the German stallion woke up with an enormous erection. Judith got off the couch, gave Sophya a shake and pointed with a trembling hand in the direction of his phallus which was standing to attention in the morning light.

'My sweet Lord,' was all she could say.

Judith would have liked to take a shower after sleeping during the night, but the German was not in the mood to wait. He took her onto his bed, pulled up her skirt and separated her legs so that he more easily see what was waiting for him.

He went almost berserk, waving his hands around and yelling.

'I'm rock hard. Rock hard for ever! Noow!!

He threw himself over Judith and drilled his huge limb into her without warning. Sophya sat beside him, stroking his back, and saying kind words, while he fucked Judith like a madman on his dying day.

'Everything will be alright. Everything will be fine; your mother loves you.' Sophya went on saying nice things until he finally came. Uncontrollably, with all the energy he could summon. Judith almost flew up into the air with the pressure, as he emptied himself inside her body.

'Judith,' he said moments later, 'I want you to give me a little kiss on the cheek please.'

The following morning, in one of the conference rooms, a young, smartly dressed Swedish business executive with a pony tail, addressed the gathering of distinguished businessmen.

***

'Today I would like to begin by welcoming all of the directors, and especially our honoured guest from Germany, to the first Board meeting of TASSEN AB.'

'Point 1. Has the notification for the meeting been conducted in an appropriate manner? I find that it has! Point 2. Election of Chairman. I would like to propose Henrik Rubin. Point 3. Election of deputies. I propose Karl Adam Faukberg and Berit Grynman, and now, on to point 4, choice of... blablabla.'

Gerardh Drott slept through the procedures and discussions throughout the Board meeting. During the long evening, Judith had worked him hard and got the better of him. Her younger age had given her the upper hand.

No one at the meeting dared to wake him and eventually the meeting came to an end. At this point, Drott finally stirred himself, stood up and stretched himself to his full height and asked if it was time for lunch.

Chapter 30

THE PARTY

Rave had been out training in the gym that morning and the phone was ringing when he got home. It was Jan.

'We need to meet. Tonight, for a walk in the Old Town.'

As they walked through the Old Town, past the German church, it was dark and raining once again. Jan said that their intelligence services had flagged that there was ahigh risk of an imminent attack on Stockholm. They were not really sure who might be behind it.

'It's important that you urgently start building a relationship with the priests. They have connections with all sorts of dangerous groups and might be involved in some way with any possible attack. You never know. We know that you're working closely with a couple of women who are Russian spybabes and we want you to use them. No-one's as hungry for women, alcohol and drugs as those priests! So try to get them interested in the girls and set up a honey trap at the Grand Hotel!'

Having outlined what he had in mind, Jan was silent

for a few seconds as Rave digested what he'd just been told. Since Rave had no questions, Jan wished Rave goodnight, turned and walked away before turning into a small alleyway and disappearing.

Rave returned home having decided to set up a meeting with the ladies as soon as possible. All Jan wanted was for them to squeeze some drinks into the priests. Nothing too difficult about that.

Rave met Judith and Sophya, and explained the assignment. Orders from the top. Together they could set the perfect trap. Judith checked with Kovalchuk and got the green light. 'If Sweden wants to do something with these priests, then we're in.'

Judith was instructed to assist the Swedes in every possible way. She planned an evening with booze and drugs since she knew that was what they liked. It would be a private party at the Grand Hotel, 'everything included', in the women's regular suite.

'So, our boss wants us to get the priests together for a meeting at the hotel 'where they can have a glass or two in the spirit of good fellowship and comradeship,' Judith commented. 'And my orders are very clear. Get the priests to the Grand Hotel, whatever you have to promise them!'

Sophya, who had assured Rave that she was his but also totally loyal to her organization and her country, lowered her eyes whereas Judith, with her easy smile, and well-built figure, gave Rave a worldly look.

'Well, at least we won't have to sit on that German pig again. That's a bonus to begin with!' Judith joked and Sophya laughed with her.

Rave looked at the two girls. What jobs they had. Whores and nothing else. But they were prisoners too. If they wanted to quit, they'd be shot because they couldn't be allowed to talk or even less write their memoirs.

The Russian security service was highly allergic to former agents who appeared on TV or talked to the newspapers and then sold their stories to a publisher. The only way these girls could ever get out of the business was when they were no longer sexually attractive. Yet, when that happened, they would most likely get a bullet in the head for precisely that reason.

What did Judith really think, Rave wondered. The German was quite violent with her. Did she like it? Probably, or she was too indifferent to care any longer. But can a woman turn on and turn off her sexuality just like that? Maybe they can, he thought, in which case these ladies carry live ammunition between their legs that's for sure.

***

The next day, Rave made his way to the Grand Hotel and sat in his usual place, closest to the exit at the bar, the place where he'd met Sophya for the first time. A lot had happened since then. He had been converted from someone in finance to a person who collected important information for the best interests of the state. How strange. No one would believe him and his stories. Many of the events involving murder, expulsions and the like had never been reported in the so-called free press. The Swedish government had total control of the news flows they wanted their citizens to read, and the news they had been covered up so no-one would have to worry.

Rave disliked the priests. They were a collection of arrogant East German intellectuals who believed they had the answers to all life's questions, politically as well as spiritually. Defectors, informers, intrigue-makers; the list could be made long. The former social democratic government had good contacts with the East, but not only East Germany. The priests were invited to the Black Sea by the politburo to exchange political information with the other Comecon countries and to drink and screw little girls in working hours as representatives of their party. Rave Alexander didn't know why he had been asked to gather the priests together. Perhaps there would be information for the whole group later in the evening, and answers to a few questions. They would see. His job was just to gather them together and have a 'nice' evening.

A waiter approached. He stopped in front of Rave, bowed his head slightly and presented himself as Klas. Klas looked like an over-correct gay from the ranks of the social democrats. He was excessively polite in a snobby way, maybe a must if you were to get a job at the hotel. He was someone who would fit in.

'I have been tasked by MUST to be your waiter tonight. There will be a lot of champagne and brandy. I've seen the order. Are you celebrating something special? '

Rave felt straight away that 'the waiter' knew more than he was letting on. Rave didn't know that a MUST agent would be operating as a waiter. No-one had mentioned anybody to him called 'Klas'. He hated not having the full picture - not having full control, and wriggled around in the armchair feeling somewhat perturbed. But he showed none of that to Klas. He nodded knowingly as if he'd been fully briefed everything concerning the evening's events.

'Yes, as a matter of fact we are. We're celebrating that everything is going so well for us,' said Rave sounding as convincing as possible with his improvised response.

The waiter turned on his heels, walked smartly over to the elevator and rode up to the party suite and started preparing for the evening.

Two hours later, Wolfgang and his two arrogant priest friends appeared in the bar. They greeted Rave and the girls politely, and after the usual small talk, the company left the bar to take the elevator up to the suite for the night's activities.

Klas, the waiter, stood firmly to attention beside a table of half-full champagne glasses as the guests arrived and helped themselves. Rave could only hear the camera recording inside the suite very faintly.

Sophya put on some music, and began to move a little in time with the music. As she did so, her dress began to swirl as she spun around and the eyes of the priests lit up as they witnessed the sight of her sexy body in motion.

The evening was going well with plenty of food and drink being consumed, especially the latter. Klas ran in and out with more drinks from the bar, everyone was dancing, and the Germans were warming to the girls as the party stared to swing, laughing and even pulling at their clothes.

Wolfgang walked over to Sophya and stood right in front of her. When she stopped dancing, he pulled her blouse straight up and over her head, exposing her firm, impertinent breasts to everyone in the room. Sophya raised her hands in the air and continued to dance with her breasts dancing and hopping up and down in time with the beat. Rave pretended to laugh but actually he clenched his fists in his trouser pocket. He decided there and then that if he got the chance to do away with Wolfgang, he would take it. But now it was dangerous to show anything. Instead, he stepped over to Wolfgang and draped his arm across his shoulder and pointed towards Sophya.

'She's really something extra, isn't she?'

Sophya was the best kind of spybabe. She could turn anybody's head and get the information she needed in the service of her country.

Now it was Judith's turn. When her blouse was torn away, her breasts were liberated to the sound of raucous cheers; quite a bit larger than Sophya's but still firm and 'the real thing' for all the admirers. She stretched her limbs and moved with the music; she laughed and flirted with the priests who, by now, were getting very drunk.

'Excuse me a moment.' One of Wolfgang's minions staggered out to the bathroom and emptied the contents of his stomach onto the floor before slipping down onto the floor in a drunken stupor. Then he started to creep back into the room, with his clothes in disarray and stained with his own vomit.

Everyone was stoned now. Rave knew that, oddly enough, he was much clearer in his head than the others, even though he had been drinking from the same bottles. 'Of course, it's Klas,' he realised. 'Klas has laced the priests' drinks but not mine! That's why Klas smiled like he did, downstairs in the bar. Klas must have had orders from MUST to secretly lace the drinks,' Rave thought.

It was really late and the room looked like a battlefield. Wolfgang tottered around and tried to dance. He danced in some rare state of solitude. He was in his own bubble and the girls smiled at him. It was hot and the girls moved slowly around him, weaving their spells.

Prostrate on the floor, Gunter and Ulrich were completely gone and were either asleep or unconscious. The windows were open to the street and the park but, despite that, it was hot and sticky inside the room. From the dining room downstairs, music and the sound of conversation could be heard. People were laughing and joking loudly in the bar. Wolfgang was thinking with his half brain; if only his wife would come and fetch him in her big car and take him home!

Wolfgang understood nothing, but he didn't feel good at all. He decided that he needed to get himself onto a bed and quickly. He staggered into the bedroom and fell face down onto the bed with his strength ebbing away.

The girls, the night, the food, the drinks, the music, the drugs; it as all too much and he lay there in a semi-comatose state and twisted over and over on the bed.

He turned face up, and Sophya was there, suddenly standing naked and straddling him wide-legged and smiling, with her hands on her hips. Her eyes were big as chicken eggs, her smile was cold and twisted, and she looked down on him from her great height.

Without taking her eyes off him, she bent over and unbuttoned his trousers and pulled them down on the floor. His cock was wet and soft like that of a small child and it moved a little when she began to stroke it. Behind her stood Rave, filming with a video camera.

Wolfgang heard someone crying desperately. He couldn't tell if it was Gunter or Ulrich or someone else. Perhaps it was him.

His first cry of 'No' was followed immediately by a second 'No'.

And then he passed out.

Klas at that point, punched a number into his mobile phone and spoke two words before ending the call.

'Come now.'

Within minutes, there was a knock on the door. Rave opened it and in came Arhan, the proprietor of one of the city's largest carpet stores, followed by his assistant.

'Excuse the late hour, but I have been ordered to deliver three authentic Bokhara carpets to this suite tonight.'

He looked around, at the men on the floor and on the bed, and at the two naked girls. Without a word they leaned the carpets against the wall and waited.

'We might want the carpets to be moved out again tonight,' Klas said, 'So wait downstairs in case I need to call you.'

Arhan waved and shut the door behind him.

'Roll each of them up in a carpet. Lay out the carpets

here. We'll roll Wolfgang up first.' Klas said as he took command of the situation.

Rave and the girls did as they were told and began by rolling out the first carpet. Then they lay Wolfgang down onto it and rolled it up again. They repeated the procedure with the two other men and then carried the carpets out into the corridor, one at a time.

Klas phoned downstairs to Arhan. 'We want the carpets cleaned and we'd like you to fetch them immediately from our suite.'

Next Klas turned to Rave.

'Your instructions are to accompany the mat dealer out to Bromma Airport, now, in his truck. Drive to the gate in section C. You will find that it is unlocked. There is a Gulfstream ready to take-off on the runway. Drive up beside the plane on its left side.'

Then Klas went out into the hotel corridor and took the elevator to the basement and was gone.

Chapter 31

AN EARLY DEPARTURE

As always, Görel Nilsdottir was awake at the crack of dawn. Today was a big day for her cat, Nils, who was to be neutered shortly so as to make him over into a more 'cuddly' cat. Nils was to be a nice stay-at-home and purr-in-Görel's-lap cat.

Two hours later, Goyan was back home again, feeling as happy as a lark. She got out of her 12-year-old Audi with the cat purring away in her arms, its genital region extensively bandaged.

'No sulking now Nils. This is something that all male cats and middle-aged men should do for the good of society as a whole.'

Görel entered her semi-detached house in the suburb of Sollentuna on the outskirts of Stockholm. The constant din from the nearby motorway gave her a headache, so she was pleased to close the door behind her. Inside the house, with its avocado green kitchen appliances which showed that no one had invested a penny in the house since the early 80's, it was absolutely quiet.

Görel opened all the cupboards in the kitchen searching for something for Nils to eat, or 'Nila' as she had now decided to call her. She found an unopened tin of sardines she was saving for special occasion and thought that, today of all days, Nila deserved to enjoy a really good meal.

'I wonder why Wolfgang isn't up and having breakfast?' she said thinking aloud. 'He's an early bird, like me.'

Göreland Wolfgang had met in the 1970's, on a summer course in Greifswald, where Goyan learned about socialist culture. Wolfgang was a pacifist, a communist and a very eloquent, articulate person. They became a couple and moved to Sweden where Wolfgang got a job as a priest and was given a work permit in record fast time.

Over the years, Görel came to understand that her husband had an insatiable appetite for both women and men. She had silently accepted it and was reconciled to spending one or two nights a week alone at home in Sollentuna, with just Nila as company.

Wolfgang became very aggressive and verbally abusive when she first confronted him with his infidelity, as Swedish women do.

'You're too dry and too small. You can't move in time with me and you're as lifeless as a dead snake. I need to have a real woman, and really great lays. So you can choose. Either you close your eyes and accept my life-style or you can leave.' She had closed her eyes.

For Görel, Wolfgang was her whole identity. All those communist friends. His house in Greifswald. The big parties with friends there during the summer. Wolfgang's ample cock, which she could at least take care of occasionally with what she had to offer. So Görel turned the other cheek.

But now the bed was empty. No Wolfgang had slept there during the night. Görel wondered what to do next. It was 10 o'clock in the morning. He should be at home, she thought. He doesn't have a job to go to any more. He had been fired as a teacher and priest after years of rumours that he had connections with Stasi. She began to get worried.

At one o'clock she made her way to the local police station.

'My name is Görel Nilsdottir, I want to report that my husband is missing.'

Her hair was in disarray and her eyes were filled with tears.

'My husband was at a get-together at the Grand Hotel yesterday with some friends in the priesthood. They meet quite regularly to discuss sermons and so on, and have a beer or two afterwards. He usually comes home at a reasonable hour.

The female police officer was a 40-year-old woman originally from Egypt. Her name was Gulnara. She looked at Görel as if she might have an idea about what had happened, and showed her into a small, more private, back office.

'Come in and sit down so we can make out a proper report.'

Gulnara looked calm and concerned about Görel who sat sobbing and wringing her hands.

'Let's start from the beginning. Why are you afraid that something has happened? Does he usually stay away all night long? With other women? Has he ever been involved with alcohol and drugs? Is there reason to believe that he has links with other countries' security services or the underworld?'

Görel sat there with her face in her hands. Completely destroyed. She understood that the police officer had seen through the situation immediately. Her face was grey with grief and humiliation.

***

In the afternoon on the same day, the criminal team led by the senior officer in charge, Erik Blind, gathered for a briefing. Gulnara and a second officer who had interviewed a second woman in a suburb south of the city, reported that a total of three men were now missing. All three had worked as priests in Sweden. They had originally come from East Germany, were married to Swedes and, it seemed, had not encountered any problems getting entry permits and work permits in Sweden. Someone has blessed their immigration.

And they all had possible links to the East German intelligence service, Stasi.

'Let's concentrate our focus on the Grand Hotel. We'll question all the staff and try to interview all the customers who were in the hotel last night. Talk to all the taxi drivers who usually wait outside for a fare. If we find any rooms or places in the restaurant that they might have been in, seal them off immediately. I'll speak to the hotel manager, myself,' said Blind. 'Report back here to me in 4 hours.'

The room emptied in seconds when everyone rushed away on their respective assignments. This was a sensitive case since the government had made considerable concessions in recent years to become friends with the East.

Blind's theory was that the men, at that moment, were in someone's cabin in the woods with some women, alcohol and drugs. 'We must find them and deal with them quickly,' he told Gulnara, 'Before the media find out and go public - which happens all too often in cases like these. We have to locate them fast and find out what happened at the party at the Grand yesterday and who was present at the time.'

Erik Blind was a third generation Stockholmer. Born

and raised in Gröndal, a former working-class district in the south of Stockholm. A devout social democrat who was pleased to pay his taxes and who didn't go to prostitutes. A man of integrity who felt personally responsible for keeping the Social Democratic party's banner clean. Erik understood that this had to be dealt with quickly.

***

'They met last night for 'an evening of pleasure' in one of suites at the Grand Hotel. The three men, a couple of girls from an Eastern country and a Swedish person, Rave Alexander, about whom we know nothing. The party went on into the small hours according to the receptionist. A lot of booze was ordered. We've now sealed off the suite. It looked like a pigsty. Spirits, drugs, blood, and sperm on the carpets and the furniture.'

Blind looked around at the other police officers. His face showed nothing but disgust for the men who had so poisoned the socialist cause and wanted more than ever to catch them before a major scandal was a fact.

'Rave Alexander. Let's find out all we can about this man. Any possible links he might have to other security services.'

Another female officer entered the room with a piece of new information for the group.

'It seems that, late last night, a carpet dealer called Arhan turned up at the hotel with his so-called assistant. They spoke to the guy on the Reception Desk and said that they had been instructed to deliver three Bokhara mats up to one of the suites.'

'Perhaps someone was planning to ride away on them,' someone said from the back of the room.

A wave of giggling broke out and Blind glared angrily around the room with an ice-cold look. The giggling ended instantly.

'Both Arhan and the assistant are missing. Their wives have reported their disappearance. All the spirits and everything that was delivered up to the suite was ordered by one particular waiter. His name is Klas. He doesn't work at Grand Hotel but he was responsible for all the serving between the kitchen and the suite in line with the customer's wishes. The bill for entire party amounted to SEK 230,000 and was paid by an investment company based in Ljubljana, the capital of Slovenia. We don't know yet who the company's owners are but, given some more time, we should be able to find out more.

Blind sat quietly thinking to himself. To an old fox like me, he thought, this smells like a trap. Perhaps a trap set by someone in our national security service

'Let's find out all we can about Rave Alexander, Klas and the girls who were there. Let's bring them in, give them a grilling and hopefully get a better picture about what's going on.'

Everyone left the room. Blind remained, looking pensive. Who's really behind this and calling the moves? He asked himself.

***

One hour later, Blind's phone rang. A police officer in Bromma.

'We have witnesses who saw a van drive onto the Bromma runway at 0400 this morning. The vehicle belongs to a mat dealer in Stockholm. A plane, a two-engine private jet, was waiting with its engines running. Minutes later it took off and was seen flying in an easterly direction over the city and out towards the Baltic Sea. Later we found a man who we believe was the mat dealer's assistant, shot in the back of the head several times with an automatic weapon. His body is now in the mortuary.'

Blind was furious and ready to explode. What was this? A professional contract killing? A kidnapping? An extradition to another country? What was going on? All hell would break loose if the media got onto it before they had things under control.

'Kvällsbladet is on the line, boss. They want to talk to you. They say that they've interviewed several residents in Bromma and they'd like us to tell them what's happening.'

'They're fucking blood suckers. Always wanting more and more. Well, they'll have to wait until we know more. Keep them happy but in the dark for the next 10 hours, if that's possible?'

* * *

'We know all about you, so it's a waste of time trying to bullshit us. That will only make things worse. If you withhold anything from us now and we find out later that you knew all along, then I will personally make sure that you spend a good many years behind bars. Do you hear what I am saying? We know for a fact that you were at the Grand Hotel. Why were you there? Is it your job to fix women for private parties?'

'How do you know the priests? You don't come from a German family, but is there anyone in your family who has links with East Germany?'

Rave looked calmly at Blind, said nothing, and shuffled around in his chair before resettling. The room had no outside windows but there was a large mirror on one of the walls behind which sat a small group who monitored every question from the interrogator and every response from Rave. His nervous movements, his way of constantly moving one leg over the other, his facial expressions. Everything was registered.

An elderly man with a beard knocked briefly at the door before entering and sitting down beside the others. As he did so, the men almost 'came to attention' and turned to listen to what he had to say.

'Erik, you can break off the interrogation for a while and come in to us. There is someone here who wants to talk to you.'

***

Later that evening, Blind spoke to his team in the operations room.

'You've done a good job so far during the time we've been working on this case. Thanks for your efforts. You've been really professional. But now the case has taken on a more international dimension and it's been decided that it would be best to leave the rest of the investigation to our colleagues at MUST. So, MUST is now taking over the entire investigation and you will be assigned new tasks tomorrow. Thank you.'

Blind took a deep breath and scanned the room. No-one had left. No-one had moved.

A young officer called Binga was the first to speak. 'This is disgusting. It stinks. MUST goes in to cover up for someone at the top who must be protected at all costs. It makes me physically sick to be treated like this and so bloody humiliated.'

Young Binga was a successful, young, black, female police office with high ambitions, but not enough sense about when to speak up and when to shut up. Soon she would be redeployed back to traffic duties again. That's how it worked.

Blind stood up and left the room without another word. Out on the street he got into his old SAAB 95.

'At least I can go and play inner bandy tonight,' he said out loud as he pulled out into the traffic.

Chapter 32

FLYING CARPETS

Rave had been standing in the hotel corridor as Arhan and his assistant cleared the way from the elevator and the suite. Arhan was sweating and his hands were shaking. Without a word, they lifted the first carpet and carried it into to the elevator. Rave joined them.

Down in the foyer it was quiet and deserted. The night was over and the evening's guests had gone home. The male receptionist didn't bother to look up, but carried on watching a film on his computer screen. Long-serving hotel employees have seen and heard everything. He belonged to the category of people who had seen it all before.

The sound of a moan emanated from the rolled-up carpet. Arhan stopped in his tracks and looked at Rave, who pointed towards the side door and nudged Arhan in that direction. Outside, they walked over to Arhan's van. It was chilly in the early morning light and the only thing to be seen was the odd taxi driving past.

'Lay the carpet on the floor without unfolding them. I'll wait here while you go and pick up the other two.'

Rave let the night air cool him off a little. His jacket was open, his shirt unbuttoned. After a hard evening with too much to drink even for him, it felt good to have the first carpet loaded into the van. Nothing moved and no sound came from the carpet any longer. The streets were empty which was lucky. Rave waited for what seemed like an eternity before the second carpet arrived and was placed into the back of the van beside the first. He wanted to leave the area as soon as he could. After another 10 minutes, the third carpet was finally loaded into the van and they all jumped in.

'This is wrong! I can't do it! They're going to die! I know they are.'Arhan broke down behind the wheel, shaking with fear.

Rave bent down and pulled out his Glock pistol from its ankle strap and, in one continuous movement, he fired a shot into the side of Arhan's head. Arhan was thrown violently against the car door, blood spurting from his nose and temple, his head was almost split in two. He was stone dead.

'Throw him behind the carpets and come here and drive'. Rave aimed the pistol at Arhan's assistant. 'And no funny tricks, or else....'

Arhan's body slid down like soft-boiled macaroni between the front seats and the carpets in the rear of the van, and they drove off at speed through the empty, rain-swept streets of Stockholm. Neither of them said anything or even looked at each other. The drive took them out of the city, over a bridge and into the residential suburb of Bromma; a journey which took about 20 minutes before the high security fences surrounding the airport came into sight.

'Drive to gate C,' Rave ordered.

Gate C was unlocked and open, the airport was closed and the runway lights were turned off for the night. The only visible light came from a small airplane on the runway with its engines running, ready for take-off.

They drove onto the runway and stopped on the left side of the aircraft, then got out of the van with the carpets still in the back, and began to walk back towards the gate.

'Leave the area immediately,' someone said behind Rave in heavily broken English, which was quite unnecessary because he was already on his way, walking as fast as he dared without appearing scared.

Suddenly a shot echoed out and Rave threw himself to the ground and looked back over his shoulder towards the plane. Arhan's assistant had fallen to the ground. Blood was pouring from his chest.

A man walked forward, put a gun to the assistant's forehead and fired off another round. Once again, the night was shattered with a sound like that of a bottle being thrown against a brick wall. His face was now gone and he was unrecognisable.

Rave scrambled up and ran across the grass towards gate C. Once out through the gate, he carried on running until he came to the main road leading back into the city. He had to get away. Someone must have called the police after the shots which had echoed across the airfield.

The small two-engine Gulf Stream plane thundered over his head as it headed due east, out over the Baltic Sea. The FSB takes back its agents. That's good. Very good.

'I want a taxi to pick me up outside Bromma Airport. I'm waiting opposite the filling station. As soon as you can, please.'
Rave stuffed his phone back into his jacket pocket and went to a bus shelter to get away from the chilly wind while he waited for the taxi to pick him up.

Soon, the area would be teeming with police officers. He knew he needed to be far away when that happened.

Half an hour later, Rave stepped out of the taxi and made his way into his apartment. He knew Sophya would be waiting for him there, but she'd probably be asleep.

It was getting light now. Sophya's clothes were thrown everywhere, the TV was still on, the lights were lit and Sophya was lying in bed asleep beneath her duvet. The bedroom smelt of 'woman', of a female body and her perfume. All was as it should be.

Rave suddenly realised that he was actually rather tired now that the night's mission had been completed. He had delivered what was required of him. MUST would take care of Arhan and his assistant, and explain events in terms of gang killings in the middle of the night most probably.

 A week or so later, the whole thing would be forgotten. He lay down beside Sophya, closed his eyes, embraced her from behind and floated away in a deep sleep.

***

Meanwhile, dawn was breaking over Lappeenranta,

a small Finnish town close to the Russian border. It had a small airfield mainly for private planes, but at this time of day, the airfield was closed.

A Gaselle van was parked at the side of the runway. It had Russian plates. Two men in black leather jackets and Adidas bottoms were leaning against the van smoking. One of them, a man in his 30s, with pig eyes, a flat head, a fleshy face and at least 20 kilos of fat around his waist, was playing with something that looked like a small sub-machine gun. It was an Uzi.

When the heard the sound of the small jet plane making its descent prior to landing they climbed in and drove down to a spot half way down the runway.

Once down on the ground, the plane braked, taxied towards the parked van and then came to a complete standstill. The two Russians were beside it within seconds.

The carpets were quickly unloaded and carried into the van. It was light by now and the town would be starting to wake up so the men were in a hurry to get away. One of the Russians spotted a woman in her forties standing on the other side of the perimeter fence which surrounded the airfield. She had a small dog, a poodle, by her side on a lead and presumably they were out for the dog's morning walk. She stood watching the men and had seen what they were up to.

'Fuck! Get her! Now before she gets away.'

The man with pig eyes ran over towards the fence, sub-machine gun in hand, and shouted at her to stand still. She stopped immediately, clearly frightened, but the dog ran away from her, dragging the lead from her hand.

The man then walked over to the fence, said 'good morning' and sprayed her full of lead. He emptied the entire magazine into her to be on the safe side. The woman collapsed in her own pool of blood, with one of her beautiful long legs protruding at a strange angle.

After admiring his work, he ran quickly back to the vehicle, before driving away from the airfield area at high speed and heading straight for the border crossing where Russian personnel had already been informed about the transport.

Happy with themselves, they looked at each other and smoked their cigarettes.

'Ha! She was a good-looking woman. I should have danced with her while she was still alive. We're always in such a fucking hurry.' Both of them laughed at the funny joke.

The first plane to take off at Lappeenranta airport that morning was the small Gulf Stream plane which turned in the sky after taking off, steered due west over Helsinki and the Baltic Sea, and headed back to its home airfield in Stockholm.

Chapter 33

ONE TEA

Sophya and I were dining 'in' that night. We'd bought the food together, prepared it and cooked it together, enjoyed it together and now we were sitting finishing off our wine together, small talking across the table.

'This is so nice. Rave. Just you and me and a romantic candle-light dinner.'

'Yes, it is. it really is, Sophya. It's been a great day. Walking around at the market together, hand in hand, buying the food for tonight.'

'Yes, that's right. It gave me a lovely feeling as well. We're together again. And your cooking was magnificent Rave. Baked salmon with chanterelle sauce, king prawns and green-lipped mussels from New Zealand with avocado and Rhode Island sauce. My God, what a feast!'

I put on some bossa nova background music and sat down next to Sophya on the sofa. We were both in a good mood and I was pretty sure that we were both in the mood for some love-making.

'The wine has made me feel really sexy,' Sophya said as she hooked her arms around my shoulders. So why don't you just kiss me?' she whispered in my ear.

I did exactly as she wanted. I kissed her long and passionately and neither of us wanted it to end.

'Oh Rave, you kiss so well. Like before.'

'Well, you know, don't you? I'm enchanted by your beauty, like before.'

'That's wonderful. You're such a romantic animal. And now it's time to behave like one. Here and now. Take me hard and take me deep.'

'But of course, Sophya. Anything you say.'

The kissing began again and showed no sign of ending. I lifted her dress over her head and let it fall to the floor. Sophya pulled my shirt up, unbuttoned it and dropped it on top of her dress.

I kissed Sophya's neck and held her buttocks in my hands as I became aroused. I loved her ass. It was so delicious, so smooth. The perfect shape and size. So beautiful and so sexy.

Sophya shivered a little as I kissed her neck and she started to lick my ear, which made me pull away a little. My ears were really sensitive to licking and sucking.

Sophya knew this and it was her well-proven trick to get me where she wanted me. We knew each other bodies and each other's triggers inside out.

Sophya then pulled my pants down, took hold of my cock and wrapped her beautiful lips around it.

I was already rock hard; aroused by the ear-licking.

Sophya quickly pulled her panties down.

'You're so hot, Sophya. So sexy.'

'And, Rave, you have such a lovely cock.'

Sophya pushed me higher up the bed and lay on top of me.

'Your skin is so smooth.' I said, as I moved my hands across her back and onto her breasts.

'You do this so well, Rave. Don't stop, will you?'

Sophya kissed me again and began to creep still higher on me. She knew it made me crazy.

'Wait, Sophya, wait, not my ears again.'

'OK, let's wait a while.'

Sophya sat on top of me and slowly eased my cock into her already wet pussy.

'Oh my God, Sophya, you are so horny tonight.'

'Just keep going. Don't talk so much. I want you. I want you inside me. I want you to come inside me. Deep inside.'

'Yes, yes, yes, Sophya ...'

Sophya rocked gently on me at first then she got faster. I could feel her gripping me. Only Sophya could do such a thing. She was wonderful.

'Now Rave, take me, take me now. I can feel your heat.'

I sat up and embraced her fully in my arms and held her long and hard. When I moved towards the edge of the bed, she hooked her legs around my waist as I stood up. She was hanging from me.

'Rave, I feel I'm floating. As if I'm weightless.'

And then we both climaxed together in a perfect moment of bliss.

**

When they had both come back down to earth, they lay on their backs, silent in their own thoughts. Rave was the first to speak.

'What a night it was at the Grand Hotel! You danced naked in front of the priests - crawled all over them as they lay on the floor and gave them a close-up of your pussy. Don't you have a stop button on that body of yours?'

'Rave, we've been through this before. I'm a spybabe and I do my job for my country, but you must know too that I really love you. With all my heart.'

It was strange with women, thought Rave. In some situations, nothing really mattered to women and they'd let things pass without it affecting them. But, at other times, a woman could take a man to court for up-skirting her on an escalator and he'd get a hefty fine or a prison sentence. We'll never be able to understand them, he thought, but one thing is certain; Men are being criticised like never before by the state, by women, by the police, in the social media, in social circles, by their children, and even their mother-in-law's.

Rave looked at Sophya and her wise, blue eyes. How long can two people live as we do? We're still young, but - we've become bitter, cynical and manipulative. If only there was a way to get out now and live our own lives, without having to follow 'their' orders. But there isn't. Rave had been deceived so many times, cheated by his own feelings, sometimes over money but above all by his heart.

You think you know everything, Rave thought to himself. You think you have total control, but you don't. There's a lot you still don't know – yet, and I'm afraid that you'll soon be on your way.

I know for a fact that MUST have identified you for what you are and want you out of the country.

It serves you right for disappearing to Panama behind my back, but - all in good time my little beauty. Revenge is best enjoyed in the cold light of day.

***

Nothing was reported in the press or on TV about the party at the Grand Hotel or the execution of Arhan and his assistant. MUST had put the lid on everything in true totalitarian fashion.

'Rave, darling, can you make some tea for us. As I tell you all the time, we Russians are tea drinkers, you know.' She smiled at him and he saw that she loved him. She was clearly tired, but he saw true love in her face, and it hurt him.

Rave went out into the kitchen, and started making the tea. Outside on the street it was dark, cold, raining and deserted. A car was approaching. Rave saw from the number plate and the typically black German make of the car, that it was a diplomatic car. The car pulled up outside the main entrance without a noise.

Without speaking a word, he returned to the living room with a mug of tea in his hand.

'But Rave, why have you just made one cup of tea? No tea for me you naughty boy? Aren't I your favourite little pussy cat anymore?' she joked. 'Now just get yourself into the kitchen real pronto and bring me a cup of tea too.'

Rave returned to the kitchen and stood looking out the window, drinking his tea, until there was a sudden ring at the door. Sophya looked at Rave, clearly very surprised by the bell. Rave put his tea cup down on the table and walked out into the hall. Sophya followed him with hesitant steps.

'Good evening, Mr. Alexander, my name is Ove Shoot. We're from MUST.'

The two men standing at the door looked tired and scruffy in their worn-out trench coats and cheap shoes. Too much coffee and fast food at petrol stations and too many late nights and assignments that ended in family tragedies had taken their toll on their minds and bodies.

'Excuse the late hour. We know you live with Sophya Sackenova.'

Sophya stared at the men, then at Rave. He looked perfectly calm and normal. It suddenly crossed her mind that MUST and the FSB were in this together. And that it was about her work in Sweden.

'May we come in?'

The men waited for Rave to respond.

'Of course.'

Rave still remained perfectly at ease.

'Miss Sackenova, as I said before, we're from MUST, Sweden's security service. We need to ask you some questions about your situation here in Sweden. We'd like you to come with us now, right away, if you don't mind?'

Sophya nodded and tried to smile. She threw her coat over her shoulder and started walking towards the door.

'I'll be back soon,' she said to Rave, 'so don't get worried. Kovalchuk will get this sorted out in no time.'

On the way out of the door, she saw another man standing lower down on the stairs. A Russian diplomat she knew very well. He was always there in attendance when the Russians had to remove or take home one of their staff from Sweden, often to be sentenced in Russia to prison or given some mediocre office job far away in the eastern part of the country.

She realized that she'd been set up, cheated, and she now understood why Rave had just come out of the kitchen with one cup of tea. Everything was planned. He'd made love to her today better than for a long time. He'd had been spurred on by the fact that he would be getting rid of her; that she'd be sent back to Russia to face an uncertain future

'YOU FUCKING BASTARD! I loved you so much!'

She threw herself at Rave. The officers tried to stop her but she was still able to spit him in the face, scratch his cheek so it started to bleed, kick him in the crotch and thump him with her fists, before the men could get hold of her and drag her out of the apartment.

Rave turned towards the window, wiping away the spit and blood from his face. His face was expressionless. Down on the street, the diplomatic car was parked with its engine running and its lights on. The MUST officers appeared first on the pavement with Sophya, her hands cuffed behind her back, followed by the Russian diplomat. They manhandled her into the backseat and quickly drove away with their precious cargo.

Rave watched Sophya's abduction with a cold heart. At the end of the day, sex was one thing and feelings were another. At that moment, his feelings for Sophya were zero despite the sublime sex they'd had a few hours earlier. And in any case, she was a sex machine who could turn it on and turn it off. What kind of woman was that? She had taken her money and her daughter to Panama for a better life without him. She had deserted him at his moment of need; when he needed her most. No, Sophya was better out of his life and out of Sweden.

The car's rear lights disappeared around the corner and with them, Sophya. Gone from his life, but would it be for ever?

Chapter 34

SONJA AND VAL

You could set the watch by Adria's take-offs and landings. The airline was a good mix of Austrian punctuality and Italian beauty. Never any delays and none of the endless announcements you heard from other airlines at European airports. The cabin interiors and the cabin crew's uniforms were reminiscent of the 60's, when flying was the latest thing - an expensive luxury, long before the beer-drinking masses began to fly around the world.

I chose an aisle seat at the front of the cabin and read the menu for today's flight. Fish, meat, poultry, vegetarian; it was all there. If you travelled with Adria you got what you paid for and it was a lot more than a paper bag with an apple and a yogurt in it. Adria was a class airline as too was Aeroflot, at least with the new aircraft in their fleet. New planes, good menus, good service, good-looking cabin crew. Large comfortable armchair seats in business class if you could afford to fly 'business'.

Towards the end of the three-hour flight, we made a tight turn as we approached the small airport in Ljubljana. I looked through the window and saw that we were leaving the Alps behind us and would shortly be landing in this picturesque country with its well-kept farms and villages.

A man was waiting for me in the Arrivals Hall with the keys to my car which he had parked outside the terminal building. We exchanged a few words and with everything in order, I was soon on my way.

No one here knew who Rave Alexander was, simply because it wasn't my name here. I had a different identity. In my business you had to have several identities depending on what you were doing. 'A wise rat has many holes!'

My investments with Carl August, my business colleague in Ljubljana, had given me a solid foundation on which to live. Together, we had stakes in hotels, office properties, agriculture, meat production and manufacturing industries, all of which were in good financial shape. Carl August was a good partner. The question was if he knew of my other identities and what I did for MUST?

Intelligence and security services were unlike anything you could think of in the 'real world'. Everyone had a cover identity and outwardly could work as a businessman, or a doctor or teacher; basically, anything that would allow them to lead a double life. It was an occupational hazard to see double identities in everybody, everywhere. The word paranoia didn't even begin to describe the life style.

***

It was a wonderful day. A clear, blue sky, warm yellow spring sunshine, and the snow finally melting. I sat behind the wheel of my white Range Rover, feeling as pleased as punch, having completed my assignment with MUST. The security industry was raw and dirty. It was difficult to succeed, and even harder to leave once you were inside. But here I was, away from Sweden. Away from all the shit.

The drive took me along twisty roads in the alpine countryside. They were well maintained and lined with tall fir trees and pine trees. Hardly any other cars on the road. It was just a normal day up here, and the few people who lived here were probably busy at work.

This part of Europe had seen many wars, civil wars and internal conflicts between the people who live here. Many had conquered and ruled the country over thousands of years. 'The more beautiful the landscape, the more dangerous the people,' I said out loud to myself.

When I thought back over my times in Stockholm and Saint Petersburg, I remembered them quite favourably. I thought of the happy times that had given me pleasure. I pushed the bad things to the back of my mind in the hope that they would eventually wade away.

'The man who takes himself too seriously will be lost.'

***

Rave drove further on through the forests. After a long straight stretch by the banks of a lake, he turned onto a small gravel road. The road was smooth, without any potholes, and was bordered by willow trees that led to a large semi-timbered house. The architecture was typical for houses in this part of Slovenia. A white-washed first floor, timber higher up, balconies with flower boxes, ornate wooden shutters, windows wide-open with bed clothes hanging out waiting to be shaken.

He drove up to the house, stopped the car and got out.

'Ah, Val, Val! Ja ckychala.Val, I've missed you so much for so long.'

A young, blond woman in her thirties, tall, with rosy cheeks and dressed in national costume for the day, came rushing out of the house. She ran up to him, stopped and looked at him closely, laughed, and without any hesitation, threw herself headlong in his arms.

'Welcome home Val. You've been away so long. We've missed you so much and the children have asked for you every single day.'

'Sonja majaljobimaja, my love. You're more beautiful than ever.'

He held her hard, kissed her lips but said nothing. Sonja smiled at him. She trembled with excitement, shed a tear and turned away from him for a second.

'PAPA! PAPA!'

Two little boys, one six and the other eight, ran up to Rave where he was standing with his wife in his arms. He sat on his haunches, opened his arms and embraced the boys as they hurled themselves at him, almost knocking him backwards.

'What big boys you are! I have missed you so much.'

They remained like that for quite a time, all four of them, together in a small group, enjoying the touch and smell of each other.

Sonja broke away and went into the house, before coming out again onto the porch to say that the food was ready.

Presents. There were always presents when Dad came home. The children received their presents and sat down, each in an armchair, deeply focused on getting the paper off and seeing what was inside. Sonja sat quietly and enjoyed the family scene as only a mother could do. She signalled to the housekeeper to come and take care of the children, then stood up and walked past Rave. As she did so, she touched his leg and smiled seductively at him before walking up the stairs.

Rave stood up and followed her up into the bedroom. When he opened the door, Sonja had already taken off her costume and removed her blouse and underwear. She had tied a red silk ribbon several times around her neck to show him that she was his gift.

Rave looked at her and removed his shirt as she walked up to him, put a hand behind his neck, and gently, silently closed the bedroom door.

EXTRACT FROM *BREAKOUT* – BOOK 2 IN THE RAVE TRILOGY

DUE TO BE PUBLISHED SHORTLY

Chapter 35

'Most merciful God,

We confess that we have sinned against you in thought, word, and deed, by what we have done, and by what we have left undone.

We have not loved you with our whole heart; we have not loved our neighbours as ourselves.

We are truly sorry and we humbly repent, for the sake of your Son Jesus Christ, have mercy on us and forgive us; that we may delight in your will, and walk in your ways, to the glory of your Name.

Amen'

The priest turned to the women who were standing facing him, heads bowed, and raised his arms above his head.

The congregation consisted of women who had murdered, women who had been sex workers, women who had committed serious crimes, who had stolen and, in many different ways, betrayed their fellow human beings.

The small chapel in the Platinum Women's Prison was only half full for the Sunday service. Sophya and her new husband had spent their first night together in prison after the wedding ceremony the preceding day, and Vlad had been given special permission to attend the service.

Sophya had lowered her gaze, when the chapel began to shake. Slowly at first, and then with greater intensity. Icons fell to the floor, the ceiling began to collapse and falling rafters hit the priest knocking him to the ground. A second later, the shockwave from a deafening explosion threw the women across the chapel like rag dolls, ending up beneath the debris which had fallen the ceiling.

And then the roof collapsed completely above their heads. Vlad took Sophya firmly by the hand and dragged her frantically out into the prison yard, and towards the wall in the southwest corner of the yard. Sophya lost a shoe and her foot started to bleed.

'Run Sophya – run like hell!' Vlad shouted as he half pulled her across the yard.

Timed almost to the second, Rave drove his vehicle up to the foot of the wall and started hoisting a ladder, getting it quickly it into place. The ladder extended up and over the top of the wall and down on the inside of the prison wall.

Vlad was the first to climb up to the top of the wall, with Sophya right behind him on the ladder. He extended his hand towards Rave a smile crossing his face. Rave's look back was an ice-cold stare.

As the sound of the shot echoed across the yard, all the lights were turned on, and barking dogs and armed prison guards charged towards the three of them on the wall.

Vlad 's face was split in two by the bullet and he toppled backwards, headlong, straight on top of Sophya who lost her grip on the rungs of the ladder and fell back to the ground where she lay with Vlad's dead body on top of her.

The dogs throw themselves upon Sophya and the dead Vlad, growling and snarling, until they were called off by their handlers.

On the other side of the wall Rave started to run away from the prison as fast as he possibly could. Searchlights illuminated the scene and white lights criss-crossed the area tracking Rave as he ran. The first shot from one of the snipers on the wall went straight through Rave's right arm but he kept on running. The second hit him in his calf. He cried out in pain and fell to the ground.

In Moscow, lawyer Flöjel received a call that made him fly out of his armchair. Two hours later, a fish truck, a worn-out Ford Transit, arrived at the grocery store in the small town of Russian town of Platina. It was late in the evening and the last delivery for the day had been made. The fish truck then made its way to a small remote border crossing into Lithuania, where the border guard recognised them and waved them through after the usual exchange of a few friendly words and a few pieces of choice fish. They drove through the night until they arrived at Vilnius Airport.

On the runway, a specially built Gulf Stream was ready to depart. Rave was carried into the plane on a stretcher. Jan and Mr Randall stood on the tarmac to see that Rave was safely aboard. They glanced at one another, clearly worried about his condition.

The small Gulf Stream got the all-clear to take off and, once airborne, it set course for Bromma Airport.

Printed in Great Britain
by Amazon

71111792R00203